D1589658

MARIANNE MACDONALD

Die Once

NEW ENGLISH LIBRARY
Hodder & Stoughton

First published in Great Britain in 2002
by Hodder and Stoughton
This edition published in paperback in 2002
by Hodder and Stoughton
A division of Hodder Headline

1 3 5 7 9 10 8 6 4 2

A CIP catalogue record for this title
is available from the British Library

ISBN 0 340 82182 5

Printed and bound in Great Britain by
Mackays of Chatham plc, Chatham, Kent

Hodder and Stoughton
A division of Hodder Headline
338 Euston Road
London NW1 3BH

In memory of
Louis Dudek
and
Edith M Scott
. . . part-payment

ACKNOWLEDGMENTS

And once again I would like to thank all those who have been so supportive during the writing of this book, especially the 'Dido Hoare Reading Circle' – Erik Korn (who was, as always, helpful in antiquarian matters), Sandra Macdonald, Merilyn Moos, Alex Wagstaff; and most especially Andrew Korn for his hard work and extensive suggestions during the final stages of revisions. Thanks are also due to my agents and editors on both sides of the Atlantic, who have always been helpful – and forbearing too: Jacqueline Korn and Wendy Schmalz, Carolyn Mays, Sara Hulse, Ruth Cavin, Julie Sullivan – not to mention Carolyn Marino, for her good conversation, and Dona Helmer of Anchorage.

'A man can die but once . . . and, let it go
which way it will,
he that dies this year is quit for the next.'
– Shakespeare

'You only die once, and it's for such a long time.'
– Molière

I

The Good Customer

Timothy Curwen walked into my shop one day nearly two years ago. It was probably a Saturday afternoon, because we were so busy at the time that I barely noticed his arrival. (My customers are a mixed lot. The most unlikely-looking people collect books, and my shop sells books to collectors: Dido Hoare ~ Antiquarian Books and Prints, that is.) But I was paying attention to this one by the time he left.

For starters: he was the most elegant man I've ever seen outside the pictures in ancient copies of the *Tatler*, from his impeccably tailored charcoal-grey suit with its faint pin-stripe, and the monogrammed handkerchief in the breast pocket, to the tips of his gleaming black boots. Even the white-and-green golfing umbrella which he furled as he entered was a sort of fashion statement. I wondered at the time how he had made his way to my shop in its back street: I would have expected to see a man like that lounging along Piccadilly, or languidly descending the steps of the Garrick Club with an old-fashioned look on his face. Somebody might have recommended us. Maybe it was chance.

Second, Curwen bought one of the best books in the shop that day – a first edition of Trollope's *Barchester Towers* – using a platinum credit card to pay the marked price of £1,895 without so much as the murmur of an attempt to haggle. The card company promptly approved the purchase. I wrote the number on the slip, wrapped the three volumes with their calf bindings in bubble-wrap, and slid them gently into one of my gold-and-blue carrier bags. I told him truth-fully that it had been a pleasure doing business with him and that I hoped to see him again soon.

And I did, irregularly but often, usually on Saturday after-noons. He would poke around the shelves and talk about books, nothing but books – I got the idea that he had just started collecting and was eager to learn. Not that he was unfriendly: but he was strictly business, and there are lots of browsers on Saturdays, so that I tend to be a little distracted, watching for buyers. And thieves. He asked a lot of questions about buying and caring for old books, about book auctions – that kind of thing. The only personal information he ever offered was when he dropped the comment, during one unusually rushed visit late that spring, that he was in a hurry because he was on his way to a ghastly, ghastly garden party at Buckingham Palace. Had I caught a flicker of guile in his face? Anyway, he paid *cash* for a first edition of *The Way We Live Now*, which I had got for him from an Edinburgh dealer. I think I might have raised my eyebrows. He looked at me, smiled broadly, said, 'Birthday present,' and asked me to send it to his flat. I said, 'Happy birthday,' and slid forty-two £50 notes nervously into my cash-box, the one I'd lost the key to a few months before.

My father, Barnabas, overheard him and reacted coolly. 'To the best of my knowledge,' he commented stiffly as he stared through the display window to where Curwen was climbing into his waiting cab, 'Buckingham Palace does not hold garden parties on Saturdays.'

I should have been paying attention. It was a long time before I knew even half the truth about my good customer.

Curwen collected Victoriana, especially Trollope and Meredith. He bought at least one book on each of his visits, even the last one: always first editions or early association copies in excellent condition, and usually again for cash. Like the bottomless purse in the fairytale, his wallet had an inexhaustible supply of twenties and fifties. We went on talking about collecting. Perhaps I thought that Victoriana was an odd area of interest for a young man who was certainly no academic, but he seemed to read his books with interest and affection. Carefully, I assumed, since they were valuable. But of course, Timothy Curwen was a very careful man.

The most remarkable thing about his appearance, apart from the old-fashioned, formal clothing, was his hair: a thick, white-blond shock that fell over his forehead and occasionally had to be brushed back out of astonishing violet-blue eyes. His face was pale, as though he spent more time in nightclubs than on golf courses; his lips were full, and they formed that wide, sweet smile whenever I managed to produce some book that especially pleased him. He was never, ever less than impeccably courteous and beautifully dressed; and my father, Professor Barnabas Hoare, late of Oxford University (whose education in these matters reaches levels that I never particularly wanted to attain), assured me one day after my good customer had left that the suit was certainly Savile Row, the shirts were Jermyn Street, and the shoes looked hand made. I was a little impressed.

The last time he turned up was at the beginning of September. It was a brief visit which he concluded by buying one small volume. He had been looking along the literature shelves when his eyes fell on a copy of Charles Dickens' last Christmas Book, *The Haunted Man and The Ghost's Bargain*; the title seemed to tickle him. I was asking £200, and this time he paid for it with a cheque which I deposited in the night safe of my bank that evening, along with the rest of the day's takings. On the following Thursday morning, an envelope arrived with the cancelled cheque, which his own bank had bounced.

I wasn't surprised. I'd had my fingers crossed ever since I'd noticed an item on an inside news page in the late edition of Wednesday's *Evening Standard*: the body of Timothy Curwen, aged thirty-nine, had been found in the basement area outside Abbey House in Mayfair, where he had lived. It described him as a 'Burlington Bertie figure', which in these circumstances seemed unnecessarily cruel, and said that he had jumped from the balcony of his flat some time on Tuesday night or early Wednesday morning.

2

Chasing the Ghost

For some reason, I hadn't been expecting to hear the dead man's voice.

'Hello,' it said, still alive and personal in my ear. 'This is Timothy Curwen's answering machine. Sorry, Tim is unavailable at the moment. Leave him a message.'

I stammered and pulled myself together and started the speech I'd been planning: 'This is a message for Timothy Curwen's legal representative . . . his executor. My name is Dido Hoare. Mr Curwen bought a number of books from my shop over the past few months. Last week, he took a copy of a book by Charles Dickens and paid with a cheque, but his bank has just refused payment. I'd like to get my book back and return the cheque. Please contact me as soon as possible.' I left the name and number of the business, and hung up feeling queasy. There is something about speaking into a dead man's ear which feels like chucking a letter in a bottle into the sea. My message would probably sink without trace.

Therefore I was sitting at the computer writing a back-up letter when a whisper from the little Nepalese bell on the shop door warned me that somebody had arrived. I deleted two sentences and looked up at the thin figure silhouetted against the light from the street. My father stepped inside, carrying a rolled-up newspaper under his arm. He stopped and looked around, as I had two hours ago, making sure that everything was in order. Then he saw me looking at him.

'The new window display looks well.'

I said, 'I know. Now that it's September, and the sun doesn't shine in the window for half of every morning, I thought it was time to put out something pretty. I've spent the morning shifting books around.' And deciding what to do about the little Dickens problem.

We exchanged business chitchat while he joined me in the office, placed his newspaper on the desk, and folded his lanky body into the visitor's chair. I watched him covertly. I do that all the time, although I am trying not to. Neither the thick white hair, nor the sharp grey eyes, nor the intelligent, thin face seem to have changed much since the heart attack that nearly killed him a couple of years ago, but something in me still anticipates the worst.

Belatedly I noticed that he was staring back. He said, 'What is it?' It had taken him about thirty seconds to notice.

I told him that I'd just heard a dead man talking, and explained what I was up to. His eyebrows twitched. Well, for me it was the obvious thing to do; but my father was inclined to argue, demonstrating for the thousandth time that our standards of etiquette differ.

I said defensively, 'The book wasn't paid for. It's a nice book, and I gave Jim Murphy a hundred and twenty for it last winter. If somebody wants it, they only have to pay me. If they don't want to pay, I'll take it back. I don't see what's so difficult!'

Barnabas was still looking at me with a shadow of paternal disapproval. 'You should have left it until after the funeral.'

Then he glanced at the newspaper on the desk. He had left it open at the death notices, and I could see Curwen's name. I picked it up and scanned the brief item, finding it as uninformative as the dead man had always seemed. It said, essentially, that my customer had died 'suddenly at home', aged thirty-nine. 'Enquiries to Messrs Price Rankin Burke of St James's, SW1.'

'What that really means,' I interpreted (never slow to state the obvious), 'is that anyone who is owed money should put in a claim. I'll send these people a copy of the invoice and the returned cheque. I'll just ask them to let me have the book back; I don't see that there's a problem.'

I watched my father continue to look as though I were committing some kind of social *faux pas*. But there had been no mention of surviving relatives in the obituary notice, so I assumed that the dead man was unattached: no wife, no old mother, no orphaned child to be offended by my greed. What I hadn't yet told him was that there might be a problem if I left things any longer. It was only by chance that I'd noticed the date stamp on the back of the cheque. They had refused to honour it *before* the news of Curwen's death would have reached them. Rapidly putting two and two together while I was working on the window display, I had started to wonder whether a high-spending socialite like Tim Curwen might, if he found himself broke, just decide that he couldn't face the world as a bankrupt. That was sad, but it also suggested that I ought to retrieve my property before some other creditor beat me to it.

I left my father to his own devices and started a letter to Price Rankin Burke. When I thought I'd explained things adequately, I printed out two copies with my letterhead, which naturally includes the information that I am a respectable member of both the big antiquarian book dealers' associations, and then copied the invoice and the dis-honoured cheque on the scanner and printed them out. Finally, I folded everything into two envelopes and addressed the first to the solicitors. Just to cover all possibilities, I marked the second envelope 'For the attention of the heirs and executors of Mr T. Curwen', and looked up his address on my database: Flat 502, Abbey House, W1. Then I remem-bered that I was out of first-class stamps, not to mention milk, so I grabbed my shoulder bag and stuffed both the envelopes inside.

Barnabas looked up from a pile of books on which he was working. He still prefers to list our purchases by hand, then let me or my part-timer, Ernie Weekes, enter them into the computer database.

'Shopping,' I said, accurately but evasively. 'We're out of stamps. Back in ten minutes.'

After I'd dropped the first envelope into the box in the post office, I hesitated. I was still holding the one with Curwen's home address on it when I wandered back out into the street. The clock on the tower of St Mary's church across the road said it was nearly half twelve. The morning was gone, I had a pile of more or less urgent paperwork that I didn't feel like tackling, and it was still almost five hours before I was due to pick up Ben from nursery. I reminded myself that my big MPV was parked in the residents' bay outside the shop and under Barnabas's cynical gaze. My hand shot out of its own accord, and a black taxi slid to a halt. On a kind of guilty, curious, truant impulse, I scrambled in and gave the driver Tim Curwen's address. As we pulled away, I noticed that I was feeling oddly relieved. I would phone Barnabas on my mobile and reassure him that I hadn't been hit by a car on the pedestrian crossing, but that could wait for five minutes. I'd probably be evasive, because this journey made very little sense, even to me.

Maybe it was the weather? After an early spring, the summer had been cool and wet, and it had shaded into September leaving me feeling dissatisfied and restless. Maybe it was Ben, my son, two-years-eight-months-full of energy, who could be blamed for my chronic sleep deficit. Somebody claims that being a single mother is the hardest job in the world: they do not lie. Maybe it was the business? There was nothing wrong with the business. We were putting out a good postal catalogue regularly every two months, and had a website which was also starting to sell books. It was all nice and increasingly profitable nowadays, and it made me feel reliable, bored, responsible and older than my age.

The taxi turned a corner. For the moment we were running through a patch of sunlight under a break in the clouds. A weak ray of light hit my face, so that I saw my reflection in the window glass: a white oval with expressionless dark eyes, surrounded by a bush of disorderly brown curls. Maybe I should get a haircut. Maybe I'd buy a dress. Maybe I'd do something else now.

The taxi dropped me at the door of Abbey House. That turned out to be an Edwardian building just off one of the garden squares north of Oxford Street. I would have said this was Marylebone, not Mayfair, whatever the writer of the death notice thought. Curwen had spent his last days in a grand red-brick building, the kind of old-fashioned mansion flats that seem designed for comfortable widows. The entrance was up a shallow flight of steps from the pavement. When I looked through the glazed door panels, I could see a porter's desk, unmanned. I pushed inside and found a rank of old-fashioned brass letterboxes on a side wall. The door swung shut, muffling the sounds of the traffic, and in the quiet I was suddenly aware of my intrusive footsteps clattering on the tiles as I crossed the empty lobby and pushed my envelope into the box marked 502. There was already something inside, visible through the little glass window. But somebody would be bound to clear the dead man's mail sooner or later.

In the rear wall of the lobby were swing-doors leading to a hallway, and the folding brass gates over an ancient, open lift shaft. As I watched, the cables in the shaft began to move and the weight came inching up from the basement. I turned away.

Back outside, I wandered aimlessly along the iron railings, looking through them into a shallow sunken area. Judging by the windows in the basement there, that floor must contain a couple of flats as well as various storage spaces, boiler rooms and maintenance sections. Something blue and white was flapping on the railings ahead. When I reached the place, I found a tangle of police tape still stretched across an iron gate above a flight of four steps leading down to a door and a row of dustbins. When Abbey House had been built, this might have been an entrance for servants and deliveries. Nowadays, the sign beside the door just read 'Flat A – Porter'. Gingerly I leaned against the railings and stared, prepared for bloodstains; but there was nothing to see except a sheet of newspaper which had blown down the street, and an abandoned metal sign on a folding stand which read 'Metropolitan Police CRIME SCENE Do Not Enter'. So this was indeed the exact spot where my good customer had died.

I looked up, counting the rows of stone-framed windows and shallow balconies. Curwen's flat must be on the top floor. There was nothing up there now that marked the spot where he had thrown a leg over his balustrade, hesitated, and finally plunged forward, diving through the air.

I couldn't have said what I was thinking at that moment, except that he had been only a few years older than me, and in my mind's eye I could still see his jaunty smile, giving nothing away. Ghosts. I wished now that I'd thought to bring a flower to throw down on to the cement floor where he died.

Somebody was watching me. As I was turning away towards Oxford Street and its cruising taxis, my eyes fell on a window just above head height. Old-fashioned net curtains had been parted, and the white face of a child, maybe ten years old, was pressed close against the pane. He wore glasses with small circular lenses. We stared at each other for a moment; there was something intense but unfocused in his gaze. After a moment, he looked down into the area below his window, then back at me. He seemed to know why I was standing here. I walked away.

3

Serendipity

It was still raining. This was a Tuesday, and there were no appointments in the book so no need to open the shop. Returning from walking Ben to his nursery school, I was planning to pick up the morning's mail, go upstairs, drink coffee, and do paperwork in the comfort of my sitting room while I listened to my new *Underworld* CD. If I felt in the mood, I would break off for a hot bath. Considering the weather, I was pretty sure that I was in the mood; but catalogues always come first – you never know what you're going to find in booksellers' catalogues, overlooked and underpriced. Serendipity, Barnabas calls it.

I ignored the red light flashing on the answering machine as I sorted the post on the office desk: junk mail in the bin, smaller envelopes in a heap to be dealt with soon, and three big envelopes with today's new book catalogues – the urgent pile. The phone started to ring. I grabbed the catalogues and fled as the answering machine switched itself on once again.

At the top of the stairs, I turned right into the sitting room and dropped everything on to the coffee table. Mr Spock, our resident ginger tabby, twitched an ear and went on sleeping in the middle of the settee. I spread my damp jacket over the back of a chair, switched on the CD player, pulled off my trainers and dumped them by the door, and then wandered off towards the kitchen. Spock overtook me halfway down the hall, sprinting towards his food bowl. Somebody had emptied it during my absence. I conceded an extra lump of tuna from the tin in the fridge, refilled my coffee mug, yawned, and wandered back to tear open the first of the big envelopes with a feeling of pleasant anticipation. It was from Finch . . . a catalogue of nineteenth-century literature which reminded me of Tim Curwen again. It was five days since I had turned away from the home he'd abandoned so abruptly.

I shook myself and concentrated: Arnold . . . Ashe . . . Austen . . . I checked that the phone was within reach and wrote a question mark in the margin beside a copy of *Lavengro*, which I was pretty sure somebody had been asking for. And I blanked out everything else.

Half an hour later I needed to go downstairs to the office to search my database. As I was unlocking the shop door, I could hear the answering machine switch off. It was the time for my father's daily phone call; having reached the machine here, he would now be trying again upstairs. I turned the computer on, left it, pressed the Play button and listened to three or four recorded messages.

The next to last was a woman's voice speaking rapidly: 'I'm trying to reach Miss Hoare: will she please ring Dona Helmer regarding her recent letter.' She spelled out her name, which seemed to have dropped one of the usual consonants, and gave the name of a company with an inner London phone number, which I scribbled down obediently on an unopened envelope. The final message, as I'd expected, was from Barnabas, sounding peevish: 'You appear to be elsewhere,' it said. 'I am just leaving for the British Library. How is Ben today?'

I was tempted to ring back and leave a message on his machine in turn, saying that the nursery had just realised that Ben was a genius and had therefore entered his name (only fifteen years early) for Oxford entrance; instead I dialled the mystery number.

'Price Rankin Burke.'

Suddenly I remembered. I snapped to attention and

explained that I was returning Dona Helmer's call, and a second afterwards was introducing myself to the confident voice.

It said, 'Ah. It's about your letter of September twenty-first. I'm dealing with Mr Curwen's estate.' There was an audible hesitation. 'I have to apologise for taking a while to get back to you – we've been having problems, though they seem to be resolved now. I wonder whether I could meet you? You have a shop? Could I come there?'

I told her that she could and offered some practical advice about parking; we agreed on two o'clock, which would give me a chance to finish the more urgent business matters, and I hung up and wasted ten minutes trying to guess what she had meant by 'problems'.

The clock function in the computer pinged; at the same instant I stuck down a length of tape on the parcel I was wrapping and heard a metallic tapping noise coming from the front of the shop. The tapper was a woman of about thirty, with expensively cut brown hair, highlighted and shaped smoothly around her jawline, wearing a trouser suit which was just as expensively cut as her hair, and high heels. She held a slim briefcase in one hand and was rapping on the glass of my locked door with a bunch of keys. And she was on time for our appointment – to the second. I went to let her in and directed her towards the office while I locked up again. We settled on opposite sides of the desk.

I said, 'What problems?'

She looked blank for a second. 'Oh – yes! It's just that we weren't able to get access to Mr Curwen's flat for a while.' I asked the obvious question. She shrugged. 'I've no idea, but the police were still "pursuing enquiries".'

I digested that information. A week seemed a long time to be enquiring about a suicide. 'Is something wrong?'

She hesitated. 'You haven't heard? Well, I don't know why you would. There do seem to be some questions. However, they contacted us yesterday to say that they'd cleared up in the flat and we could pick up Mr Curwen's keys from them. My boss popped over first thing this morning to get them and have a quick look around. He wants us to begin work on the probate, and I'm supposed to go over and check the inventory, look for unpaid bills, and find out what we need to clear.'

I let her see that I was puzzled.

'The probate? Mr Curwen's book collection? Well, Mr Burke saw a whole room full of books, so he thought I'd better come and get your advice. If you and I go and pick up your Charles Dickens thing, do you think you could just cast your eyes over his shelves and tell me whether it's worth asking you to do a probate valuation?'

I looked at her. 'If you'll trust me not to make an offer of five hundred pounds for the lot . . .'

She smiled faintly. 'I should warn you that Mr Burke does know about old books himself. He's also a collector. He told me to contact the Antiquarian Booksellers Association and check that you're reputable.'

'And I am?' I asked with interest.

She glanced at me, obviously amused. 'Mr Burke says that I can give you the Charles Dickens right away, if you'll just let us have the original documents of the sale; and he's authorised me to ask you to quote for doing the valuation, since the collection may be worth something. You *do* probate valuations?'

My first impulse was to say that I didn't, although I used to in the old days when business was slower. But it looked like a way for me to get my property back, and I might even decide to make them an offer for some of the other books in his collection. I reminded myself that the fee should be easy money for a couple of hours' work, since I already knew the current values of the kind of books Curwen had liked. I decided to say,

'I can probably give you a rough estimate on the spot. If you decide that you want a formal valuation, I can tell you what I'd charge when I've seen how much work is involved. I know that Curwen bought some books from other people as well as me.'

She nodded. 'Are you free to come with me now?'

I couldn't see why not. Definitely.

4

Gone Away

The porter was still absent when we got to Abbey House. Ms Helmer looked through the inner doors into the hallway, hesitated briefly, shrugged and muttered, 'Just a second.'

I buzzed for the lift while she went over to the bank of letter-boxes, produced a leather key-holder from her briefcase, and unlocked Curwen's box. When she turned back, she was holding two envelopes, one of them mine. She and the lift reached me simultaneously, and we started a slow journey to the top floor. I noticed her reading the safety certificate framed above the emergency button. She was probably checking that it was still valid. I did that too.

The hallway which ran the length of the top floor was wide, clean, thickly carpeted, brightly lit, and punctuated by solid mahogany doors with polished brass numbers. Outside the door marked 502 at the end of the corridor, she produced the key-holder again. Then I noticed her hesitate, and made a guess.

'They did say that they'd cleared the place up?'

She nodded and grimaced, unlocked the heavy door and stepped forward into a square, shadowy space. I followed. The air was stuffy, full of a smell like a mixture of glue and dead plants, a little unpleasant. On the telephone table to our right was a vase with flower stems, surrounded by a drift of dried lily petals. Beside the table, a longcase clock stood silent, its hands stuck at twenty to six.

'We might open a window or two,' she said.

'If we're going to be in here for long,' I agreed politely. I suddenly decided I would tell her that I didn't do probate valuations any more – not this one, anyway. It was just my imagination, of course, but this stuffy old place disturbed me. I only wanted to find my Dickens and get out.

We were standing in a big, square entrance hall. Eight or nine of those heavy mahogany doors were dotted around the walls. The one immediately to our left obviously opened into a cupboard. The next two gave us glimpses of bathroom tiles and a separate WC.

'Shall we?' my companion suggested. She was sounding more subdued with every passing minute.

We went across and poked our heads through the door of a narrow old kitchen, with a wall of cupboards behind old-fashioned glazed doors, a sink, a modern electric cooker, a little fitted fridge, and a tall, narrow window at the far end which opened on to a light well. There was nowhere to sit and eat, and the place looked as though nobody had been doing much cooking here, either. The room next to it was a bedroom, cheaply furnished and unused. It might originally have been the maid's quarters. Next to it we found a big, stuffy room filled with an old-fashioned maple dining suite.

The rooms that stretched along the front of the building were another matter: the doors opened one after the other on to a master bedroom, remarkably tidy by my standards if you ignored the unmade bed; a wide reception room with a thick cream-coloured carpet square laid on parquet and upholstered furniture with down-filled cushions in matching silk; and finally a little study.

This was the place: its walls were lined with books, and an old-fashioned leather-topped desk sat in the middle of the carpet, holding a desk lamp, a blotter and a pile of papers. The room was lit by a pair of big French windows opening on to a shallow balcony. I averted my eyes.

'All right,' I said reluctantly. 'Do you mind if I simply . . . ?'

She shrugged. 'Make yourself at home. I'm here to pick up documents: records, bank statements, bills – that kind of thing. If you come across anything like that, can you point it out to me? With luck, though, it'll be in the desk. Then I just have to check the inventory.'

'Inventory?'

She looked at me. 'It's a rented flat, it belongs to an old lady in New Zealand. I have to check the agents' inventory before we negotiate with them about the balance of the lease.'

'That explains it.'

She looked around us and smiled faintly. 'I think it's nice,' she said. 'It reminds me of my grandparents' house.'

I said, 'I'll just find my book, and then I'll give you an idea about the rest; but I can't do your valuation. There's a lot more stuff here than I was expecting, and I don't really have time. I'll recommend somebody, if you like.' She looked at me with a trace of amusement. I didn't particularly want to tell her that the place felt creepy, so I heard myself point out defensively, 'I have a little boy, and a business to run. Incidentally, I have to be at the nursery to pick him up at five, so if you don't mind . . .' That wasn't strictly true, because Ben's nursery doesn't close until seven; but I usually try to pick him up by five, and it gave me a good excuse to get away.

I was already scanning the spines of the books in the first case. There were six identical modern bookcases in here, plainly built of blond wood which matched nothing else in the flat, so I guessed that they had been Curwen's own property. Each stood six feet high and was nearly three feet wide, and was crammed tight with books: hardback and paperback, old and newish. This might take a little time after all.

Papers rustled. 'He was writing a book.'

I turned and found her holding some of the typed sheets that had been lying on the desk.

After a moment, she added, 'It's a book of etiquette. Would you imagine?'

I went over and found myself staring at a typed sheet headed 'VII. INVITATIONS AND OTHER SOCIAL CORRES-PONDANCE'. The first paragraph began: 'Courtesy demands that a written card or letter should be answered in writing. A telephone call is not' – the text stopped there.

We looked at each other in amazement. I shook my head and she tidied the typescript and placed it in a pile on one corner of the desktop before she opened the shallow central drawer. I caught a glimpse of the usual desk clutter before I turned away.

Six tall bookcases hold a surprising number of books: I'd guess an average of about twenty hardbacks to the shelf, or as many as four dozen paperbacks. Here, the two were mixed in together. In fact, as I saw almost at once, Curwen's collection was so obviously shelved in random order that I had to wonder whether the police had moved every single volume while they were here. The dead man had owned a lot of paperback fiction, most of it old and well read. Those volumes were now scattered amongst thirty-year-old hardbacks, with and without their dust jackets. There were a few volumes by nineteenth-century authors too: I found Carlyle's *Letters on Literature* rubbing covers with a two-volume Browning on one side and a cheap edition of *Jude the Obscure* on the other.

It took me about five minutes to be entirely sure what I was up against.

'Is something wrong?' Ms Helmer asked.

I shrugged. 'This makes no sense. I'm going to have to look along every single shelf until I come across my *Haunted Man*.'

'Your what?'

I laughed at her tone. 'That's the title.'

After a pause, she laughed too. 'I forgot. He wasn't very organised.' She had removed the shallow top drawer and placed it on the desk in order to examine a tangle of bills, papers, ballpoints and credit card slips. Apparently these had benefited from the same organisational methodology as the books. She started sorting things into piles; it was going to take her a while.

'Funny,' she muttered. 'He seems so neat in his living arrangements, and so messy in all this.' She made a rueful face, and we turned to our separate tasks. At one point she left the room, and I heard her opening and closing drawers in the sitting room. By this time I'd more or less come to a halt. When she returned, I watched her transfer a collection of papers and scraps from the desktop to some folders in her briefcase. Then she looked at the envelopes she had retrieved from the letterbox. She added their contents to the collection. One was my letter; the other looked like a phone bill.

She stared at that. 'This is weird: he made exactly two phone calls in the last quarter. Well, I guess this bill won't break the bank.'

'Wait until you find the one for his mobile,' I warned from personal experience, and she laughed.

She produced another folder containing a typed list – the letting agent's inventory – found a pen, and started to move from room to room. I sat down in the chair at the desk and leaned back, trying to decide what to say to her. I swivelled and let my eyes drift over the shelves one more time, though I'd really seen more than enough. I was just trying to avoid admitting the truth to myself. I hadn't found the Dickens. I had found a paperback copy of *Barchester Towers*, though not the first edition which I had sold to Curwen the year before; not *The Way We Live Now*, not the Christmas book, not any of the other books he'd had from me. Not one.

My companion eventually reappeared, replaced the inventory sheets in her briefcase, snapped it shut and looked at me. 'I'm done. Any luck?'

I said, 'I must be missing something. Did *you* see any books in the other rooms?'

She shook her head.

I couldn't work this out, but I'd had enough for the moment. I said, 'I'm sorry, I'm expected at home. I'll have to come back. I'd better call a cab.'

Even then, I knew I should just say, No way, but I hesitated because the whole situation looked so interestingly peculiar. I told her, 'I may as well do the probate valuation for you, but I think I'll need to make several visits – the books are in a mess, and I don't want to miss anything out. I'll probably have to sort and reshelve all the books, and I'll need to be able to come and go in my own time. If that's acceptable, I'll charge your firm three hundred pounds, payable on delivery of my written report. I could finish it in a few days.'

I held my breath. I'd named a sum that was obviously too high for what there seemed to be here: an inflated fee for a job that I half wanted to avoid. I expected her to laugh.

Instead, she shrugged. 'If you'll put that proposal in writing and fax it to the office . . .'

I nodded, tight lipped.

She said, 'Well, I'd better get back and see what I've got here. Can I drop you off at Oxford Circus?'

By late afternoon in the West End, that was probably going to be the quickest way for me to get home: four stations to the Angel via Euston. I said, 'Fine.'

When I got out of her Honda at the Underground, we had reached an understanding. She dropped Tim Curwen's key case into my hand and then drove off down Regent Street. I pushed down the steps into the station, which by this time was swarming with bodies and shopping bags. I was so deep in thought that I'd reached the automatic gates before I remembered that I didn't have a ticket, or change for the machines, and had to turn around and fight my way to the end of the lengthening queue at the ticket window. Waiting there gave me a chance to wonder why I was so uneasy. I could feel the hard lump of Curwen's key case in my pocket. I pulled it out and unsnapped it. It held half a dozen spring clips, with keys attached to three of them: two for the doors of the flat and of the building itself, and the little one for the letterbox in the lobby. The clips seemed to be gold plated: the colour had rubbed away on the edges of the ones that held the three keys, but equally on the inner curves of two of the empty ones. The solicitors or the police must have kept some keys to other parts of Curwen's life. It was *not* my business.

When my turn at the window came, I bought my ticket and then pushed back towards the escalators. I was already fed up – mostly with myself for getting involved in this business, whatever this business might be.

5

What Seems Clear

Barnabas put his teacup on the lamp table by the settee and remarked that it all seemed quite clear to him. When he thought he had kept me waiting for long enough, he added: 'The Dickens isn't there.'

I disagreed with him automatically. 'It could have been on some high shelf where I didn't notice it, or fallen down behind some of the other books, or possibly there's a bookshelf in another room where he kept the best stuff.'

'Possibly.'

But not likely. So then my books had all gone walkabout – including the one he had only just acquired – either before or just after he had killed himself? My mind flickered back to the tiny matter of two missing keys: perhaps he'd had another home – say, a country mansion? Dona Helmer should know. At least I could prove I had sold these books to him, because I had the records.

'You have a theory,' Barnabas noticed, 'or a problem?'

'Is my face so transparent?' I hedged.

'Very nearly. You were thinking . . . ?'

'He killed himself. He was rich, he spent cash like water, and he killed himself. He may have sold all his good books because he was skint.'

'And how long would this debonair young man have been able to live on the proceeds?'

Not long, because he wasn't a professional book dealer and I assumed he'd have no idea where to get the best prices for his collection. A thought struck me. 'He didn't buy all those books from me. He may have dealt with lots of people.'

Barnabas nodded. 'Nevertheless, he couldn't have expected to enrich himself by selling *any* number of books, large or small. What would another dealer have offered for such books? Half of *your* marked prices, possibly? He would have been selling them at a loss. Such a practice would be quite irrational.'

'So it was an emergency.'

'Gambling debts? Something of that sort?'

I could see that a gambler might easily find himself in sudden, desperate need of cash. The problem with this, oddly enough, seemed to be Charles Dickens. It hadn't been a particularly valuable book, and he couldn't really have bought it with the idea of cashing it in. So I began speculating again about that dishonoured cheque. I would ask Ms Helmer whether Curwen had been comprehensively broke when he died.

'Anyway,' I said aloud, 'if worse comes to worst, Price Rankin Burke will be paying me. I've quoted them three hundred pounds for doing the probate. It won't take long to finish, not unless I missed something when I was there. I suppose I'll feel better about this when I get some money, and it will give me a chance—'

'A chance?' Barnabas enquired coolly.

After a second I said, 'A chance to make sure *The Haunted Man* really isn't tucked away somewhere there.' I'd very nearly blurted out, 'A chance to find out what was going on.'

All those missing books were annoying me. It wasn't any of my business, I was just *annoyed*. If I went over there alone I'd be able to poke around; and if that didn't produce any more books I'd ask Dona Helmer whether the solicitors could throw any light on the problem, since my valuation was obviously going to be incomplete.

Barnabas wouldn't appreciate hearing any of this. I know from long experience that my father disapproves deeply whenever I get involved in other people's affairs, and there wouldn't be much use telling him this really wasn't what I intended. He would say that it never is. But this time, I told myself, it was different. This was business. I'd be in and out with my book, or at the worst some compensation, or maybe both. A focused effort. A surgical strike. No messing.

6

If at First

Ernie was half an hour late when he finally arrived with his rucksack in one hand and a takeaway kebab in the other. I beckoned frantically from the office door as he walked in, and he picked up his pace and dodged around the middle-aged history lecturer from a Midlands university who was browsing through the children's books. I noticed without surprise that our customer shrank back.

At first sight my friend and employee, Ernie Weekes, comes across as a hard man. People who do not know him tend to look for the baseball bat. He is black, short, young, broad and very fit, with hair bleached at the moment to an unlikely apricot blond; his dress tends to the baggy military style. This results in his being stopped in the street by the police a little too often, which he takes in better humour than I would. In fact he has never been found carrying anything more illegal than his textbooks – Ernie has started a degree course in computer studies at the university up the road. He works Friday and Saturday nights as a bouncer at a club in Holloway, and he does look more like a security man than an assistant in an antiquarian bookshop. He also works at least two half-days a week in the shop, mostly at my computer, being as underfunded as the next student.

He grinned at me sheepishly. 'Hey, Dido! Sorry – hadda talk to my tutor about my project.' He leaned forward and gave me a resounding kiss, as is his custom nowadays.

I returned it and said, 'I want to pop down to the West End for a while. All right?'

''Course,' he said briefly. 'I only gotta bit o' work to do on our website, no problem. Will I get Ben for you?'

I thought about it. 'If I'm not back before five, yes. I'll leave the keys to the flat in the top drawer here. But I may be back in time.' I hesitated and decided to say it. 'If my father comes in, you have no idea where I am.'

I could see his ears prick up, and for a moment I was tempted to turf my customer out, lock up, and take him with me. Ernie would have been a cheerful presence in Curwen's gloomy flat, not to mention muscle if I needed some bookcases moved. However, evicting one's paying customers is no way to run a business. I shook my head regretfully, told him to give Ben some milk and a biscuit if they did get back before me, grabbed my shoulder bag and ran. I knew he was watching my back. Ernie is getting as sharp as Barnabas at knowing when I'm up to something.

Back at Abbey House, I creaked up to the top floor in the old lift and let myself in to 502. When I flipped the wall switch inside the door, I discovered that the electricity was off. Ms Helmer must have been busy cancelling the utilities. No problem, to quote Ernie. I grabbed the dried remains of the yellow lilies and carried them into the kitchen. The cupboard under the sink held a rubbish bin. Somebody had removed the liner, but I crammed in the rotting vegetation anyway, drained the green slime into the sink and left the vase soaking. The window agreed to stay open. I marched across the hall to the study, dropped my bag on to the desk, dug out a lined pad and a couple of pens, and looked around for somewhere to rest them. A thought struck me, and I went back into the hall, dumped the phone on the floor and carried the little table to a convenient place in front of the first bookcase. Having positioned my pad and pens for action, I glanced at my watch. Nearly 2.30: that was all right.

By the time I'd finished the first bookcase, I knew I was looking at the most unpromising collection of old tat outside of the charity shops.

There were three parts to this job I had planned. I was making only a rough count of the paperbacks. Given the questions that were likely to arise, though, I had decided to list all the hardbacks by author, title and publication date. I found two books in the first case that were worth five pounds each, and made sure that nothing was lurking out of sight behind the rows or between other volumes, because the Dickens is a small volume, easy to miss. As for my Dickens, when I started, I still thought there was just an outside chance that I might find it. By the time I'd gone through five bookcases and wasted five sheets of my paper, I knew it wasn't going to happen. *The Haunted Man* had vanished as completely as though I'd imagined Tim Curwen and all his deeds. I stood with the hairs rising on the back of my neck. Maybe Ms Helmer . . . ? No, she didn't seem to know anything about collectibles; and anyway, there was no sign that they had ever been here.

There was, of course, one obvious place to look for a record of the missing volumes. None of the drawers in the big desk was even locked. Dona Helmer seemed to have removed all the papers, and there wasn't much else. The shallow drawer still contained pens, a couple of coloured pencils, typewriter erasing fluid, and a pocket calculator. The deep filing drawer on the right was empty except for a *Roget* and a dictionary, which I added to my list. The drawers on the left were entirely empty, barring half a ream of expensive typing paper. This seemed to be par for the course.

Eventually I went downstairs to feed the parking meter and came back with a large coffee from a sandwich shop along the road. Then I took another minute off to drink it, standing at the French window, and to ring the shop on my mobile to tell

Ernie that I probably wouldn't manage to get back in time for
Ben after all. I stood there for a while, looking over the edge
of the little balcony with its pots of ivy, thinking of my dead
customer, wondering what he had been up to – because I was
starting to believe he had been up to *something*.

This whole situation made no sense.

When I dropped my empty cup into the wastepaper basket,
it hit the bare metal of the bottom with a sharp thump. I looked
in. Apart from my cup, the wastepaper basket was empty. Just
as the kitchen bin had been.

There was another bin in the bathroom. That had also been
cleared. I went back into the kitchen, looked in the cupboards
and opened the door of the fridge. I wasn't prepared for all the
empty shelves in it, or the smell which was coming from two
cardboard boxes that contained frozen prepared meals.
Somebody had torn both of them open and then crammed
them back into the defrosted ice-making compartment. The
food inside was just starting to grow fuzz.

Curwen had obviously not been a cook. Aside from the
rotting emergency meals, some tea bags and a tin of sardines
– and the half-loaf in the bread bin which had dried into a
lightweight white brick – there was no food. While the police
or the lawyers would have removed all interesting papers, they
wouldn't have carted off packets of herbs, or vinegar, or tinned
tomatoes. At least, I didn't think so. So he must have been
eating out. Well, maybe he belonged to a gentleman's club.

There was, almost literally, nothing except the furniture in
either the smaller bedroom or the dining room. If Curwen had
been born with a silver spoon in his mouth, he hadn't kept it
in his cutlery drawer, which now held two old stainless-steel
forks, three knives and a teaspoon. The shelves in the sideboard revealed two clean glass ashtrays and a pressed-glass
bud vase, all pushed back – and an unopened packet of paper
plates.

In the master bedroom, on the other hand, the chest of drawers was crammed with about three dozen clean white shirts and eight pairs of striped pyjamas. They were all professionally laundered and ironed, protected by clear wrappers, but looked as though they had been thrown into the drawers from a distance. It also appeared that somebody had reached in and stirred the monogrammed handkerchiefs and rolled pairs of black silk socks with a hasty hand. Helmer, yesterday? Had she *really* been counting his socks? Scary. A box on top of the bureau revealed plain cuff links and a tie stud – probably gold plated. A set of real bristle brushes sat beside it. That was all.

I opened one of the mirrored doors of the big mahogany wardrobe and was faced by a rail of those elegant suits and monogrammed blazers that Curwen had been wearing every time I saw him. Somebody had shoved them apart, to both sides, and left them crammed into two tight bunches. I checked the top shelf to see whether any books were hiding there, and found it empty. There wasn't even any dust. This man had so much space in his life that he had an entirely *unused* shelf in his *wardrobe*? I thought coldly of the state of my own cupboards. Then I climbed up on the bed and looked across at the top of the wardrobe. That held a fine layer of reassuring dust, but no books, no boxes or suitcases. I still had nothing.

So I went nosing along, looking for books in drawers, in the living-room sideboard and the tall corner cupboard there, climbing on chairs to look at the tops of the furniture, lying on the carpet to peer under the big sofas. Most of Curwen's drawers and shelves were empty, and I kept seeing tiny signs everywhere that anything which was there had been stirred around by a careless hand.

The place had been searched.

Well, Dido, *of course* it had! The crime scene officers must have done it while they were here. They'd been here for days, according to Helmer. She had said something about them 'clearing up'.

I sank absent-mindedly on to one of the sofas and found myself pleasantly engulfed by down-filled cushions, so that it didn't seem worth struggling up again. I stretched my legs out in front of me and focused on my toes. I wasn't the first person who had looked carefully through Tim Curwen's drawers, but how many others had been here before me? Helmer might have done some of it while she was checking the inventory, but she hadn't taken anything away except papers, or I would have noticed. But why would the police have removed all his possessions? And if they hadn't, then had Curwen been robbed recently by somebody with a key to the place?

Then I remembered seeing one other place where he might have hidden something. I struggled out of my nest and went to discover that the cupboard by the front door did indeed hold not just hooks and coats but lots of other things as well. It would have been nice if the light in there had still been working – I stumbled over a vacuum cleaner hose, regained my balance at the cost of a bruised elbow, and backed out. There was a tiny electric torch on my key-ring, intended for locating keyholes on dark and drunken nights; I didn't use it often these days, so the battery still worked. I went and found it in my bag and, by its faint glow, explored the hooks and shelves, turning up a collection of cleaning materials, a couple of cartons piled on top of one another in a back corner (the top one still held three unopened bottles of California Chardonnay), an empty leather suitcase, the familiar golfing umbrella, an old walking stick, and finally a smart navy Burberry and a full-length cashmere overcoat carefully arranged on hangers. A three-year-old telephone directory of central London business numbers was the nearest thing to a book of any kind. I almost didn't bother to shift the carton with the wine, but at the last minute I peeked into the box below and found the only thing that seemed even remotely interesting: some padded envelopes like the ones that I use when I post a book to a customer. The box was almost empty.

I struggled to pin down a memory. Months ago – yes, it had been some time last winter – I could remember Curwen telling me he wanted to send a book to a friend abroad. I'd given him one of my padded envelopes. When I looked at this box again, I saw that it had come from the same chain of office suppliers that I use. He had actually bought a whole box full of these things – one hundred big, padded envelopes?

There were eleven left.

After a while, I put everything back in place and tried to erase the signs of my search. I shut the door of the cupboard and then thought of fingerprints, my fingerprints everywhere, if anybody wanted to test for them. Only why would they? The police had finished all that business. It couldn't matter. Anyway, if challenged I'd lie.

I pulled myself together. The point was, he had used eighty-nine padded bags. Or even more – there might have been other boxes.

The problem was that I couldn't see where I was going with this discovery. Logic suggested that Curwen had packed up all his best books, at least four or five times the number that I had ever sold him, and sent them . . . somewhere. Logic also said . . .

Dido, my inner critic pointed out, suddenly springing to life and speaking as usual in the voice of my older sister, Pat, *logic – if that's what you'd call what you claim you're using – also says that there is no reason why you should bother about this. It's all gone, even the Dickens. Let's just finish up, get out of this expensive, miserable dump, send in the inventory with an invoice, and hope that the solicitors don't object to paying something for nothing.*

So I decided to give up. And then the doorbell rang in my ear. I squeaked, and froze. After a while, it rang again.

It's the porter. Or Dona Helmer, come to see how the inventory is going. Or maybe a neighbour who heard me moving around in here?

I crept over to the security peephole in the door. There were two callers. The one in front, and clearly visible in that well-lit hallway, was a stranger. Dark suit. Grey raincoat. No distinguishing features. I could just make out that a second figure was lurking behind him. I reminded myself that I had no authority to open this door to anybody, and kept quiet. Then, when the one in front looked sharply at the peephole, I realised that I was probably blocking the light, and it was too late to duck. He reached into an inside pocket. He was pulling something out and holding it up flat in front of the door.

Warrant card.

I opened up.

7

Interview

The name on the card was 'Kevin S. Smith' – S for 'suspicious'. Or maybe 'sulky'? The detective constable was a sharp-eyed, scowling thirty-year-old. His colleague was an older man with five o'clock shadow who for some strange reason barked, 'Wait!' at me and then stood around looking depressed.

I told them my name when Smith asked for it and added, 'Can I help you?' in a voice as duchess-like as I could manage. We were still in the doorway. I watched the constable's gaze dart past me, taking in the open cupboard door and looking for other signs that I'd been ransacking the place.

'You'd better tell us what you're doing here.'

I was tempted but resisted. My choice settled on the accurate but uninformative phrase 'Probate inventory'.

'Probate?' They exchanged a glance.

I said, 'The tenant here has died.'

For some reason, that annoyed them. The constable barked, 'On whose authority?'

I managed not to laugh by lifting my chin and barking back, 'Price Rankin Burke. And you? You must know why I'm here. The solicitors have been in touch with your people.'

Smith remained dubious. 'The porter gave us a ring and said that somebody was in the flat. I don't think that you should be in here. This is a crime scene. The executors are moving already?'

I thought it was time to distract the two of them and looked for respite by saying masterfully, 'Shall we go in and sit down?'

and leading the way into the sitting room. That gave me an excuse to avert my face from them while I was thinking, *Crime scene?* I directed them with a hostess-like wave to one of the settees, lowered myself into a nearby armchair, then noticed that although the older man had seated himself directly opposite me and was staring at the wall above my head, the younger one was over by the window now with his mobile phone poised.

'How do you spell that name?'

I spelled it.

'Date of birth?'

I raised my eyebrows and agreed to play along. He pushed a button. Without any greeting, he snapped, 'Smith. Run a check: D-i-d-o surname H-o-a-r-e. Female. Four, four, sixty-six.' There was a long silence while we all stared at each other. Because I was watching closely I noticed the constable's deepening frown, but that was the only sign that betrayed the fact that what he was hearing had surprised him. He snapped, 'Thanks,' and clipped the phone back on to his belt. We went on staring at each other. He hadn't been taking up my references with the solicitors, that was clear, and it made me wish I knew what my entry on the police national computer actually said. I waited them out.

Eventually Smith said to me and his companion equally, 'That's all right,' and wandered across to the settee, running his eyes around the room as he went. I'd closed the doors and drawers after my hunt. There was nothing to catch his attention.

I said stiffly, 'I don't know what you meant by "crime scene". Suicide was decriminalised years ago.'

Smith reached into a pocket and pulled out some cigarettes. Then he looked at me. 'All right if I smoke?'

I shrugged. 'Not my house. What exactly are you saying about it being a "crime scene"?'

'It is,' he pointed out, considering his half-empty pack at

length, 'the scene of an unexplained death. The investigation isn't closed, and your lot must know that.'

I hoped he was assuming that I was a real member of the law firm. He delayed things by offering his cigarettes to the two of us and lighting his own, drawing deeply, looking thoughtful.

'I was told you were finished in here,' I said carefully. 'Look, I'm having a problem – perhaps you can help me? I see that somebody's searched this place.'

He looked blank. The second man said, 'We had the forensic team in.'

Well, of course they had. I returned to the struggle. 'Did they take anything out of the study?'

They both looked at me as though I were half-witted – which put my back well up. Of course they had.

I took a deep breath and said to the space between them, 'There are some valuables missing, and I've been asked to locate them. I want to know whether your people removed a number of books from the shelves in the study.'

Smith repeated, '*Books?*' in a blank way that suggested he knew nothing about books, that he was one of those men who call magazines 'books', that he himself filled any shelves he might accidentally own with back issues of *Loaded*. The other one just went on looking at the wall.

This was hard work. 'Mr Curwen collected valuable antiquarian books,' I said very, very clearly. 'Very little of his collection is still in this flat. I am supposed to be valuing those books, and they are missing.'

'And they're worth money?'

I remarked that I wouldn't know that until I'd found them, but that it would be a question of thousands.

'So there may have been a theft,' Smith said, glancing sideways at the older man, and got to his feet with sudden enthusiasm.

I said, 'Wait! I'm not saying that this has only just happened, or that it has anything to do with your investigation, whatever that's about.'

'Why?'

I got to my feet too, playing cool. 'Because although I know he owned those books, there's no sign that they were ever even here: there are no empty spaces on the shelves, for instance.' I had just made the snap decision not to be more forthcoming, because I kept remembering that I was the person who had the keys to the place and had been casually spreading fingerprints about where they had no business. Some day I'll work out why the mere presence of a policeman always makes me feel that I've done something wrong. 'It's not as though somebody came in and knocked him over the head and then walked out with them in a suitcase. They could have gone months ago, or over a period of time.' Except the one that I knew about which had been in his possession for only a few days when he died, and that seemed to be missing too.

Smith lost some of his urgency, but remained standing. 'Mind showing us?'

I led the way to the study and turned around to look at the two men as soon as I was through the door. They both turned straight to the nearest bookcase without looking around at all, so I deduced that this wasn't the first time they had been here; they had obviously been part of the team which had investigated Curwen's death. This could explain why the police dispatcher had sent the two detectives over here – not people from the uniformed branch – when the porter phoned them about an intruder. All right. Then I remembered to say, 'You see?'

'You moved them at all?'

I said sweetly, and without pausing between my sentences, 'Of course! I told you, I'm doing the inventory. What happened when Mr Curwen died?'

Smith continued to run his eyes over the shelves. 'They must have looked at them,' he mumbled. 'You're right, there aren't any spaces.'

'Judging by the mess,' I said coldly, 'your people must have pulled everything off the shelves at some point. Do you know why he killed himself?'

His eyes slid to the desk, to my face, then back to the enigmatic bookcases. 'I hear he typed out a suicide note and then jumped off the balcony.'

I'd been given the thinnest possible outline of the published version, but the older man had a coughing fit.

'There was a note? Did he say why he did it?'

Smith shrugged. 'I think he just wrote something like "I can't stand it, I'm sorry." Look, we have to get back, but I don't know about leaving you here . . .'

'You're welcome to stay and watch,' I told the two men graciously, 'but I have my work to finish. I'll be ready to leave in a little while.' I couldn't see them carting me off in handcuffs. 'You'd better phone Price Rankin Burke, if you need them to tell you I'm authorised. Ask for Miss Helmer. But we got the keys from you people, so you should already know about all this. You *are* stationed at Seymour Street, I assume?'

There was another of those exchanges of looks, and then Smith mumbled, 'All right, I'll check with the Superintendent.' But we both knew that I was in the clear and that they had no time to hang around and be obnoxious.

When they left, I unbolted the French windows and stepped out between the pots of ivy. After a minute or two, the pair reappeared below me on the steps. The older one glanced up. I gave him a little wave. He nodded almost imperceptibly, and then the two of them walked to a car parked on double yellow lines at the corner. Smith got into the driver's seat. I went on watching until they had gone. Then I scraped a stray bit of potting compost off my shoes and went back inside. It was almost 4.30, getting too dark to do much more without having any lights to turn on, but there was only one bookcase left and I decided I'd try to get the job done. There was nothing in this dank, empty place that made me want to come back.

I moved grimly to the last shelves and started to count paperbacks on the top shelf. Four, eight, ten, a tick on the pad. And again. And again. I had given up on *The Haunted Man*: now I was just finishing the job I'd been hired to do.

I was kneeling on the carpet looking along the last shelf at the bottom of the final bookcase, and even in the deepening shadows I could see that something was wrong: the books at one end of this row were standing proud of the rest. I grabbed a handful of them, dropped them on the floor, reached in, and felt a smooth, yielding surface. It wasn't what I'd been expecting. I pulled a few more books out on to the parquet and edged out one of those padded envelopes. It was unsealed and unaddressed. When I slid my hand in and touched a book, I knew it at once. Carefully I slid the little volume with its red cloth cover and gilt spine out of its protective bag. It looked as though *The Haunted Man* had come to no harm in its hiding place on a bottom shelf – the most difficult shelves to examine unless you get down on hands and knees as I had. I heaved a sigh, pushed it back in its padded envelope and placed my recovered property safely in my bag.

And then I finished my job.

It was just after five o'clock. The low clouds over central London had brought an early nightfall, and there was no point my hanging around in the deepening gloom. I circled through the rooms for the last time, checking that I'd left nothing out of place. When I shone the tiny key light around the sitting room, it winked for a moment on metal: a pound coin lying on the settee where the two policemen had been sitting. I retrieved it and dropped it on a side table. Then I went on, taking a final look at the place where my good customer had lived and died.

I had found nothing of him here except the extravagant clothes, and I somehow thought that you couldn't count those. Clothes don't always make the man. I did wonder briefly which charity shop was going to receive the windfall.

In the kitchen, I remembered to shut the window and then stood among the empty cupboards, listening to the tap dripping in the sink. What was really strange, of course, was the impersonality of these rooms. The flat suddenly made me think of a TV set – something dressed by a film crew, not the place where a real person had been engaged in the untidy business of living. Not this place . . .

I stood still and said to the cooker, 'He didn't really live here.' There were the clothes, of course, but they only reinforced my feeling that this flat was not a home but a . . . a what? An actor's dressing room? I grappled with this insight and got nowhere.

I was halfway to the front door when I suddenly remembered where I *had* in fact seen something of Curwen himself. I turned aside into the study and picked up the thirty or forty sheets of his typescript. Tim Curwen had spent his next-to-last minutes working on a book of etiquette. As soon as I'd written up my report, I would read it and try to understand why he had sat working on this, and then got up and jumped. Which, you might even argue, was very ill mannered of him. I could drop the typescript back here on the way to deliver the keys and my paperwork to the offices of Price Rankin Burke. Nobody could possibly mind if I just borrowed it to read.

8

Something from the Horse's Mouth

Out in the corridor, I was turning back to check that the door had shut properly behind me when a voice spoke. 'He's dead.'

I whirled around, heart thumping, and recognised the round glasses of the little boy I had seen at a window on my first visit. He must have been hiding in the stairwell, and he had popped out like a ghost between me and the lift.

I said, 'I know. What's your name?'

He moved towards me then, stopping very close. 'Tim. The same as him. Isn't that interesting? What's your name?'

'Dido.'

'I've never heard of that name before,' he said, after thinking about it for a moment.

I agreed that it was quite unusual. 'You live downstairs, don't you? I saw you looking out of the window the other day. Don't you go to school?'

'Not at the moment,' he said politely. 'I'm waiting for a place.'

I looked at him hard and revised my original idea: despite a rather adult expression, he looked too small to be ten. His hair was mousey brown and neatly cut. His face was pale – unhealthy; the thick lenses magnified his eyes. He was dressed in an old-fashioned, adult-looking shirt under a V-necked pullover, and blue jeans, all unnaturally neat.

'I'm partially sighted,' he said. 'That means I'm not quite blind. I have about twenty per cent vision in my left eye, and

I can see quite a lot when the light's strong. I saw you when you came in downstairs. I can see you now.'

'That's bad luck,' I said carefully. 'Have you always had poor sight?'

'I think so.'

'And you haven't been to school yet?'

'I live with Grandma, and she teaches me. I know Braille, and I'm learning music. But there's a lot more for me to study, so I have to go. It's a boarding school. I'm not too keen. Are you the person who's been in Tim's flat all the time? Are you from Scotland Yard? Could I go inside?'

I dodged the first two questions and said, 'I'm not sure. Why do you want to? There's nothing there to see – to find, you know.'

'He was my friend,' the boy said as though that settled it.

Was he now? I thought quickly and said, 'Did the two of you spend much time together? What did you talk about?'

'He told me stories. Gangsters and criminals and big parties, how he met the Queen and how he once had to run away from his enemies and hide, and how he was going to buy a hotel on a tropical island. Things like that.'

I almost laughed at the picture of the elegant Curwen telling true-crime fairy stories, but I stopped myself because I didn't want the boy to misunderstand. 'So the two of you just talked? You didn't play any kind of games or anything?'

'What kind of games?' the boy asked. Then his tone changed. 'He wasn't a *pervert*, you know!'

Ouch! I said carefully, 'I didn't think he was. I knew him too. He used to buy books at my bookshop, and I thought he was nice.'

'He *was* nice,' the younger Tim assured me, 'and he had an awful lot of books.'

But you couldn't read them, could you, so there were the stories. I said, 'It's very dark in there now – the electricity's been turned off.' I bit my tongue. Quick thinking, Dido! I said quickly, 'I was just leaving, but you can go in with me for a second, if you like.' He nodded solemnly. I unlocked the door again, swung it open, and said, 'Go on.'

Without hesitation he turned to his right and went through the study door. I followed. He moved confidently in the dim light until he ran into the little table and reached down to touch it. 'That belongs in the hall.'

I said, 'You're right. I forgot I'd left it there. I moved it to put some papers and pens on. I was listing his books, you see, so I needed a little table.'

He stepped back and said, 'That's all right. I just didn't notice it.'

'But you're right,' I echoed politely. 'I'd better put it back where it belongs.' I stepped around him, picked the table up, and went to dump it in its old position. I was watching him so hard in the light filtering through from the corridor that I almost ran into the edge of the door. He was walking around the bookcases, the tips of his fingers trailing lightly along the spines of the books. When he came to the French windows, he stopped sharp and turned away. Then he moved over to the desk and touched it. He ran a hand lightly along the back of the chair.

I said on impulse, 'Would you like to have one of his books to remember him by?' A thin thread of light struck a couple of the shelves, and I saw something there. 'There's this one. It's called *The Thirty-Nine Steps*. It's a good story – about spies and adventures, and the hero called Richard Hannay is running away from the villains.' I grabbed the little book and put it into his hand. He clutched it. It was just a water-stained sixth impression; if Price Rankin Burke wanted to argue, I'd subtract ten pence from my bill.

'Tim was going to run away too,' the younger Tim said, 'but I guess he was too late.'

'I think he wasn't very happy,' I said. I suppressed the thought that he *had* in fact fled from whatever had been troubling him.

'He was all right,' my companion asserted, 'except just for a while before he got killed. Then he was pretty sad.'

I repeated stupidly, 'Before he got killed?' My voice sounded odd, even to me.

The boy was silent, clutching his book in both hands.

As soon as I was sure I could speak normally, I added delicately, 'You mean somebody *killed* him? I didn't know about that. How did it happen?'

He sounded reluctant when he said, 'He had a fight with some men.'

I wouldn't believe him yet. 'How do you know?'

'I heard them.'

I relaxed a little. 'Mr Curwen and somebody else?'

'Two other men.'

'When? Were they arguing?'

'The night they killed him.' The voice was growing more and more reluctant. 'They were all shouting and hitting. They said "fuckin-fuckin" all the time, "fuckin-bastard".' I could see him cock his head, waiting for my reaction. Grandma wouldn't approve of that language.

Quietly, Dido. The way you'd be with Ben. If Ben . . .

'Weren't you frightened? Where were you?'

He shifted uneasily, but I was standing between him and the open door. 'I was outside there, in the hall. In front of the door. I heard them.'

'They must have been awfully loud,' I said, trying to keep my tone neutral. 'These flats have thick doors.'

He was silent.

'But was this late at night?' I asked him, thinking harder. 'You weren't in bed?'

'It wasn't so late. I thought I'd walk around. I do quite a lot of exploring. Grandma was asleep when I came out, but I have a key. I heard Tim's big clock strike eleven o'clock while I was here.'

Clock? I remembered the longcase clock in the hallway. That was what he meant. Even if he had miscounted, even if it had chimed twelve times, or ten, he had to be roughly right about the time.

'You won't tell anybody I wasn't in bed, will you?'

'Why would I tell anybody? So you came up here to talk to Tim?'

He nodded.

'And you were outside the door, and you heard people arguing?'

'They were shouting.' He looked straight at me. 'I'm not deaf, you know, I heard them.'

I nodded, realised how useless that was, and said, 'All right. Then what did you do?'

He lowered his head and seemed to be staring at my feet. Silence.

After I'd waited for a while, I said softly, 'It scares me when men are fighting like that. I think if I'd been here I'd have wanted to run away and pretend I'd never heard anything.'

He said, 'I'd better go now. Gran may be looking for me.' I stepped aside and watched him march past me. In the hallway, he barely hesitated long enough to say, 'Thanks.' I wasn't sure whether for the book or something I'd said.

I said, 'That's all right,' and watched him walk down the corridor without hesitating and vanish into the stairwell. He was walking steadily, giving the impression that he was forcing himself to take his time.

Thinking about it, I asked myself whether it was possible to believe a word of his story. It had come from a little boy who couldn't see much, who with luck was too young to have had any experience of adult arguments, and who probably compensated for his blindness by a vivid imagination. His story fitted nothing that I knew about Curwen.

The problem, as I realised even while I was still telling myself that I'd just been treated to the lurid product of childish storytelling, was that a part of me wanted to believe his every word.

This whole business was starting to bug me.

9

In Case of Death

'What do you think you're doing?' Barnabas asked in a tone of voice that made Ben look up wide eyed from his sliced banana and yoghurt. 'I beg your pardon,' my father added hastily, though not to me.

I glared at him and said, 'I don't know.'

Oddly enough, that seemed to mollify him. He gave me something approaching a smile. 'This man – are we sure that he killed himself?'

I decided to assume he was using the royal 'we'. 'Everybody says so; but we are starting to wonder . . . well, not wonder, exactly . . . just—'

'Well, *I* have more than started,' Barnabas asserted loudly. 'His death resembles the classic suicide, and suicide was certainly what was implied by the newspaper notice. But when you inform me of the curious absence of anything that might be described as a collector's library, I become puzzled. When you throw out the speculation that an assortment of everyday items is missing from his flat, I do become curious. When you describe a conflict with two bad-tempered CID men, I become even somewhat alarmed. For a member of the middle classes, by the by, your running battle with the police continues to alarm and . . .'

'It is not a "running battle",' I muttered, and was ignored.

' . . . amaze me. But in this instance one man's attitude sounded slightly . . . curmudgeonly? Unless you forgot to mention that you had attacked them with a chair on their arrival? At any rate, while I was in the library today I thought I would see whether the newspapers offered any insight.'

'And do they?'

My father growled, 'Perhaps.'

Ben was sitting at the kitchen table, chattering about school and at the same time eating his supper, with messy consequences. I sat beside him with a cup of tea, and my father stood flattened against the sink, the only space left in this tiny room for anybody who wanted to keep Ben company and at the same time berate me. He left us abruptly, marched down the hall to the sitting room, and returned with his old briefcase, from which he was extracting a big A3 photocopy. He handed it over: a page from a newspaper displaying a small, rather fuzzy photograph of a familiar face and a large one of a familiar block of flats.

I said, 'What's this?'

'A background piece,' my father said. 'It was published two days ago. Keep it. Read it and see if it says anything to you. I'm going home.'

'You could stay,' I said slowly, my eyes on the headline, DEATH OF AN OLD-FASHIONED GENTLEMAN. 'I could cook something.'

'No – I feel the need for a little quiet thought,' my father said. 'I'd recommend it to you.'

Having won the debate, he placed a benevolent hand on Ben's head and then, to my amusement, on mine. And left.

Later on, I lay in my bed, wrapped in the duvet and listening for a break in the soft breathing across the room which would suggest that Ben was awake. I myself had woken a minute ago and switched off the lamp that was still burning on my bedside table. Oddly enough, turning out the light sometimes seems to rouse Ben. Not tonight.

I'd fallen asleep over Tim Curwen's typescript. He had

entitled it *Etiquette: a Guide to Manners in the Twenty-First Century*. But it read like a jolly jape, and I'd skimmed the pages with growing bewilderment. Curwen had roughed out six short chapters and the first lines of a seventh, covering a variety of topics in no special order under such chapter headings as 'Death and Bereavement', in which he discussed the style of dress expected of those attending funerals; 'Relations with Servants', urging courtesy for the downtrodden and humble (obviously a bad joke); and 'The Social Importance of Schooling', which basically suggested that there is no place like Eton and Harrow, although their exam results are no longer of the very highest rank, and that Oxford is a more genteel university than Cambridge. His description of life at Oxford bore no resemblance to my own experience, though we must have been undergraduates at almost the same time: it read as though he had lifted it from the pages of *Zuleika Dobson*. The whole thing seemed about as relevant to the twenty-first century as Bertie Wooster's journal. Even the spelling was dubious. Curwen had been just the kind of person for whom the modern computer's spell-checker was invented. Unfortunately, he had been using a typewriter.

After a while I got up and crept down the passage to the kitchen. There was a little coffee still warm in the machine; I made it colder by dropping in the smallest acceptable quantity of milk and carried the mug into the sitting room. The street outside was empty, wet, silent. I pulled the curtains, switched on a reading lamp, looked uselessly at my naked wrist and then at the clock over the fireplace, which had stopped, and guessed from the comparative absence of traffic noises that it must be three or four o'clock in the morning.

Barnabas's photocopy was on the desk where I had left it when I put Ben to bed. I carried it to the settee with my cool coffee. *Death of* . . .

The piece appeared over an unfamiliar byline. Its author

was somebody called Christopher Kennedy, and I wondered whether he was a freelancer, because the way he described 'man-about-town Timothy Curwen' suggested that he had been a part of Curwen's social circle. I reread four columns of nothing: Curwen's clothes, Curwen's artistic temperament, Curwen's literary ambitions, his work-in-progress on modern etiquette – with Curwen's anachronistic concern for the polite way to eat a banana, which seemed not very modern – Curwen's hand-made shoes, Curwen's taste in opera, Curwen's socialite friends and their bewilderment at his suicide – no names mentioned. There was no reference to surviving relatives. Bearing in mind the same lack in the death notice, this again suggested to me that he'd had none. Nothing was said about how Curwen had earned his living. I could only speculate that he hadn't needed to.

There were no *facts*. It was just as though my good customer had doubled in life as the Invisible Man. Actually, there was nothing either to explain why anybody had bothered to compose this particular article, much less publish it. I was beginning to think of Curwen as a kind of shadow on the wall.

When I found myself yawning uncontrollably, I surrendered. I had to be up in a couple of hours to get Ben ready for nursery. On my way home I meant to stop off at the newsagent's and photocopy Curwen's typescript before I returned the original. Call it a souvenir.

10

Next to Nothing

Price Rankin Burke occupied the whole of an elegant Georgian building just off Piccadilly. I gave my name to a woman in reception, who rang to warn Dona Helmer of my arrival and then sent me up to the third floor in a lift that was modern, smooth and totally without creaks. Helmer was waiting for me at the door. I felt in my bag, pulled out the envelope I'd prepared, and handed it over.

'You aren't going to like this. There's something I'd better explain.'

She accepted my offering and led the way along the corridor to a door which had her business card tucked into a little holder, as though her tenure was a temporary one. Her office was a modest room with blond wood furniture and a window that overlooked two rain-sodden patches of grass with a low brick wall between them, and the back of a terrace of tall buildings in the next street. We settled at the desk, and she tore open my envelope and tipped Curwen's keys on to her blotter. My invoice was attached by a paper-clip to my report.

'This is for a hundred and fifty pounds, Miss Hoare. We agreed three hundred.'

'I've knocked fifty per cent off,' I admitted sheepishly. 'For one thing, it took less time than I was expecting, and as it happens I found my book while I was there. I've put Curwen's bad cheque in the envelope with my copy of the original invoice, by the way. Aside from that, you'd better read my report.'

She blinked, frowned, smoothed one side of her nicely cut hair with an automatic gesture, and started to read what I'd written without appearing too upset. When she came to the end she looked up. 'So if it were sold, the whole collection would fetch about . . . ?'

'Nothing,' I said. That was an exaggeration, but not by much. 'Next to nothing. As I've said, almost all his good books, the books I sold him, are missing. What's still in the flat – well, there are a few dozen volumes worth a couple of pounds each, but most of it's rubbish. I've listed every book that's worth anything at all, by author and title, and I've given a conservative estimate for what they might bring. There's so much I was expecting to find that's actually missing, I thought I'd better be more detailed than I normally would. By the way, when you go back there you'll see that I've moved all those listed titles together into one bookcase. I thought that might make it easier for you. There are a couple of thousand old paperbacks as well, which I've counted. I've given them a value of fifty pounds here, but the right kind of second-hand bookshop might pay a couple of hundred, because there are lots of classics – books that students might buy.'

I watched her turn again to the sum written on the final page and take it in. She frowned. 'What happened?'

I shrugged. 'I can't say, because I found no records there at all. Was there anything about his books in those papers you took away?'

She frowned again and shook her head.

'Well, do you want to know what I think?'

She nodded.

I told her about the box of padded envelopes, and we looked at each other speculatively.

'Let me be sure I understand: you think that he packed up all the valuable books and sent them off somewhere?'

'It looked like that. You saw how the bookcases are full of

old reading copies – second-hand paperbacks, mostly.' I almost told her that I'd even started to wonder whether they had been bought specially to fill up the holes in the collection, but I had no evidence of that. Curwen, I reminded myself forcefully, *liked* reading. 'There are no empty spaces: so the one thing that he *didn't* do was pack them all up and send them off just before he killed himself. Can I ask you something?'

She nodded, not taking her eyes off my report.

'Did he have another property somewhere? A country house, or some other place where he might have kept the books?'

She dismissed that with a curt 'No'.

'Then was he broke?'

She looked up at that, and I could see her hesitate and search for words. 'I don't quite see it. He obviously spent money like water and yet, despite that, his bank account wasn't usually overdrawn, or not for more than a few days at a time. He paid his rent by standing order, on the dot – that flat costs five hundred and fifty a week. At the moment, I'm trying to trace his assets, and I've only just started looking. But I've already told my boss that something must be missing.' She paused before she added, 'He doesn't seem to have bothered keeping any records. I've even started to think that we won't have to go to probate on this.'

'Where did his money come from originally? Was it family money? There was nothing about his background in the death notice I saw. Who inherits?'

'Mr Burke says that Mr Curwen had a sister. I guess she's going to be upset when she hears about the missing books.'

Quite likely. I was glad that it wasn't down to me to explain things.

We parted in a friendly way, with my offer of help if any problems came up about my report and her promise that she would pass my invoice on to the accounts department. If she suspected me of some kind of sharp practice, she was careful not to let it show. In her place, I would have been more suspicious, especially after I'd heard that the Dickens had turned up after all. I was simply hoping there wouldn't be any unpleasantness. On the way down in the lift I had a few private moments to thank my stars one more time that I hadn't been alone when I entered Curwen's flat on that first afternoon.

You can't be lucky all the time, of course. My time on the parking meter had expired twenty minutes earlier, and there was an excess payment notice taped firmly to my windscreen. Time to call it a day with this whole Curwen business. Past time.

It wasn't until I got back to the shop that I remembered Curwen's manuscript still sitting in the bottom of my office desk, where I had also dumped the padded envelope with my Dickens. I'd been in too much of a hurry to get rid of the inventory. It looked as though I was going to have to confess my nosiness to Dona Helmer. I slammed the drawer shut on the evidence and sat there feeling stupid. Damn!

11

A Carrot for the Donkey

It was ten o'clock the next morning when I finally wandered down into the shop, and by that time the light was already winking on my answering machine.

A man's voice spoke, strong, very brisk and a little flat, with a touch of Yorkshire in it: 'Message for Miss Hoare. This is Lloyd Burke, of Price Rankin Burke, at eight thirty a.m. I'd be grateful if you'd meet me here in my office today at one fifteen sharp, Miss Hoare. You know where I am. I apologise for this short notice, but it looks urgent – thank you for your report, by the way: it's thorough. I'm in court this morning, so there's no point ringing to say you aren't available. If you haven't arrived by one twenty, I'll contact you later.' There was a little pause. 'I asked them to have your cheque waiting.'

That last sentence made me laugh: a carrot for the donkey. I spent a few minutes trying to list all the reasons why I didn't want to waste any more time on Curwen, and then admitting that I was done for. By five past one I had abandoned the van in the safety of a multistorey carpark about half a mile from my goal.

A notice on the unoccupied desk in the reception area said 'Back in five minutes'. I was just wondering how to find him when the lift door opened.

He was a big man, several inches over six foot, with broad shoulders, wonderfully bushy eyebrows and black hair that showed no traces of grey, although his tanned, lined face said he was well into middle age. He thrust out a hand. 'Miss Hoare? Glad you could make it. You haven't been waiting? I had to send the girl off to get me a document. Let's go up to my office and talk.'

He swept me into the lift, and we mounted in silence to the floor above, where Burke's office – guarded by his secretary's anteroom, also deserted at this lunch hour – took up most of the front of the building. He motioned me into a leather armchair in front of a low table, and loomed overhead.

'I'd like to offer you tea or coffee, but my secretary's at lunch. Can I get you a drink? Sherry?'

Burke was making me feel distinctly underdressed in my jeans and leather jacket. In these circumstances, there is only one thing that a lady can do. I said primly, 'I'd rather a Scotch, if you have it.'

He cast me a blank look and lumbered towards the drinks cabinet in a far corner. 'Single malt?'

'That would be fine,' I said. 'Just a drop of water, if you have it.' He produced an unopened bottle of Malvern water. Naturally. We settled with our cut-crystal whisky tumblers and looked at each other cautiously.

There was a sealed envelope on the table, my name typed on it. He gestured. 'Your cheque.'

I nodded and didn't touch it. 'Thank you. But you could have mailed it to me, so I assume you want to talk about the missing books.'

I watched my bluntness unsettle him, and couldn't imagine why. He was the one who had been making busy-busy noises. Perhaps he expected ladies to be more relaxed?

'Right, then: I'd like to hire you, on retainer, to locate Curwen's collection and, if possible, retrieve it for the estate.' I asked the obvious question, which he shrugged off impatiently. 'Because you knew Curwen and his books – or parts of his collection, anyroad, and your ideas sound sensible. You're an antiquarian book dealer, and a reputable one. I got one of your catalogues from a firm I deal with myself. I've checked up on you, you understand, otherwise I wouldn't be making this offer. So: you know the market, you know where to start looking. The police wouldn't move on this unless they knew the books were stolen, and even then they'd not know enough to get far. There's a second cheque in that envelope.' He glanced at it for the third time. 'As I said, a retainer. You'll have expenses. Keep your chits and submit your claims: I'll cover any reasonable amount. Give me a detailed progress report by . . . say, Wednesday next week? After I hear from you, I'll consider the next step. Can you do it?'

Maybe. That might depend.

'There are a few things I could try,' I told him. 'Will you answer some questions?'

He looked at his Rolex. 'Five minutes.'

'Did you handle Tim Curwen's business personally? Or did he deal with somebody else in your firm who may know something?'

'The firm acted for him in small things. Checked the lease for his flat, wrote his will – a few things. Various people dealt with him.'

'Did you ever talk to him about the books? You're also a collector?'

'We didn't discuss that. We only met once or twice.'

Apparently I had stumbled across the only two collectors in the Western world who didn't spend all their time together boasting about their bargains and moaning about their mistakes.

'In round figures, Mr Burke, what is the estate worth? Are these books likely to be a large part of its value?'

He looked at me. 'I don't see that matters here.' Translation: mind your own business.

I said without smiling, 'It's so I'll have some idea how much to charge you. If I agree to do this.'

He didn't find me funny. He looked away and said impatiently, 'At present we have no idea.'

'Then do you at least know why his bank bounced that last cheque he gave me?'

'Since you ask – yes. The manager says Curwen withdrew every penny from his account, in cash, right up to his five thousand overdraft limit, first thing on the Tuesday morning.'

I looked at him and he looked back blandly. I was wondering whether the cash had been in the flat when the police had first arrived. For a fleeting moment I also wondered why Curwen had needed so much cash to die with, but then another question bobbed up.

'I heard that his sister inherits? Do you mind if I contact her, in case she knows anything about the books?'

'I don't think Miss Helmer has been able to contact her. We may have an old address. Curwen said they weren't in touch. We'll have an address in the file. I'll tell Dona to look for it as soon as she has a minute.'

'Next, how did he earn his living?'

Burke looked at me. He hesitated. 'As far as I know, he didn't. Family money, maybe.'

Maybe? It was the sort of information you would expect an executor to have at his fingertips.

He nodded, as though to acknowledge my doubts. 'We're looking for records of investments and other bank accounts. Miss Helmer was asked to pick up all the financial documentation from the flat.' I nodded back at him: I had seen her doing it. 'Well, there wasn't much. We may have to advertise. Meantime, we'll need your report.'

'You don't think that the police might have kept some records that they removed from the flat?'

'They've given us a list of what they have. There were

no books or papers on the list, barring the suicide note.'

'Do you have any objection if I talk to them?'

He looked at me again. 'Not if you think it will help trace those books. I can give you the name of the man I dealt with.'

He took a thin black leather notebook from an inside pocket, scribbled on the top page with a slim gold pen that looked like a twig in his big hand, tore the sheet out and handed it to me. There was a name, rank and phone number. I put it down beside my envelope.

'Please, open the envelope,' he said again. He watched me lever the flap up. There were four things inside: a cheque for £150, a second one for £750, a card, and a sheet of the firm's stationery headed *To Whom It May Concern*, introducing me as representing the law firm of Price Rankin Burke and stating that they would be grateful if I could be rendered 'all possible assistance' with my enquiries on their behalf.

Ten days, he'd given me. With a bit of luck, it needn't take nearly that long to exhaust the lines of enquiry. Ernie and my computer would do most of the work; they had chased down missing books for me before now. I already had some other ideas – nothing that wasn't obvious to somebody in the trade.

'Sorry to rush you,' he said, standing up.

I stood up too, retrieved the cheques and the 'To Whom' letter, and pushed them back into the envelope. I said, 'There's one last thing. I may have to get access to the flat to check something or other. Will you contact the porter and tell him to let me in?'

He hesitated for a second, walked over to his big mahogany desk, and reached into a drawer. When he returned, he held Tim Curwen's leather key case. Taking it from him felt like shaking hands on the deal, and I still wasn't sure why I'd let myself agree unless it was so I could sneak Curwen's embarrassing typescript back where it belonged.

'I'll ring you if I have more questions?'

He said, 'I'm handling this personally. Contact me as soon as you make any progress. Keep me up to date. I've left my card in the envelope with the number of my mobile.' I looked inside; so he had.

We walked each other out of the building. I turned left, he turned right.

12

Midnight

Just before midnight, the skies opened. It had been a strange September so far, with unseasonable warmth and occasional torrential downpours; Barnabas had taken to muttering darkly about global warming and British monsoons, and reminiscing about the trip to India that he and my mother had taken the summer before my sister was born. I was still downstairs at the office computer, and it struck me how loud the rain sounded on the old flat roof of the office extension. If that were to start leaking some time when I was elsewhere . . .

My search had taken me two afternoons plus two late nights – after I'd finished talking to Ben and watching him fall asleep. My next phone bill would be staggering, and my own sleep deficit was mounting. But I had been successful – within limits.

I'd begun by searching the usual websites and putting up a wants list of my own, which consisted of four of the most valuable books that I'd sold to Curwen. I'd run his *Barchester Towers* to ground in Boston almost immediately, where it was being offered at nearly twice the money I'd got for it. Ouch. From the description of a repaired hinge and a bookseller's label, there was no doubt that this was the right copy. Ever since I'd located it, I'd been exchanging e-mails with the American dealer, explaining that I was enquiring on behalf of a third party who had sold that very copy to me a few years ago and was interested in buying it back. That was intended as an unthreatening explanation of my slightly off-centre questions; I was afraid they might become evasive if I hinted that the book could have been stolen. Eventually I learned that they had bought it at auction in New York. I said I'd speak to my customer and let them know his decision.

It looked as though two of the other volumes had also surfaced. If I was right, one of Curwen's books was now in Frankfurt and another in Chicago, and they also had been bought at auctions a few months before. Long and futile phone calls to all three of the auction houses involved had only established that none of them would divulge the name of the previous owner to anybody, not without prior permission. One of the New York voices mentioned a court order. I'd argued with various faceless people at length, and as sweetly as I could manage, but I hadn't got anywhere, and hadn't really expected to.

Then I'd phoned my friend Howard Peters, who runs a reputable antiquarian book operation in California, and asked for his help. Howie phoned some people he knew and then rang back to say that the provenance of both the volumes I'd mentioned was perfectly straightforward, and that Christie's in New York at least had been satisfied that the book had reached them from a legitimate private owner. They had unbent enough to give him one piece of new but unsurprising information: the *Barchester Towers* had been listed in the sale catalogue as 'The Property of an English Gentleman'. That was where I'd got by this evening, and it was where I was stuck.

I jerked awake, looked at my watch and found that I'd been dozing for nearly ten minutes. The raindrops sounded fainter, and there were still no noises coming from the baby alarm. I got to my feet and looked towards the street, which was quiet and wet. And I discovered that I had catnapped my way to a decision.

I could go on trying to run down Curwen's collection in my spare time, but I was never going to locate it all, especially when I didn't even know what 'all' meant. Just finding out where some of the books had gone was only a first step. The solicitors needed to know how those particular volumes had reached their current owners: whether they had been sold by Curwen or stolen from him. That meant trying to lean on several famous international auction houses until they agreed to hand over confidential information. It was just about conceivable that a formal approach through Price Rankin Burke would do the trick, but more likely somebody would need to get that court order – or police help – to establish whether the books had left a trail behind them. I seemed to be up against a brick wall.

I opened the bottom drawer of the desk. Burke's envelope was sitting there on top of Curwen's typescript and the Dickens in its padded bag. I pulled it out and found the note. Burke had given me a name, 'Sgt Robert Waites', and a central London phone number. I could ring the sergeant in the morning, after I got back from nursery, if I still felt like it by then. At the moment, my curiosity was flagging. I yawned and left.

13

A Little Light from a Red-eyed Man

Marylebone police station is a dour, flat-fronted, yellow-brick building just off Portman Square. Recklessly, I backed the van into the end of the parking bay at the main entrance, which was marked 'Police Vehicles Only', then ran up the ramp and into the lobby. The reception desk was inhabited by a fat man whose face said that he had seen everything and didn't think much of it. I gave him my name, sat down on one of the blue metal chairs bolted to the cement floor, and listened with waning interest while a man told him a long story about a £700 cheque and another man in a pub.

'Miss Hoare?' One of the doors dotted around the waiting room had opened while I wasn't looking, and a man stood there: not just any man, but somebody I knew – Smith's companion, the untidy man who had not told me 'Wait' when he appeared in the doorway of Curwen's flat, but 'Waites'. Ah. He pointed at one of the other doors and said, 'That's empty.' The plastic sign said 'Interview Room', and the red light above it was off. He swept me inside with an abrupt gesture. The room, or large cupboard, where we found ourselves was furnished with three upright chairs, a table, and what looked like a recording machine; an overhead fluorescent fitting lit the mottled grey walls, which were covered with dusty Metropolitan Police posters, presumably positioned to hide the fact that the walls badly needed fresh paint. As Dante would have muttered, 'Abandon hope all ye who enter here.'

We settled ourselves soberly on opposite sides of the table, and I pulled out my letter of introduction and pushed it over. While he was scanning it, I scanned him. Waites was a tired detective in his early fifties, with thinning brown hair cut short and a puffy, slightly florid face which spoke of too much work, too little sleep, and too many pints. He had loosened his tie so much that the knot was somewhere over his breastbone, and his eyes were bloodshot.

'All right,' he said, looking up. 'You told me on the phone that this is still about Timothy Curwen's death. How can I help you?' His tone was flat. It said that with luck I was once again merely going to waste more of his time than he could spare, while at worst I might actually make more work for him; that he was too busy for either; that what he really needed was a good night's sleep; and last but not least that I wasn't going to find this interview any easier than the last one. I made a mental note to be brief and encourage him to ask questions.

I said rapidly, 'I'm working for Curwen's solicitors: they hired me to trace some books that are missing from his flat. I've done a probate inventory, and I've come away with a lot of questions. Maybe you have some answers.' I pulled a note-book and pen out of my shoulder bag and slapped them down on the table in front of me. 'And if I have any information that you need . . . ?' I let my voice trail off. I didn't really mean much by that offer, but something had to be done to establish a more co-operative atmosphere.

'The books you were telling us about?' He reached out to a switch. 'If you don't mind, I'll save time by recording this.' I shrugged and tried not to look shifty. 'Go on.'

'Can we start with background? DC Smith said that you found a suicide note. Is there anything in the wording of the note that explains why he killed himself?'

I was expecting a curt 'No', because that was what Smith had suggested. What I wasn't expecting was silence, and a searching look. I said, 'What is it?'

He leaned against the back of his chair, still hesitating. I leaned against my own chair and allowed myself to stare back and wait him out.

Finally, he said, 'It wasn't suicide.'

I could feel my jaw drop. Part of my brain was frozen, and the other part was scurrying to work out how this could be connected with missing books. Trying to pull my thoughts together, I stammered, 'What happened? Somebody *did* kill him?'

He answered me with his own question. 'Do you know what "lividity" is?'

I had an idea where he was going, but pretended not and asked meekly for an explanation.

He stifled a yawn. 'When a body's been lying somewhere for a few hours, the blood settles into its lowest parts. It looks like bruising. You with me? When the caretaker phoned the emergency services at about five o'clock on the Wednesday morning to say that there was a body on the ground outside the block, a response car got over there in a couple of minutes and the crew took one look and called for back-up. As soon as he got there, the doctor knew that the body had been moved some time after death. But when we went into the flat we found a suicide note in his typewriter, and French windows open on to the balcony.'

I said the obvious: 'You're saying that somebody threw the corpse out of the window.' He looked at me ironically, but I was too busy adjusting my ideas to worry about sounding thick. 'So the note was a fake, and it couldn't have been suicide?'

'Not unless he beat himself around the head, shot himself, thought about it for a while, got rid of the gun somewhere else, and then came back and threw his own corpse over the railings.'

'He was *shot*?' I echoed with a sinking feeling. 'And nobody in the block heard anything? It did really happen there in his flat?'

'Does this have anything to do with *your* problem?' Waites asked fairly politely.

'Is there any reason why you can't tell me?' I returned.

He almost smiled. 'I suppose not. Well, you aren't wrong. But as it happened, the people in the next flat were out at the time. And those old places have solid walls. You'd be surprised how often people don't notice what you think must be obvious. Still – it was plain enough just where the killing happened and where the body lay.'

Quite. 'How long had he been dead when they found him?'

This time he stared hard. 'What's all this? Are you from the media?'

I opened my eyes wide, shook my head and waited, trying not to look guilty. He leaned forward and stared at me closely. 'According to the pathologist's first report, he probably died between eleven and one. Now . . . what?'

I leaned forward too. I'd made a promise, but obviously I couldn't keep it now I knew what had really happened. I made a mental apology to Tim Junior and said, 'I think he was still alive at eleven,' and told Waites about the little blind boy.

I watched him explode. 'We interviewed everybody! We bloody *asked* everybody in the building whether they'd heard anything, and nobody said a word!'

'Even if your people bothered to ask a small child,' I snapped, 'he wouldn't have told you. He was supposed to be in bed. His grandmother would be cross if she found out what he'd been doing. Even if you did bother to talk to him, she would have been there, wouldn't she?'

'Of course.'

'Well then,' I said.

'He might have made up the story.'

'Well, he might have,' I agreed a little impatiently, 'but he got the time right. He said he heard the clock in Curwen's flat striking eleven just while some men – three men, he said – were shouting at each other. "Shouting and hitting" was what he told me. You say that Curwen was beaten and shot, and then thrown over the balcony hours later? Well, if the little boy was making up his story, why does it fit the facts?'

He held up both his hands. Surrender. 'The Family Liaison officer had better talk to him right away. Kids . . .' He looked at me with an expression that seemed more annoyed than grateful. Too bad. 'If you know anything else, please . . .'

I said sharply that if I knew that I knew anything else I'd tell him about it, but I didn't actually know what I knew. That seemed to puzzle him.

I took a deep breath. Bargaining time. 'All right,' I began reasonably. 'I have a couple of questions. If you can answer them, then at least I'll be able to work out whether I do know anything that's going to be useful. All I know for certain is that Tim Curwen had a collection of antiquarian books which were worth quite a lot of money. When I was hired to do the probate valuation, I found that they weren't in the flat: and the bookcases were full of second-hand paperbacks.'

'There were hundreds of books in that study . . .' Waites said slowly.

'Not those!' I snapped. 'I *know* about these things: it's my business. Yes, the bookcases are full; but believe me, I'm not talking about what's there now. You're sure that it was a few hours after he was killed before he was thrown off the balcony?' I was thinking on my feet. 'Would that have been to give somebody a chance of getting away quietly while the neighbours were asleep, or was it a robbery that went wrong? Was somebody looking for the books – somebody who knew what they were worth? No – no, I don't think that any of them could still have been there, but somebody might have been angry about that.'

I wasn't making much sense, and I could see that we both knew it. The thought of Curwen's big cash withdrawal from his bank account flitted across my mind, but that was none of my business.

I started again. 'Look: I've been able to trace three of the missing volumes to the United States and Germany. The books were most likely sold abroad by Curwen himself over a period of time. One book went at least ten months ago. If his collection can be traced, might that tell you something about the reasons for the murder?'

Waites was thinking. He shook himself slightly and mumbled something. Then he said more loudly, 'It's hard to think this is all about old books. So Mr Curwen knew about valuable books: most people don't. Anyway . . .' His voice trailed off, and he seemed to be examining something I couldn't see.

When it was obvious that he had stopped, I went back to my point: 'The three volumes I've traced were all sold through auction houses, and auction houses keep the sellers' names confidential. If you can help me I'd like to check this information; and it sounds as though it might interest you too. And there's something else – about the flat.'

He stared at me. You could see the wheels turning.

'When I realised that the books I was supposed to be valuing weren't in the study, I naturally went looking for them. I poked into every drawer and cupboard in case he'd put them away somewhere for safe-keeping. Your forensic people must have searched the place?'

He twitched slightly. I interpreted that as agreement.

'I didn't find any books, but what I did find was empty space. I got the feeling . . .' I stopped because it was the first time I'd said this to anybody else. 'According to the solicitors, that was his home, his only home. But I believe that he didn't really live there. Unless your people emptied all his shelves and drawers and took away most of his belongings? Even his crockery? Am I making any sense?'

Waites was on his feet, and I was interested to see that he was nodding. 'Hang on,' he said. He departed so abruptly that he left the recorder running. I switched it off for him – having my breathing recorded was starting to give me the edge. He was back with a thick folder almost before I got back to my chair, slamming it down on the table and flipping through an assortment of forms and notes. He pulled out a list and read it twice. Then he said, 'Right,' and looked at me expectantly.

Oh, no – I thought not! 'So what *did* they take away?' I cooed.

He hesitated and then consulted the list again and said, 'His typewriter and the suicide note, obviously. No books at all. A passport. The contents of his pockets: mobile phone, key case with three keys, wallet with two five-pound notes. Some articles of clothing. Laxative. Contents of the rubbish bins. Some containers and a set of scales.'

'Containers of what?' I demanded reasonably. Wait a minute . . . '*Scales?*' We looked at each other. I said, 'Was he a *drug dealer*?' I could hear myself squeaking.

'Why do you say that?'

'Because I live in inner London in the twenty-first century,' I told him acidly. 'Of course, you might have meant the bathroom scales? Somebody had been weighing the corpse?'

We glared at each other until to my surprise the corner of his mouth twitched and he said, 'There were traces of cocaine.'

Cocaine is a drug used in all kinds of circles nowadays, including the highest, and Waites had only said 'traces'. Curwen might have been a user. Even so, I needed to think this over.

I pulled out the sheet of paper which I had prepared for him, with the titles of the three books I had successfully

traced and the names and addresses of the auction houses
which had sold them and of the present owners, and explained
everything. Then I thrust it across the table. 'They won't
talk to me because I have no authority. But you can make
a formal approach through the local police or the FBI or
something and find out who sent those books to auction.
I think . . . there were nearly a hundred of them, and I can't
help thinking that all those missing books must mean something.'

He was looking at my paper with a slightly puzzled air.
'These are old novels,' he said. 'They're worth that much?'

I told him that their present owners thought so.

He said, 'I'd better talk to Art and Antiquities. That's
the . . .'

I told him that I knew about the Art and Antiquities section,
and that he should invite them to contact me if they had any
questions, and they probably would. I also suggested that I'd
be ready to speak to him again, but that right now I had to get
back to open my shop. I wound up with the threat of having
some more questions for him later. My instincts said that he
probably wanted to hold me for questioning, and that the letter
of introduction from Price Rankin Burke might be the only
thing that was stopping him. But I had to think about all this
before I said any more. I might even ask Barnabas whether any
of it actually made any sense.

'Wait a minute,' he said as I was restoring my unused note-
book to a free corner of my overladen shoulder bag. 'I was
going to make a suggestion. I think you might want to talk to
Chris Kennedy.'

I stared at him. 'Who?'

'Christopher Kennedy. A journalist. He knew Curwen
personally, and he wrote—'

'A newspaper feature about his death!' I remembered
the name, now that it had been spoken in the form in which

it had appeared over the article that Barnabas had unearthed. Yes, Waites was right: talking to the author would be a good idea, and I ought to have thought of it myself. I threw him my very best smile and left him staring glumly at my back.

14

Kennedy

Christopher Kennedy turned up in the shop just before five o'clock and found me sitting cross-legged on the floor in front of the natural sciences section, hunched over a 1909 Brewster that had been hanging around for too long and debating whether to chuck it into a box of books I was taking to auction, or give it one last chance to sell by raising its price by fifty per cent – a ploy which strangely enough sometimes makes my customers appreciate an overlooked item.

I hadn't been expecting him. My lunch-time call to his newspaper had got me as far as his extension number, but I'd had to leave a message on voice mail. When a tall man with spiky red hair, hazel eyes, high cheekbones and a beaklike nose pushed open my door and loomed over me, I just assumed he was a walk-in customer.

I peered up. 'Can I help you?'

'Are you Dido Hoare?'

I confessed.

'I'm Chris Kennedy. You left me a message.'

An action man!

'Yes. Thanks for . . .' I scrambled to my feet and threw a glance towards the door of the packing room, where Ernie was sitting at the computer and listening hard. He had spent most of the afternoon surfing the trail of Curwen's book sales and he was probably ready for a break, while I wasn't yet ready to let even Ernie overhear this conversation.

I asked him whether he needed to go out and get something to eat.

He smiled reassuringly and said he was fine. Then he twigged. 'You wan' me to go get Ben for you?' he suggested.

I thought about it and looked up at Kennedy. 'It's time to pick up my son from nursery. Will you come with me while we talk?'

'Whatever you say.' (Journalists must be accustomed to holding discreet conversations on street corners.)

I avoided Ernie's reproachful gaze as I retrieved my jacket from the back room and then led the way into the street. At five foot three, I have legs which I think of as being an adequate length, while Kennedy was one of those old-fashioned, lanky, tennis-playing types who cover the ground at a lope. We hesitated, apologised to each other, and had managed to adjust our pace by the time we were around the corner and heading towards the Essex Road.

'Why did you contact me?'

'Somebody called Robert Waites gave me your name.'

'Oh!' He hesitated. 'I've known him for a while. He spoke to me last week about an article I wrote.'

'About Tim Curwen? I read it. It was quite interesting.'

'A literary critic! Thank you for your endorsement,' he said.

Right. I stopped. When he noticed that I wasn't with him and turned around, I was waiting. 'This isn't about your ego,' I said.

He looked down at me, amused. 'What is it about, exactly?'

I said, 'It's about Tim Curwen's murder. Waites says that you knew him personally.'

His face froze. I started walking again. He swung into step just behind my left shoulder and said hesitantly, 'Being paranoid, I thought you were taking a crack at me for some reason. What makes you call it "murder"?'

'I called it by its name,' I said, suddenly feeling sour.

We walked silently past the last of the shops.

'So Marylebone have decided that it's murder?'

I said snappishly that Marylebone had known it was murder from the very first day.

He said, 'Whoa!' This time he was the one who stopped.

I waited for him. When he reappeared at the edge of my field of vision I told him, 'I meant that your piece read as though you were holding something back. You were writing a human-interest story about Curwen without saying anything that made him sound very interesting. I couldn't work out what the piece was for. When Waites said I should talk to you, I assumed he meant that you could tell me what's going on.'

'Where do you come in?'

I said, 'First, just tell me one thing: did you know Tim Curwen very well?'

'We moved in the same circles. I was fond of him.'

I stored that away. 'Well, I've known him for the past eighteen months or so,' I said in return, and described his first appearance in the shop, and his regular purchases.

He nodded. 'I knew about the collecting. I thought it was a funny thing for him to take up out of the blue, but he told me he'd always liked reading. I'm not sure where he was coming from.'

'I was never sure either,' I admitted. 'Why books? Maybe I was underestimating him, because he did read them, they weren't just for show. Mr Kennedy—'

'Call me Chris.'

'Call me Dido,' I returned sharply. If this was going anywhere, I needed to move it on. 'Can we get to the point? Why did Waites tell me to contact you?'

'Interesting. I'm not sure whether he wants you to check me out, or just get me off his back. I'm an investigative journalist, and a stubborn bastard. I'm going to keep on at them until they get to the bottom of this death, even if I have to make myself a bloody nuisance. Did you know that the Met are twenty per cent understaffed at the moment?'

I took in his apparent non sequitur. 'You're a nuisance? You mean, professionally?'

'I try to be. When necessary. That's how I earn my living.'

'Ah,' I said appreciatively, 'blackmail?'

He mumbled something that I didn't quite catch.

'Did you call me a smartarse?' I demanded unsteadily.

We stopped and considered each other cautiously. When he started to smile, it lit his eyes and cracked me up. He held out a hand. I shook it. When we went on, I was giggling. This was fairly unexpected, and the woman who had been walking along the pavement towards us nearly got herself killed by turning sharply and crossing to the other side of the road without looking both ways.

Since he had told me about his own interest, it seemed reasonable to tell him about mine. The business of explaining events in a more or less logical fashion pulled me up short.

'So,' he summarised when I fell silent, 'you started by trying to get your book back; then you got sucked in, mostly because you kept seeing things over there that you couldn't understand; and now you're working for his solicitor.' He looked sideways at me. It was a fair summary, and it sounded a little daft.

'One thing led to another. So why was Curwen murdered? I presume that you heard how he died?'

'I heard—' He stopped. 'Where did you hear it was murder?'

'He was beaten up. And shot. You read in the newspapers about race-hate crimes, or young men being battered by drunken yobs and left dying in the streets. But how does that fit here? By the way, that's the nursery just there.'

Chris stopped in his tracks. When I looked up, I caught a flash of his uneasiness. 'Didn't Waites tell you their theory? I don't know if it's still the working theory, but it was at the beginning.'

'The traces of cocaine?'

'Yes. No.'

Yes-no? I took a deep breath. 'He was selling drugs?'

'No, that's not it. They said at first that it was probably a hate killing. I don't know if you knew that Tim was gay. They were talking about him picking somebody up and taking him back to the flat and . . .' He broke off and shrugged.

So: nothing to do with drugs, nothing to do with money or books, just homophobia and bad luck? I said cautiously, 'Does that make sense to you?'

'No.' His voice was flat. 'They're lying. That kind of killing doesn't involve guns. Besides, he didn't just pick people up in pubs. Guns say drugs to me. I suppose he might have had a private buyer, but I've never known him to sell drugs in his own flat either. To begin with, Tim was more on the whole-sale side.'

That seemed to me to be a reasonable background for a murder. But what did I know about it? We finished our walk in silence.

Outside the old house where the nursery is, I stopped and played for time. 'I'd better go straight in and get Ben. Will you come back with us for a cup of tea?'

He laughed mirthlessly. 'I'm a newspaperman,' he said.

I chose to misunderstand him. 'Then you can have some of my vodka instead,' I said, 'or even some of my father's Irish whiskey.'

'I'd be honoured,' he said. But his expression was uneasy.

The three of us had been back in the flat for twenty minutes when my phone rang. It was a miracle that I heard it, because Ben and our visitor had rolled up some crumpled newspaper and taped it into a rough sphere and were having a loud and disjointed conversation mixed with a game of football up and down the passage between the sitting room and the kitchen, while I boiled the kettle. I slipped between them cautiously and went to pick up the phone.

It was Ernie, ringing from downstairs, speaking loudly and sounding anxious. 'Dido, you all right?'

'It's Chelsea versus Arsenal up here,' I told him. 'Ben and Mr Kennedy. Don't worry. Are you finished?'

Ernie explained that he wouldn't mind getting off because he was meeting somebody in the pub on the corner and didn't want to keep her waiting. I said, 'Hang on,' wove back through the football match to the door of the flat, signalling 'two minutes' to the players, and galloped down the stairs to the street. Ernie was just switching off lights and putting on his black jacket when I reached the shop.

'Football?' he said.

I said, 'More or less,' and then noticed that Ernie's expression was a mixture of suspicion, curiosity and self-satisfaction.

'You know that guy?'

'A friend of Tim Curwen,' I said smoothly. 'The police gave me his name. I'll tell you all about it on Saturday. You *are* coming in on Saturday?'

Ernie nodded.

'Any customers?' I asked then.

'Some. Mrs Acker.' He didn't have to say anything else. She's a regular. 'I maybe found another book in New York,' he added. 'I left a note beside the keyboard. Only I'm not sure, but it might be.'

I had already made up my mind. The fact was that Curwen's books hadn't been outstanding. They had been good collectibles, yes – the kind of books that any dealer will tell you are 'as good as cash', meaning not too rare but interesting to lots of collectors and libraries, always sellable. Therefore, nobody was going to get any farther until they traced the route that even one single book had taken to its present owner. From that they might be able to work out whether the deal was connected with Curwen's death. It was Waites who had to follow this up, not me.

'Good,' I said to Ernie. 'I'll look. But leave that for now. By the way, have you heard anything from my father today?'

'The Perfessor phoned just after you went out. He said to tell you he's been at the library an' he'll try you later. He was talking about Sidney.'

Sir Philip Sidney, presumably, not the city in Australia. Barnabas was showing signs of a new research project. Some people never really retire.

By the time I'd locked up, set the alarm and gone upstairs again, the football had disintegrated into a shower of paper scraps, and the players were on their hands and knees trying to repair the damage.

'Milk?' I suggested. 'Alcohol?'

Ben looked up agreeably and said, 'Alc-ol.'

'A glass of milk for me,' Kennedy said with a straight face. I poured two glasses of milk, handed them over, and watched them being drunk. He said, 'I'd better go. I have some work on this evening. Look, what do you want me to do about this?'

Assuming that he wasn't offering to sweep up the last scraps of paper, I pursued a new idea. 'I have something that I need to drop in at Curwen's flat. If you're free some time soon, how would you feel about coming with me before I have to give the keys back?'

He placed his empty tumbler on the coffee table and got to his feet slowly. 'Why?'

'You knew him personally, and I'd like you to take a look at the state of that flat, tell me what it says to you, because I'm finding it odd. Could we talk about this later?'

He nodded slowly. His face had gone blank again. 'All right. When would suit you? Tomorrow?'

It would depend on organising Barnabas to shop-sit, which meant I'd have to speak to him before I could be sure. I explained.

Kennedy nodded. 'You have my number,' he said, and saw himself out.

'Supper,' I said to Ben at that point. 'What about some baked beans?'

'Is he coming back?' Ben demanded.

I told him I didn't know.

15

The Dust off His Feet

We walked back out through the double doors of Abbey House and halted on the steps, sharing a moment of baffled silence. I'd managed to slip Curwen's embarrassing typescript into a drawer of the desk, but that apart this hadn't been one of my better ideas. I could no longer even remember why I'd thought that it might be.

We had made a lightning tour of Flat 502. I had followed Kennedy from room to room, seeing from his actions that he really was familiar with the place, although how significant that was seemed uncertain. By now, he was looking as uneasy as I felt.

I had to stop and sneeze the dust of the place out of my lungs. 'Any ideas?'

'Remember that I haven't been here for a couple of months, and all I can say is that it wasn't empty like that last spring.'

Chasing a fleeting notion, I asked him, 'Had the two of you quarrelled?'

He shook his head slightly and looked evasive. 'Now that I look back, I'd say that Tim became withdrawn months ago. I thought he was having money problems, and the state of that place makes me think I was right. But I wonder if he was simply in the middle of moving out?'

'Throwing things away and packing?' *Or preparing to die.* 'That would explain it. But he didn't tell you what his problem was?'

He shrugged.

I found myself suddenly remembering the fairy story, the one about the man who was running away from his enemies, escaping to a desert island.

'I'd better get back,' I heard myself saying. I had left Barnabas in the shop, so it wasn't as though my business was closed down, but it seemed like days since I had paid attention even to routine matters. A few hundred pounds from Price Rankin Burke was looking increasingly irrelevant. How had I let myself get sucked in?

Kennedy said flatly, 'Keep in touch.'

I said, 'I'll phone you if anything comes up,' and watched him start off towards the square, where he had parked.

My own van was on a meter a couple of streets to the east. I was a few yards from it when my mobile warbled and I switched on.

'Ms Hoare?' I recognised Dona Helmer's voice and snapped to attention. 'I hope you don't mind my ringing you on this number – I tried the shop and got it from your father.'

I said, 'Of course not,' and asked whether there was a problem.

'Not really,' she said, and then qualified that with: 'Just a small one. The letting agents have found a new tenant for the flat. Curwen's lease isn't up, but these people will take over the balance if they can move in on Sunday, the first of the month. Otherwise, we may have to go on paying the rent out of what looks like a non-existent estate until something else comes along. It's all happened very quickly, and I have to arrange for his things to be stored and get the cleaners in. I've been told to give it my personal attention. Mr Burke said he gave you the keys? Look, I hope this won't inconvenience you. I was going to drive over to Islington, but Professor Hoare says you're out on business.'

I didn't have to stop and think. 'You're welcome. I've done everything I can. It just so happens that I'm leaving Curwen's place now, and I'm in a rush, so I'll go straight home—'

'Couldn't you leave the keys with the porter? It would be much quicker for me to go there.'

For once, the old man had been at his desk this morning, so I could say, 'Of course: I'll take them back right now.'

I heard the half-suppressed sigh. 'Thanks. I have a lot on my plate today. See you later.'

I went on and picked up the van, drove it back to Abbey House, and pulled in on the yellow lines just across the street from the entrance.

The old porter was still in the lobby. He saw me, hesitated, croaked, 'Oh, miss, I just let the gentleman in. I don't think he knew you were coming back.'

'The gentleman?' I echoed.

'The gentleman who was here with you.'

I opened my mouth and stammered something – about how he must have forgotten something. 'I'll go and lock up,' I babbled. 'We'll be down in a moment. Don't go away, please, because I'm supposed to leave the keys with you. Miss Helmer is coming to pick them up – you know, from the solicitors?' I stabbed three or four times at the button while I was babbling, and the lift responded to my urgency and heaved into a crawl.

The door of the flat was closed. I eased the key into the lock and turned it gently. He wasn't in the entrance hall. I stepped inside on a rush of adrenaline, leaving the door wide open behind me. I didn't think for one second that Kennedy had any legitimate business here. It would be a good idea to catch him in the act – whatever act it was that he had omitted to tell me about.

A draught was blowing from the study. I edged across and peered through the door. The French windows were standing open wide, but I couldn't see him at first because the desk was in the way. When I crept closer, I found him outside on the balcony. He had a hand on the ivy that was growing in one of the ceramic pots, and I watched him tug at the plant lightly and haul out a tangle of roots, stare at them and then at the hole where they had been, then stuff the plant back. I watched him repeat the operation with the second pot. Then he seemed to be thinking. When he looked up, I was in plain sight.

'Gardening?' I commented. Then I noticed, a little late, that I was standing about ten feet away from a man who was up to no good. I made myself back away a couple of steps.

'Oh, shit! Wait . . . can you please wait for a minute? I'd better wash my hands. Don't go, please.'

I was deciding whether I ought to scream or run or something. He must have seen it, and he dealt with it by letting me back into the hallway before he moved. He followed, but veered away into the bathroom without even looking at me, and I heard the water running: he was apparently . . . well, washing his hands. He stayed there for what felt like five minutes while I pulled myself together, noticed how clever he was being, and wondered what I was going to do. When he came out and saw that I was still there, hovering just inside the door to the hallway, his relief was visible. He halted ten feet away – I could easily escape if I wanted to, he was giving me that space for my reassurance.

'What are you doing?' My voice sounded more or less normal, though not particularly friendly.

'Looking for something, but I think somebody else got to it first. A kilo of cocaine, if you really want to know. Are you OK?'

No, I wasn't, so I said I was just fine. Then I said that we'd better get out now, because somebody from the solicitors was on her way to pick up the keys. He nodded; a nerve was jumping under his left eye. We walked to the lift, keeping a few feet apart, and rode down in silence.

Dona Helmer's Honda was just rolling past the front of Abbey House as we came out for the second time that morning. At that moment I remembered the French windows were still standing open on to the balcony up there. Well, that could be explained – if she asked – although other things couldn't. I stomped down the steps and plunged across the road behind the Honda. Helmer was driving slowly, on the lookout for a parking space. I ran to the van without hesitating. Kennedy called out, but I'd taken him by surprise. As I pulled away from the kerb, I could see him standing on the pavement staring after me.

16

The Rain on His Head

By the time I arrived outside the shop, I had come to the wise decision to think about other things. There could of course be some acceptable explanation for what had just happened. I could even imagine working out what that explanation might be, given a long, long time and nothing better to do with it.

When I had started my drive home along the Marylebone Road, I was telling myself that it was impossible for a police search to have overlooked a kilo of cocaine, so Kennedy's entire story was rubbish. Around King's Cross, I spent many uneasy minutes constructing theories to explain why even a lying journalist would smuggle himself into the very empty flat of a dead friend. Most of the theories centred around the cocaine, if it had ever been there: an attempt to steal it, or perhaps just remove some evidence that incriminated both himself and Curwen. Driving north from Islington Green, I mused briefly on the only thing that appeared unarguable by now: I knew the real reason for Curwen's murder. I know that drug dealers don't make old bones. As for Mr Christopher Kennedy, he clearly knew more about Curwen's death than he ought to, and it wasn't impossible that he had been involved, although on the other hand . . . I couldn't work out how I felt about him. Wary, certainly. Frightened, probably not.

Five lunch-time customers were scattered around the shop in various stages of search and discovery when I arrived. Barnabas was down by the illustrated books, so deep in conversation with two fat, elderly men that he barely registered my arrival. The phrase '. . . but on the other hand, the Piranesi plates . . .' floated over to me. I wandered up the other aisle to make a proprietorial survey of a student type who was sitting on the floor reading Descartes, and a couple of familiar faces turned towards the classics and the early children's books, concentrating hard. Everybody was getting on just fine without my help, and it all looked so ordinary that I could sense my tension oozing away – more tension than I'd known I had.

I ducked into the office, switched on the computer, listened to the hard drive making a chugging noise which I really must remember to ask Ernie about, and then abandoned it temporarily for the morning's post.

Barnabas had made a start. He had removed half a dozen orders from their envelopes and tucked them into the appropriate volumes, unearthed from the shelves and stacked on the corner of the packing table ready for paperwork and wrapping – a nice, mindless task that would suit me well today. A shallow pile of invoices and cheques was waiting for details to be entered into the spreadsheet. It all looked so normal that I flung myself into the big swivel chair, pulled the telephone within reach, and started checking catalogues. The rest could wait.

At 2.30, with the shop temporarily empty, I looked up to find my father lowering himself on to the other chair and staring at me hard.

I said, 'I've ordered a second-edition *Robinson Crusoe*. It sounds quite good.'

He said, 'Ah?' Defoe did not interest him just now. 'You were gone for some time. You were socialising with the journalist?'

I hesitated. 'You could call it that.'

'What happened?'

A simple chronological account of events left my father alarmed.

'Dido, you—'

'Stop! You don't have to say it!' Suddenly I was angry with everybody, especially him.

He looked at me closely. 'He wasn't pulling your leg?'

I pushed my chair back on its castors so hard that it bounced against the filing cabinet. 'I didn't ask! I just locked up and left.'

'He threatened you?'

I considered that suggestion at length and recognised once more that Kennedy had been clever enough to do just the reverse. 'No. He was very careful. As soon as he saw me, he backed off. I didn't feel in any physical danger.'

'Well, that's something at least. Dido, what exactly do you think of the man? This business has clearly upset you. He hasn't, er, made a pass at you?'

I tried hard not to laugh.

'What?'

I said, 'I think he's gay. There was some kind of relationship with Curwen . . . I haven't worked it out yet, but I believe that the drugs may have had something to do with their breaking up.'

My father leaned back in his chair, said, 'Well,' and closed his eyes. 'Get out of this! Probate valuation be damned! Tell the police what happened today, and then keep away.'

I groaned at him. 'I keep trying to convince you that I'm not dim! I am going to write a letter to the solicitors and tell them that I don't expect to be able to do anything more for them. I'll repeat, in words of one syllable, that the police are the only ones who can get them any more information about the books I've traced to those auction houses.'

'And you will tell the police about Kennedy, who has some explaining to do?'

'Barnabas, they already know all about the cocaine because Waites told me. They already know Kennedy – he's been in contact with them, and remember that it was Waites who suggested that I should talk to him. I was startled by what happened. I don't really trust any of these people, and I don't understand what's going on. I wonder whether I'm somehow being used? I'm going to return the retainer the solicitors gave me. They've paid for the valuation, there's no problem about that, but they're not paying me for anything else. I'll write the letter now and mail it on my way to pick up Ben.'

'And you'll forget about the whole business?'

'Of course I'll forget about it,' I lied. What he meant was that I couldn't risk involving myself any further in anything so dangerous as hard drugs. That was also what I meant.

After a moment he muttered, 'I suppose I should go and lie down for half an hour. Busy morning.'

I said, 'I'll make us a cup of tea at about four o'clock,' and watched him walk slowly down the aisle to the door and along, past the display window, towards the door to the flat. It was starting to rain again.

The afternoon dragged. I used up a good part of an hour writing and rewriting my letter of resignation until it said why only the police could take my enquiries farther, in terms that any five-year-old could understand. I printed out a final version, signed it with a rush of relief, and found a paper-clip to attach copies of the details of the books I'd already traced and my cheque for the value of the retainer. I sealed the whole lot in a large envelope, addressed it to the solicitors' offices, and stuffed it into my shoulder bag. I couldn't wait to get rid of it, possibly because this seemed so much like surrendering that I wasn't sure that I'd do it if I didn't act at once. At five to four I stuck a notice on the door for any stray customer who might turn up, slipped upstairs to wake Barnabas with a cup of tea, and then borrowed his big umbrella to walk across Upper Street to the post office. This particular letter was going by recorded delivery.

By a quarter to five I was approaching the nursery school.

As soon as Ben was ready, we ambled back through the rain, talking about elephants. The lights were on in the shop, and I could see through the window display to where Barnabas was talking to one of our regulars, pointing at something. Ben and I went upstairs, greeted Mr Spock, and took off our wet shoes and coats.

The phone rang just before 5.30.

'Dido,' my father said without preamble, 'have you looked out your front window of late? He came in asking for you a few minutes ago, and I invited him to leave. However, he seems to be stuck out there.'

I mumbled at him, put the phone down, and crossed the sitting room. From the window, I saw what he was talking about: an old but immaculate Jaguar convertible parked directly across the road, and Kennedy leaning against the car in the falling rain, his hands in the pockets of his jeans. He was wearing a black leather jacket but getting wet anyway. It looked as though he had been there for a little while, because the rain had darkened his hair, and I saw him wipe a hand abruptly across his forehead. He could have been waiting for his recovery service, but somehow I thought not.

I pulled the window up with a bang, leaned into the rainy wind, and said quietly, 'Go away!'

He hunched his shoulders and said, 'Dido, you—' I shut the window, returned to the phone and said, 'Don't worry about it.'

'It appears to be a demonstration,' my father noted, 'or a picket line. Shall I . . . ?'

'No,' I said. 'He'll leave when he gets wet enough. It's very wet out there.'

'Indeed,' my father agreed pleasantly. 'This is just the kind of thing that *you* might do, isn't it?'

A few minutes later, Barnabas gave my bell a warning blip, and came climbing slowly up the stairs. Ben and I were in the kitchen by then, dishing up his supper. When my father appeared in the doorway, I asked whether it was still raining.

He looked at me ironically. 'Let's say that I must remember to retrieve my umbrella from you before I leave. Dido, I think the man is mad.'

I didn't, but I was prepared to accept that he had his own way of getting what he wanted. I grabbed Barnabas's umbrella and marched down the stairs. In fact, the rain was beginning to let up. I walked across the road, handed Kennedy the umbrella, and turned away without saying a word.

'We do have to talk,' he called after me.

Although he was standing there with water dripping off the spiky ends of his hair, he managed to look not at all pathetic. In the circumstances, I was impressed. Not only that, but I was afraid he might be right. My heart sank. Back in the shelter of the doorway I turned around and said, 'All right.'

Then he raised the umbrella ceremoniously and followed me across the road.

17

Talk

Sitting at the kitchen table in his pyjamas, Ben looked up. 'You're wet,' he remarked as calmly as though he were used to men turning up just before his bedtime, dripping all over the carpet.

'Do you think I could borrow a towel?' Kennedy asked him gravely.

'I think so,' Ben said, and returned to his chicken stew, keeping his eyes fixed on the visitor.

'Bathroom,' I said flatly. 'Help yourself.'

In his temporary absence, I turned my own gaze to Barnabas, who was radiating disapproval.

I muttered, 'He said we have to talk. He's right.'

Barnabas looked ugly. 'A threat?'

You could read it that way, but I said, 'If it is, this is a good chance to find out. He's no danger here and now. If I take him into the living room, could you stay with Ben while he's eating?'

'Make him sit on a folded towel,' Barnabas flung after my back. Grumpy. Cheap shot.

I stood at the open bathroom door and watched our visitor using Ben's already damp bath towel to dry himself down. When the worst had been dealt with, he looked at me out of the corner of his eye and asked, 'Well, should I sit on a folded towel, d'you think?'

Wordlessly I pointed towards the sitting room, where he assessed the situation and chose to settle on the relatively waterproof wooden chair in front of the writing desk. I sprawled on the settee, tired of it all.

'Talk, then,' I commanded. 'You can start almost anywhere. I don't suppose you've said anything to me so far that isn't a lie. Try again. Keep it simple. Start with the cocaine. Yours?'

'Use your head.'

We exchanged glares, and I said, 'I am. As my father always says, start at the beginning. How long did you know Tim Curwen, was he really a dealer, was that why he was murdered, and why did you sneak back into his flat this morning? And everything in between.'

He was looking cagey.

'I'll make the time to listen,' I told him sweetly. 'I'll even let you finish by telling me what you're doing here, after my father told you to buzz off. Presumably you've come to beg me not to tell the police about today? How do you know that I haven't reported it already?'

He turned half away from me and said, 'Have you? All right, all right. I met Curwen last year at Karl's Place in Soho. A trendy club, very trendy just then, full of us media hacks.'

'Was Curwen a "media hack"?'

He laughed. 'Tim was a rich brat, but he liked to hang out. You know that he wanted to be a writer? He was working on a book, and he liked talking about it, when he wasn't bending ears about having a lot of connections in the Home Counties: old family and not much money, I assumed. He was interested in social class and . . .'

'Etiquette,' I supplied. 'I've read his manuscript, remember.'

'. . . and a bit of a hustler, I was going to say. But that's not all there was to him. You must know that: didn't you tell me you found yourself liking him too? He was good company. He talked to me because he knew I was with a newspaper, and he wanted me to get him work freelancing, but we hit it off despite that. Shall we leave it?'

'He asked you for work? What kind of work?'

'Reviews, pieces about art, collecting.' He looked at me. 'He wanted me to give him some writing tips, some contacts. I'm an established journalist, you know. Almost respectable.'

I said, 'Really?' In rapid succession I saw that I could easily check that part of his story, that he must know I would, that he was perhaps a more serious newspaperman than I'd understood, and that he was being much more open than I'd expected. He was making it very difficult for himself if he intended me any harm. I adjusted my ideas and added, 'Is that how you got away with publishing that peculiar, empty "human interest" piece, "The Death of a Gentleman" or whatever it was called?'

'I traded on my reputation.' He looked at me ironically. 'After I'd known him for a couple of months, I found out what was going on – caught him in the act, and discovered a bit too late that he'd actually supplied cocaine to some people I knew. He called it "a favour". He was perfectly open after that. He used to joke that anybody with an endless supply of one-gram deals can get an invitation to any party in London. But he didn't make a regular thing out of it, so it took me a long time to realise there was a lot more involved. He was a middleman. That was how he earned his living. It took me a while to understand, probably because I didn't want to, that his whole social persona was a kind of act, a caricature. You must have noticed what I mean: that old lady's flat, the clothes, the name-dropping of people you'd never heard of – "my aunt, Lady Hester", "Sir Alan Whatsit", racing tips from "a National Hunt jockey I know". I began to see that it was all just a disguise. But the charm was real, you know.'

'What did you do?'

'Asked him to stop.'

'What did he do?'

'Said that he couldn't, that he knew too many names and faces. I think he was acting as a kind of errand-boy to somebody very big, an importer. In those circumstances, I could believe that they'd make sure he never got a chance to betray them.'

'Was he telling the truth about that? I suppose he was.'

Kennedy hesitated. 'I thought so at the time. He said that he couldn't just walk out – I could see that. He said that if I wasn't all right with it, I'd better back off.'

'And?'

'I backed off. I'll tell you some time how I feel about hard drugs and why. I kept worrying about him, but I took care not to see him except at a distance for about six months.'

'So you don't know if something happened to him?'

'I didn't say that. When we bumped into each other at a friend's house early last December, something had gone wrong.' He looked at me. 'Suddenly, he was saying that he knew he couldn't go on, that somebody was crowding him and sooner or later there'd be an accident and he'd either be killed or banged up. He was afraid of spending time in prison: he really thought he'd be murdered if he even got that far. He was close to losing it altogether. Then he started to hint that he'd found somebody who might help him, who might be able to get him out of the mess; he just needed time to make some arrangements.'

'You believed him?'

'Well, something had changed. But I let it go. I shouldn't have.'

'Why do you say that?' I demanded, fascinated.

He shrugged. 'If I'd understood the situation fully, perhaps I could have made sure that he did get out when he wanted to. I keep wondering what I should have done.'

'About today—'

'I don't want to go into that.'

I looked at him coldly. 'You think I'm giving you any choice? You're trying to tell me that there could still have been a kilo of cocaine hidden in that flat after a police forensic team had searched it, not to mention me and one of the lawyers? I accept that you went there today because you somehow needed to have a look and you realised I could get you inside the place; but that doesn't explain why you thought his stuff might still be there, or what you were going to do if it was.'

He said slowly, 'It must have been there at some point, because I knew he had an errand to do on the Monday – we spoke on the phone that afternoon, and he told me he couldn't meet me because he had some "business" on that night. As a matter of fact, he also said that it was going to be the last time. I wanted to believe him. Listen, I don't suppose that he ever kept anything in that place for a minute longer than was absolutely necessary. It would have worked like this: Tim would have picked up the goods from somewhere, probably the importer's contact, and passed them on down the line as fast as he could. He might have taken it back to the flat just for long enough to cut the stuff, take a slice for himself, weigh it up into one or two smaller orders . . . You understand that the whole reason for that flat is that it was the most unlikely place you could imagine for what he was doing, and the reason for those big ceramic pots of ivy out on the balcony . . .'

'Yes?'

'Until he could get the stuff off the premises, he hid it under the ivy. When we were up there today, I looked out and saw that his plants were starting to die, and then I noticed a trace of mud on the floor of the balcony. I needed to find out whether anything was still there. If it had gone, then that would have suggested one possible scenario for the night he died. I don't think the police found anything, because there hasn't been a whisper about it, though of course there are some coppers who regularly pocket any drugs they think they can get away with.'

I considered all this. 'Then that was what the killers were after, and it isn't there now. Why did they kill him if he gave it to them?'

He hesitated. 'Actually, I keep thinking that somebody discovered that he was planning to get out.'

What is the wholesale cost of a kilo or two of cocaine? Ten times the price of my *Barchester Towers*? Twenty times? Oh, they would have been asking, all right, assuming they knew about it. 'Shouting and hitting', to quote my witness. I persisted, 'What were you going to do if you found it there?'

I took note of his hesitation. Eventually he said, 'I don't think you'd want to know.'

'Then I don't think you know me very well.'

He still hesitated.

'You thought you'd make some quick money?'

He stared at me so bleakly that I felt embarrassed. 'I thought there was a chance that I could use it to bait a trap.'

I laughed. 'Oh yes? A trap? You are jumping to one hell of a lot of conclusions, Superman! Any sane person would have told me he was going to take it straight to the police. Do you really think I'm such an idiot?'

'No, but I know that you're out of your depth. If I'd let it be known that I had Tim's stuff—'

I glared. 'You say it's *me* who's out of my depth? What makes *you* into Scotland Yard?' I heard myself and stopped. Apart from the fact that I was beginning to sound like Barnabas, suddenly I wondered. 'You *aren't* . . . ?'

'No, and I'm not a secret agent for MI6 or Interpol, either, for Christ's sake! You know exactly who I am! I'm an investigative journalist who specialises in criminal and political stories: a professional information-gatherer doing my job.' His voice was hoarse. 'One thing that Tim did say, months ago, is that he was working directly for a senior man, some flash geezer who runs one of the big operations. He said his boss was smart, he was safe, he's never been nicked or even identified, and yet he's one of the biggest players: into a dozen games over the years. It sounded as though this man was seriously rich and seriously paranoid, and if he heard that his consignment had been found, he'd send somebody to get it. It could have been a way into the whole business. If Tim was telling me the truth.

'We were both stinking at the time, or he wouldn't have said that much, even for a laugh, and by the next day he was pretending it had all been a big joke, a story for his newspaper mates. But when I went over there with you this morning and saw that the ivy looked sick, I had to take a look. As for spilling my heart out to the police – frankly, I wouldn't risk it. There's nothing to say that the police aren't in this themselves. It's happened before now. If I draw their attention before I take precautions, I could be in deep shit. When you walked in on me, I thought for a minute that you were part of the problem. Those people are . . . I hope you've never met any people like this.'

The voice from the doorway said soberly, 'I would agree with you there, at least.'

I jumped and squeaked, 'Barnabas, have you been listening?'

'I made no promise not to overhear your excessively heated conversation,' Barnabas remarked coldly. 'Ben is playing in the bedroom, and I expect that he would like to see his mother now. Dido, have you done what you promised?'

I made a quick guess at what he meant and said, 'I mailed the letter this afternoon on the way to pick up Ben.'

'There's just one thing that I've come here to say,' Kennedy interrupted. 'Dido, you have to forget everything you've been thinking, everything you've found out. I've only told you this to make you understand what's involved, so you'll get off my back. This isn't fun, and what I'm doing doesn't concern you.'

'There, too, you and I are in total agreement,' my father said icily.

'I am way ahead of you both,' I growled. I looked straight at my damp visitor. 'I'll even tell you that I'm no longer employed to investigate missing books; I've told both the police and the solicitor everything I've found out, and I resigned today on the grounds that I can't do any more. I'm out.' That was it, but there was something in his face that made me say, 'I'm sorry about Tim Curwen. What are you going to do now?'

'Ask around. I'm looking to develop a book about Tim, did I tell you? My usual colourful, investigative stuff.' His expression was unreadable. 'Who knows? If I act nosey enough and naive enough, something may crawl out of the woodwork. I'll talk to Waites tomorrow. Carefully. He's pretty honest, and pretty smart, and I've known him for a couple of years. That doesn't mean I trust him, but I can ask a few innocent questions, throw out some hints, and try to push him in the direction of the drugs thing.'

I said, 'You'd better be careful.'

'Oh, I'm a professional coward,' he said harshly. 'Believe me, if I hear anything moving in the bushes, I'll go to my editor and get help.'

'I wonder whether you might be able to give me a lift to the bus stop?' Barnabas asked loudly. 'I'm afraid it's still raining quite heavily.'

I said nothing, despite knowing that, as Barnabas normally takes a minicab home in bad weather, he was intent on manoeuvring this dangerous man out of my presence. I decided to let him follow his impulse. I was tired and I couldn't make any sense of anything. And when they were gone, Mr Spock and I went into the bedroom and sat there with Ben while he was falling asleep.

18

Glitches

The note landed on my desk late on Saturday morning, courtesy of a large figure in motorcycling leathers and a big black helmet with its visor pulled down over the face. I called, 'Don't you need a signature?' after the retreating figure, but it seemed that its ears were insulated by the helmet and it ploughed straight on down the aisle and vanished into the street.

Barnabas, who was dissuading Ben from exploring some valuable illustrated books at that moment, asked, 'What was that?'

I said, 'Courier,' in the same second as Ernie, who was having trouble with the computer, muttered, 'Darth Vader,' and added aloud, 'Dido, we got problems, I'm gonna back up the hard drive,' and a would-be customer approached me waving a cheque book. We were in business.

Sale completed and the cheque tucked away, I grabbed the envelope which had just been delivered and read the return address: Price Rankin Burke. Oh? I slid it in among the rest of the morning's as yet unopened mail, picked up the whole pile, and proposed tactfully that I should take both the post and my restless son upstairs for a little while and leave the other two to get on without our help.

What I had received turned out to be a single sheet of the firm's letterhead with a few words scrawled above Burke's signature: 'Miss Helmer found this', and a name and address: 'Mrs Theresa Clark, 253 Lavender Way, E9'. I was thrown for a moment, partly because I failed to remember what this name meant, having tried to stop thinking about Tim Curwen, and mostly by the discovery that Burke had decided to ignore my letter of resignation. But the note had yesterday's date at the top, so I realised that our communications must have crossed. Then of course I remembered asking him about Curwen's sister's address, although I didn't need it any more. On the other hand . . . Kennedy might. I left a message on his voice mail.

While I was at it, I phoned Price Rankin Burke to leave a message asking Dona Helmer to contact me, and found myself switched through to her so rapidly that it took my breath away.

'Miss Hoare! Thank you for ringing back.'

I wasn't, so there must have been a message on the machine downstairs. I said weakly, 'Can I help you?'

'I don't suppose so. Well, just . . . I wanted to ask you—' This meant more trouble. I waited. 'You didn't . . . ? I don't know how to say this, and of course I'm not accusing you of anything; and I know myself that Mr Curwen's study wasn't in such a mess when I saw it yesterday, but I started to wonder . . .' Her voice faded into an awkward silence.

I blinked. 'What is it? Look, I think I might have forgotten to shut a window there when I left the keys.'

'Yes. Oh, I mean, no. Yes, I noticed and I closed it. It was this morning. I went to let the movers in and show them what to pack up before the cleaners came, and . . . everything was . . . All the books were scattered all over the floor, and of course I *know* it wasn't like that yesterday when you left. I can't understand it.'

I wanted to say 'Join the club'. But somebody had. I thought about it. 'The porter must have let somebody else in.' Again.

'He swore not. He was very indignant.'

Indignant? I stifled a snort and said, 'Then could somebody have got in from the balcony?'

'I left the French windows bolted.'

I told her that I couldn't imagine what had happened, which was not precisely true. Somebody had a second set of keys. I was picturing those two empty, worn clips in Curwen's key case. 'Is anything missing?'

'Well, I haven't checked every book you listed . . .'

'If any of those books is missing, don't worry about it. I promise, it's not worth bothering about.'

I listened to silence. In the end, she said faintly, 'Of course, you're right. You know, I'm going to be glad when this is finished. I'm sorry I disturbed you.'

'Any time,' I said, and we exchanged goodbyes. When I'd hung up, I remembered why I'd phoned, and that I'd actually forgotten to say anything about the couriered message and my resignation. Never mind, too late. I started my usual juggling act, giving half my attention to Ben and half to sorting out the rest of the mail.

By six o'clock the last of our customers had gone, the day's takings had been tabulated by hand, and Barnabas was safely out of the way upstairs with his grandson while Ernie and I conferred over the computer's corpse. Ernie was giving a very detailed technical analysis of what had gone wrong and how many extra gigabytes we ought to have anyway, as well as which new bells and whistles he wanted to install to make the machine not just work again, but work faster and better than ever. I was pretending to understand him and forming the idea that the safest thing might be to give Ernie the old computer to dismantle and then go out and buy a new one when my mobile phone trilled.

'Is it safe?' Kennedy's voice asked. 'I can't see your father.'

I noted with interest and even alarm that the sound of his voice was cheering me up, and threw a startled look through the display in the window. The Jaguar was out there in the road, lights on and engine running for a quick getaway.

'What are you doing?' I demanded. 'Don't be stupid.'

'Thank you,' he said, and cut the connection. The head-lights blinked off, and then he was loping across the pavement towards my door. As he came down the aisle towards the office, he was already talking. 'He never mentioned a sister. You say you've got her address? I need to find her.'

'He left everything to her, but they weren't supposed to have been in contact for a while. The lawyer sent the address over this morning.'

'Keeping her away from his drugs business?' Chris specu-lated. 'Have you . . . ?'

I pulled Burke's note out of a drawer and passed it over.

'E9? That's Hackney – Homerton or Victoria Park or there-abouts.'

I thought about that for the first time. It seemed a little odd that somebody like Tim Curwen's sister was living in what was, notoriously, one of the more deprived inner-city areas in London.

'Some streets over there have been coming up for the past couple of years,' Kennedy said, obviously reading my mind. 'Look – I'll take this and be off.'

'And do what?' I asked, snatching the paper back while he was searching for an answer. When he reached for it again, Ernie moved forward. The three of us had a stand-off.

'I'm going to go and talk to her.'

'Now? Just like that?'

'I thought I wouldn't make an appointment,' he said simply.

'I'm coming with you.'

Eyebrows rose – understandably.

'Notorious curiosity,' I admitted. 'I've never been able to mind my own business.' It sounded lame. I looked quickly for another excuse and found one. 'Maybe she'd feel easier about talking to a stranger if there's another woman there.'

'I was going straight away.'

'I know,' I said. I was already reaching for my jacket and for the large envelope I'd left on top of the desk. 'Luckily, we've just closed. Ernie, could you tell my father that I've gone on an errand and I'll pay the day's takings in at the night safe on my way back?'

'You need a baby-sitter?' Ernie asked. 'Me an' Naomi could sort of stay around till you get back.'

Naomi? I told him I thought Barnabas was all right, but maybe he should check with him before he left. Then I told Kennedy that I was ready.

His car was a very dark blue Jaguar XJS, maybe twelve years old, with a cream-coloured soft top and an interior which was largely lined with cream leather. It was smaller and cosier inside than I'd imagined, with bucket seats set into low-slung wells; I was surrounded by cherry wood and leather. Suddenly I understood that I wanted to hijack this car. In order to distract myself from the discovery, I volunteered to navigate.

We drove eastwards along Balls Pond Road, which seemed quieter than usual in a rainstorm which had washed most of the pedestrians off the streets and thinned out the traffic. It took us twenty minutes to find Lavender Way: a long, straight, featureless street lined with old brick terraces, running between Lower Clapton Road and the Hackney Marshes. We rolled eastwards slowly, looking for house numbers in the gloom.

Number 253, when we found it at last, was on the north side of the road: a two-storey, end-of-terrace house with a little paved front yard in which a car was sitting. The streetlamp on the corner was out, and we shot past and braked halfway down the dark block.

'There were no lights on,' I pointed out.

'I think it's worse than that. Do you want to sit here and keep dry?'

Without waiting for my answer, he got out and started back,

his shoulders hunched against the rain. I scrambled out and joined him at a low brick wall at the corner of the property. He was right: it was worse. Sheets of chipboard covered the ground-floor windows, and another had been screwed across most of the front door, leaving gaps about a foot high at the top and bottom. The car I had noticed had no wheels and was sitting on cement blocks. Both the house and the car looked as though they had been like that for a long time.

A narrow footpath strewn with rubbish led down the side of the house between the wall and a rickety wooden fence. 'We could look round back,' I suggested without much enthusiasm.

'I will,' Chris said, and in view of the darkness and the mucky state of the path I allowed him to go alone. He returned quickly, shaking his head. 'I'll contact the housing office on Monday – this looks like a council property. They may have a forwarding address.'

I said, 'Why was Tim Curwen's sister living in a council house in Hackney?'

'Logically . . .' he said.

'Logically,' I chimed, 'it's a fake address.'

'I won't speculate,' he said.

I'd heard the tone of his voice. 'What is it?'

He shook his head and remained silent until we were back in the car and rolling towards Islington. By then I had an armload of ideas, none of which made much sense although they all looked interesting. Kennedy had told me about a man who was a chancer; but it would be crazy to build a structure of theories on that and on an address belonging to a sister who seemed to have gone away long ago, if she had ever lived there anyway.

We were about halfway back when he suddenly repeated, 'I'll make the time to get over there on Monday morning and ask at the housing office. If the sister has moved recently, that could be connected with Tim's problems. She may have been involved. Or she may be in trouble herself now.'

'Or she may never even have existed?' I scoffed. Because this friend of Tim's had never heard of her; but I wanted to find out.

We were chewing on that one when I realised that we were back in Upper Street and passing my bank. I shouted, 'Stop! Drop me here! I need to get to the night safe.'

'If you'll be all right . . .'

I said I always had been before, gathered myself and my belongings, and hesitated. Oh, to hell with it. 'Phone me on Monday evening,' I suggested, 'and let me know what's going on?'

'I'll let you know what I've found out,' he quibbled. 'If it's that easy to find out what's going on, I'd be silent with astonishment.'

'Make sure you aren't,' I urged him uneasily, and stood at the kerb watching the Jaguar continue southward towards Islington Green.

When I got back, I found the shop in darkness and the security alarm blinking peacefully above the display window. Checking upstairs, I located Mr Spock in the kitchen, absorbed in a double helping of Super Cat, and Barnabas and Ben in the sitting room. Ben was reading *The Cat in the Hat* aloud; he knew the book by heart and was turning the pages at the correct points in the story. Barnabas, I was interested to see, was too deeply absorbed in my photocopy of Tim Curwen's book to remember to comment on my abrupt departure.

'This man,' he observed without any other greeting when I appeared in the doorway, 'says, or rather implies, that he was up at Oxford. Of course, he may not have graduated, but he was presumably matriculated. How can he be semi-literate?'

I stopped, momentarily trapped in the sleeves of my jacket. 'Semi-literate?'

My father looked up from under his eyebrows. 'That's what I said. I thought you'd read this? The spelling is comical, the vocabulary extraordinarily limited, and the style almost confined to the simple sentence; his punctuation consists of dashes and full stops which he uses fairly randomly, and the paragraphing is more or less absent – ergo, semi-literate. I'd deduce an A-level grade of D at best.'

I had no answer.

'Of course,' Barnabas conceded, 'these days a great many people do graduate and even aspire to be writers without necessarily . . .' He fixed his eyes on me. 'Where have you been?'

'Hackney,' I said, and told him about it.

He heard me out and then seemed to change the subject by asking about dinner.

'Dinner,' Ben agreed, dropping the book abruptly and sliding off the settee. 'Granpa's staying.'

'Then it will have to be a Chinese takeaway,' I warned them.

'That will do,' my father agreed. His tone was curiously placid.

I phoned out the order. While we were waiting for delivery, he demanded and received the note containing the missing sister's address.

'Sunday morning,' he was saying when the doorbell rang, 'though not too early, would be a good time to find the neighbours at home. Shall we say that you will pick me up at eleven?'

This was an astonishing about-turn, apparently based on Tim Curwen's weak spelling, but unfortunately I chose not to object.

19

Staying Cheerful

By one o'clock Ben and I were hungry and cranky, so I was relieved to see my father striding towards us. Being tall, purple, and large enough to hold either a ton or two of books or up to eight passengers, my MPV had been rejected by Barnabas as far too conspicuous. Therefore he had made me park it out of sight around two corners from the house in Lavender Way, towards which he had set off alone on foot.

Ben had grown bored of being shut up, even in a spacious van and even with a couple of his toys, and we had gone for a long, dull walk through empty, litter-strewn streets that offered very little amusement until we came across a corner shop. Though closed and protected by graffiti-sprayed metal shutters, it had a fascinating coin-operated vending machine chained to a drainpipe by the door. It offered us brightly coloured sweets and a few little scrolls in plastic envelopes which promised to tell our fortunes. *You will suffer a serious disappointment but must try to remain cheerful,* we were advised by the one that popped out in exchange for my last coin. Penniless, we each unwrapped a red sweet, took one another by the hand, and strolled back via Lavender Way, sucking hard.

I'd caught a brief glimpse of my father standing at a doorway in the side passage of one of the houses there. He was deep in conversation with a fat man in a sagging black-and-white shell suit and appeared to be clutching a five-pound note. It had seemed tactless to hang about, so we had walked on; but I'd been waiting for him to turn up.

Barnabas climbed into the passenger seat looking thoughtful and already talking. 'I don't know . . . Most of the people I spoke to agreed that house has been empty for more than a year. One was sure that a family called either Herring or Harris used to live there. It is indeed council property, by the way, and remains empty pending a new roof – I have heard a good deal about the financial problems of Hackney Council. I asked everyone whether they knew of a woman called Theresa Clark. I said she had loaned you five pounds one night recently in a pub, and you'd asked me to return it for you without, obviously, having recalled the address correctly. Almost everybody professed ignorance.'

I woke up. 'Almost?'

'One person said he might have heard the name. He said he wasn't sure where she lives. He offered to pass your money on to Mrs Clark the first time he saw her around; according to him, she has never lived at the address you were given, but he sees her sometimes "at the shop" or "down the pub".'

'But he doesn't know where she lives?'

'I couldn't feel confident,' my father commented drily, 'that it is Theresa Clark, rather than the five-pound note, with which he was actually acquainted. Although I thought I perhaps did note a furtive gleam of recognition when I mentioned the name.'

'You didn't ask when he last saw her?'

'I asked,' Barnabas said, 'but he was vague. Recently, he thought. When I pushed for a description, he said I will know her by her very short white hair.'

'*White?*'

'Possibly very blond. Not an elderly lady, no. About forty, he said.'

I was puzzled. 'That sounds specific enough. Why did you doubt him?'

Barnabas considered my question and eventually said, 'I can't say, except that there was something rather knowing about his manner, as when somebody is aware what present you are getting for Christmas, but isn't going to tell you.'

'Kennedy may be able to find something out from the council.'

'True. In the meantime . . .'

'I'm *hungry*,' Ben whined.

Barnabas looked at him. 'So am I. Would you like spaghetti, young man?'

When the young man said that he would, my father uttered the command, 'To Rocca's, then.' His favourite, family-run Italian restaurant was some distance away in Bloomsbury; but it would certainly be a good place for a cheering Sunday lunch; as buying food had been one of the many things I had forgotten to do this week, I wouldn't even attempt to object. I really should find time to get in some groceries.

I drove south along Mare Street, turned right towards the West End, and went on considering the morning's non-events. I wondered whether I could blame Barnabas, for once. My feeling of disappointment burst out as we were crossing the lights at Old Street.

'How is she supposed to receive the proceeds of Curwen's estate if she's disappeared?'

'Didn't you say that they had lost touch? Well, she will eventually be found by advertisement or a professional enquiry. Just now, the thing that worries me most is the stray yet insistent thought that we may actually have a fictitious heiress. However, if as you have explained there is nothing for her to inherit, I suppose that idea should be abandoned.'

I opened my mouth, closed it again, and considered the truth of his statement. By now it did seem unlikely that there was anything to be gained – barring some very nice used clothes and some much less nice used books, all of which might with luck sell for enough to pay Curwen's rent up to Tuesday midnight.

I drove on, puzzled: *no heir and also no inheritance?* It didn't appear that Price Rankin Burke, in their smart St James's offices, would earn the kind of fees from handling Curwen's affairs that they must have been hoping for; but they were taking a lot of trouble over it anyway. I'd better remember to phone Burke in the morning, tell him that the sister had moved away, and remind him very loudly that this business no longer concerned me. If my assessment was correct, he ought to thank me for bowing out and returning their money.

I couldn't get rid of the feeling that there was something I'd missed.

'You said something?' my father suggested.

I denied that.

20

Exchanges

Monday mornings being what they are, I had divided mine between the big supermarket up the Holloway Road, my kitchen cupboards, and the launderette around the corner.

At lunch-time, suffering from a housework overdose, I heated up a ready-made lasagne in the microwave and ate it at the kitchen table with a glass of Chilean red. Then I went into the bedroom to fold a mountain of clean clothes and sheets, and put them away. The state of my own cupboards by comparison with Tim Curwen's hit me for the zillionth time and was, in accordance with recent vows, quickly pushed away. I flopped on to the bed when everything was as tidy as it would ever be here, closed my eyes, and the thought came back uninvited: the virtues of space . . . empty, lovely space. I may have dozed.

At any rate, it was mid-afternoon before I finally got into the shop, picked up the day's two mail deliveries from the floor at the door, dropped the envelopes on to the desk and pushed the button on the answering machine.

Chris Kennedy's distant voice spoke without a greeting: 'I thought I'd just let you know – I've been to the housing offices. It's a dead end. That place has been empty for nearly two years, and the last people who lived there were called "Harris". So . . . I thought you'd like to know.' There was a silence, during which I listened to the sound of an open line.

In the end he said, 'See you later,' and hung up.

The Londoner's farewell: it means this year, next year, any time, never.

I sat in the swivel chair, contemplated the screen of the dead computer, and felt relief wash over me. Or rather . . . not exactly relief. I reminded myself sharply that when the question of hard drugs comes up, you are talking about very bad men doing very bad things, and therefore any sane person will be very, very afraid and will certainly duck and run. Unless, of course, you are talking about some poor sod in the police force who can't. So why was I suddenly swept by this wave of disappointment, dissatisfaction and unfocused discontent?

It struck me suddenly that, after all the fuss I'd been making for the past couple of weeks, I'd just left *The Haunted Man* sitting in the bottom drawer of the desk: ridiculous. I pushed my questions about Kennedy and his motives to the back of my mind and dug under half an inch of assorted papers for the padded envelope. The book emerged. I checked to see whether my £200 price was still pencilled on the flyleaf and paused, looking at it, to wonder whether I ought to raise it a bit now. It was, I reminded myself, really quite a nice, fresh copy.

When I riffled through the leaves of the volume, however, I was brought up short. This book no longer qualified as nice and fresh. I found myself suddenly thinking ill of the dead, because Mr Curwen had used a blank leaf to make a list of some of his favourite passages. Fortunately, he had done his scribbling in pencil, and with some care I could probably erase it, but it would take hard work to get the paper looking like that of the other pages. I focused on the top line, the inscription 'Pages nos'. I knew that Curwen read his books, but on this occasion he had gone too far. I flung the book and its envelope back into the drawer in disgust. I keep throwing things in there to deal with later, and I was aware that I should have a sort-out some time. Soon. When I had a moment. Right now, there was something else to clear up.

When I phoned the solicitors' offices, an unfamiliar voice explained that Mr Burke was not expected today. I considered leaving a message, but that seemed too casual to make my point, so I asked for Dona Helmer instead. Unless it was just my imagination, she sounded wary as she asked me, 'How are you?'

'Don't ask,' I muttered. 'I've just discovered a lot of scribblings in my *Haunted Man*. That isn't why I'm phoning, though. I wanted to make sure that Mr Burke got the letter that I posted to him a couple of days ago. I told him that I couldn't find out anything more about Curwen's missing books, or anything. I sent back the retainer he gave me. But he sent me a note that seems to suggest he hadn't got my letter.'

'Is it important?'

I told her that it was important but not urgent, and got her to promise to ask her boss to contact me if my letter had gone astray, and then I hung up feeling relieved. The feeling faded. I dialled Kennedy and reached his voice mail.

I said, 'It's Dido Hoare. So tell me this: why did Tim Curwen choose to give Mr Burke the address of an empty council house over in Hackney for a sister who doesn't exist? Why there, not anywhere else? He must have known that address, somehow. And why did he invent a sister at all? And why did he name an imaginary person as beneficiary in his will?'

I hung up.

Then, without realising what I was doing, I bashed the computer screen with my fist and knocked the monitor off the far side of the desk. I could hear something smash as it hit the floor. That was stupid of me – I'd bruised my hand and there had been nothing wrong with the monitor, as Ernie had already assured me. Then I went out to the van with my credit card and drove back up the Holloway Road to the big computer shop there and bought the biggest, blackest PC they had in stock; it was as thin as Kate Moss and as beautiful as a design by Philippe Starck, with the largest conceivable hard drive and a modem so fast that telephone lines wouldn't be able to cope for another five years at least. Ernie was going to be in seventh heaven.

Then I carried the boxes with all the bits of my new system from the van, through the shop and into the office, and started the business of unpacking: polystyrene foam, shapely black plastic and a stack of manuals out; polystyrene packing with the old keyboard, the tower, the cracked monitor in . . . At some point, the flap of the letterbox clattered, and I glanced over my shoulder just in time to see something lying on the floor by the door and glimpse a figure hurrying past the window – someone with blond hair and a purple jacket, certainly not our usual postman.

Without any haste, I went to pick up the packet. At first I thought the big, thin, brown envelope was some kind of junk mail, a sample, because it had no address. Then I noticed that someone had pencilled the initials "DH" in the corner where the postage stamps would have been stuck if there were any – so, no, it probably wasn't junk and, yes, it was meant for me. I slid a fingertip under the flap and peeled it open. One look sent me scrambling to the door, although I knew even before I'd moved that the person I'd seen outside was long gone.

I went back and dipped into the envelope, pulling out a handful of notes: £5, £10 and £20 notes, neither new nor very old. I guessed without bothering to count that they added up to £200. At first I thought they had come without a word of explanation, and then I discovered the slip which had been enclosed – an unused lottery slip on which somebody had printed in blue ballpoint the words: '4 the book sorry abt the check'.

Somebody thought they were being funny.

21

Trouble

It was raining hard. Come to think of it, it had been raining all day and all weekend, not to mention most of the week before. October had begun before I'd even seen it coming – nights drawing in, global warming set to deliver autumnal floods, the news broadcasts promising trouble in the Middle East, and Serbia, and the presidential elections in America . . .

I was in the office, listening to the six o'clock news on my little radio and trying to plug the cables into the correct ports on various pieces of computer and peripherals. The shop was in darkness; and in that darkness both there and in the street beyond, I saw the headlights on high beam sweeping down the street. A car that I didn't recognise was pulling up, with a scrape of dodgy brakes, on the yellow line under the streetlight in front of the door. I watched the driver jump out, glance at the sign above the window, and then walk across the pavement to peer through the glass of the door and ring the bell. He had his back to the light, and I didn't recognise him; but the lights in the office were on and I knew he could see me. He rang a second time, an urgent, prolonged buzz, and I stalked down the darkened aisle to send whoever it was on his way.

When I reached the door I saw his face, so I opened up instead.

'Sergeant Waites?'

'Can I come in for a minute? I see you're closed, but this won't take long.'

I couldn't think of any reason to refuse, so I stood aside,

waved him in, and relocked the door. He looked toward the door of the lighted office. I looked at him. Even in the dim light, I could tell that nothing had got any better for him since we had last talked.

'I'm busy setting up a new computer,' I said. 'Can I make you a cup of tea?'

'That would . . .' he started, then stopped. He looked down at me. 'I could use a pint. Can I buy you a drink?'

Can you *what*? as I just managed not to babble aloud. He was waiting, so I thought fast.

In the office, in plain sight on my desk, sat £200 in small-denomination banknotes on top of their envelope, along with the lottery-ticket message. I'd been staring at them from time to time while I worked, wondering who to tell, or whether I shouldn't, for example, just bury it all at midnight in St Mary's churchyard around the corner. I reminded myself quickly that there was nothing incriminating about cash, nothing traceable. Which was, presumably, the point about this particular cash. Even so, I was thinking about Kennedy's hints. Could it be Waites who was heading up some huge drugs gang, with all the corruption and protection that would imply? He was stationed in the area where Curwen had been operating. On the other hand, could I see this cranky detective sergeant as a crime boss? If he were involved at all, it was more likely that he worked for the big man. Either way, I was irrationally afraid that my bundle of inexplicable cash might attract his attention. This is called guilt. Or to put it more sanely, I just wasn't up to having Waites anywhere near my desk. It made me feel nervous just being alone with him, and I needed to get him off my premises.

The news was still running on the radio, which meant that it wasn't yet 6.30 and that Barnabas, having dropped in to spend some time with his grandson upstairs, would probably not even notice a short absence. 'There's a pub around the corner on Upper Street,' I said. 'The Crown.'

'Saw it. Good.'

I said, 'I'll just get my coat,' and slipped off down the aisle. He made no attempt to follow. I switched off the lights first, then by touch I opened the bottom drawer and dropped the money in on top of the book which it seemed to be intended to pay for. I retrieved my jacket and keys, had to go back again to switch off the radio, set the security system as I passed the box, and met him by the front door. It seemed that he hadn't moved. Asleep on his feet?

My local doesn't get into its stride until well after seven, so we found a free table in a quiet, half-empty section of the front bar, and Waites went away and returned quickly with his pint and my vodka and tonic. His beer slopped on the table as he put his glass down, and I watched him settling opposite me. First impressions had been right: the bags under the eyes were truly impressive this evening.

I poured my tonic over the ice cubes and said, 'Cheers.'

He blinked and nodded and said without preliminaries, 'I wanted to thank you for the tip. We've heard from the FBI. Those books are recorded as coming from Curwen. There were others, too. Forty-odd. The auction house is faxing over the full list.'

'All from Curwen?' I hesitated, but I could only ask. 'Over what period of time?'

'Nearly a year.'

It seemed to be the moment to raise the question. 'You told me that they found traces of drugs in the flat.'

He looked at me, nodded, and let about a third of his pint slide down his throat.

'Was he laundering drugs money?'

He put the glass down and looked at me. He seemed to have woken up. 'We wondered, but I can't understand it. I haven't heard of anyone using that method. Betting shops, foreign currency exchange booths, minicab businesses, Chinese restaurants – but *books*? You tell me: why would anybody do it that way?'

I couldn't answer his question, except . . . I repeated what I'd already told others: the loopholes that allow an international trade in most British books to be conducted more or less without regulation. 'Unless you're a business, and have to make tax returns,' I added, 'it's unlikely that anybody would even notice. Private owners can sell ordinary books abroad any time they want to without paying tax. It's all legal and simple and quiet. If the Inland Revenue noticed you doing it on a regular basis they might decide you're trading as a business; but it isn't likely that would happen for years. Did Curwen pay income tax? But even if he did . . .'

'Good point,' Waites said. His eyes were fixed on his glass.

I waited. When he stayed mum I said, 'I keep worrying about something. You see, there are two problems. He could have realised a fair amount of money this way, at any rate by most people's standards, but nothing like the hundreds of thousands of pounds that they talk about in the newspapers when they write about the international drugs trade. I don't understand how he could do it on such a scale that it would cope with really vast sums. I suppose he was just a minor player? But the second thing is, where did the money go after he was paid for the books? You see, it's not just money laundering, it's a way of sending money abroad as well as giving it a respectable history. In the book trade, we'd say that it has a provenance.'

I could see him thinking about it. 'It's easier just to put cash into a brown envelope,' he said eventually. 'I don't see it yet. Well, it's under investigation. They'll get there.'

I hesitated because I'd noticed the pronoun. All right. I decided to ask, 'When is the inquest? I'd like to attend.'

He looked at me, obviously startled. 'You would?'

I nodded. Yes, I would. I waited.

He said eventually, 'No date's been set.'

'Isn't that a bit slow?'

He stared at me. 'The investigations aren't complete.'

I thought, but you don't have to *complete* investigations for an inquest, you can just present evidence of who the victim is and what killed him, and then the proceedings can be adjourned. Even I know that. I let him see that I was watching him, with my questions multiplying.

'There are unresolved problems.'

I waited.

'Thanks for your help, anyway. They'll probably get in touch with you later.'

I said tensely, 'That's the second time you've said "they". Are you off the case?'

'We've been stood down – Marylebone. We've closed operations and handed over what we had to a different department. We're all overstretched these days, so my boss is happy.'

I thought about that. 'What other department?'

'Something called the Crimes Operation Group. Our Chief Superintendent got in touch with them a few days ago. It was the drugs connection.'

Bingo. They'd known about the drugs and they'd made a decision to pass the problem on. Unless somebody in Scotland Yard had decided for them. Waites might be complaining about being overstretched but something was broadcasting the message that he wasn't very happy about this.

After a pause, he said, 'I'm going to have another. Will you . . . ?'

I glanced discreetly at my watch and said, 'I'll buy this one. Unless you're on expenses?'

He smiled faintly. 'I'm not on duty, you know. Thanks – I'm driving, but I'll risk one more.'

I walked to the bar, and leaned there without any great feeling of urgency about attracting the attention of the serving staff, because I was thinking. So: Waites had come around in his own time, off duty, to . . . to what? Thank me for my assistance? Yet according to his story, he was out of the picture now. This was begging for an explanation.

A face appeared in front of me, and I ordered and paid for the round, and carried it back to the table wondering whether I was going to get any hint of what he really wanted.

He was drinking fast. I said tentatively, 'I meant to ask you whether you heard anything useful from the little blind boy I told you about. Or is it the others who dealt with him?'

He shook his head slightly. 'I went over there the same day. You told me his name was Tim, but the porter knew him. It's Daniel – Danny Thompson. I did wonder why you told me "Tim"?'

I didn't hesitate. 'Because he told me that was his name. I don't know why, unless it was because he was fond of Curwen and wanted to relate to him. To pretend. Who knows? Curwen was a sweet man. I mean, that's how I found him.' He looked at me, obviously startled, and I added with a shrug, 'No, Tim . . . Daniel also said that Curwen wasn't a "pervert"; he's a sophisticated little kid. Did he tell you anything new?'

'He repeated what you said. It sounded like the truth. You gave him one of Curwen's books?'

I nodded. So sue me. 'It wasn't valuable.'

'He appreciates it. He's off to school next weekend. Mrs Thompson seemed relieved he'll be out of our reach, not that he will be if they need to speak to him again.'

I said stiffly that it seemed unlikely he could know much more than he'd already said, and then changed the subject by thanking Waites for putting me in touch with Kennedy. I told him I'd found Kennedy very interesting.

Waites looked at me and almost smiled. 'I've known him for a couple of years. He's a bloody nuisance,' he said. I noticed that he and Kennedy were in agreement on that point.

What I didn't say aloud was that to me the whole business was looking more and more weird, and Waites – or perhaps the Met in general – was obviously up to something, but equally obviously he didn't intend to tell me what it was. They never do. We finished our drinks almost silently. I said I'd better get back to my son, and Waites said that he supposed his wife wouldn't really object to his getting home for his tea, although he gave the impression that he wasn't very sure of it. We walked out into the wet evening, and I turned the collar of my jacket up. Waites didn't bother. He may not even have noticed it was raining.

We stopped outside the shop while I thanked him. I still didn't know why he had come. I said, 'If I can help . . .'

He nodded. He said something I almost didn't catch, and then, more loudly, 'I'll see you later.' In this case, I was afraid he meant it.

I stood at the door and watched while he got into his car and drove off: I was making sure that he really had left, partly because I was starting to think that what he had just muttered under his breath was 'Be careful'. Maybe that was what he had dropped by to say. My instincts recognise trouble even when my brain can't identify its source. Then I let myself in and climbed the stairs towards the light and warmth of the flat and the sound of my father and my son having a friendly family argument. That somehow reinforced the message that I should be careful, very careful, about anything I chose to do from now on. *As far as you're concerned*, I was telling myself as persuasively as I could, *forgetting all about this business would be a really good notion*.

But on the other hand I have a contact in SO 11, the Met's Criminal Intelligence unit: an old friend. And not only did he owe me a big favour, but he knew that he did. How do I get myself into these things?

22

Criminal Intelligence

When the familiar voice at the other end of the line snapped, 'Timothy Curwen?' I knew I'd struck gold.

Paul Grant and I had played a lot of games over the past three years, ranging from those in which one bed or another had figured to the kind that get distorted by mistrust and competitiveness. Things had started souring even before that evening last winter when our cautious relationship had blown apart. This was a man who owed me. It had been all right at first, but some people can't stand being indebted. I hadn't seen him recently, though we had spoken on the phone: 'Have you been keeping well?', 'We must have dinner some time.' That kind of coolness.

I tried to play the waiting game.

'Dido, I can't talk right now. I'll ring you back.'

I said quickly, 'I have a customer coming in at ten o'clock. A dealer from Chicago. Big spender. He'll probably be here all day.'

'So you won't be alone? Good.'

I felt my stomach clench up. 'Paul—?'

'I need to check some things. Look, I'll do my best.' Was it my imagination, or did his voice sound really edgy? 'Stay there. Sell him lots of books. If you do have to go out, take your mobile.' He was hesitating again. 'In case you need to get hold of me in an emergency, let me give you the number of my new phone. Don't use it unless it's important. Programme it into your own mobile right now.'

He recited his number. I obeyed instructions. I was just opening my mouth when he beat me to it with, 'See you later,' and broke the connection.

That phrase was starting to bother me. The whole conversation was bothering me.

It was just after ten o'clock when a black cab stopped outside the shop and a middle-aged man with a lumberjack's bushy beard emerged, holding a laptop computer case out in front of him like an offering. I hurried to unlock the door for Bernard Teran. I'd met him earlier in the year, at the big June book fair, and my original impressions proved justified when he refused my offer of coffee with gentle American courtesy, commandeered my little folding display table, set it up by the window where he would get the best light, switched his laptop on, and started methodically and silently at one end of my shelves. I carried the visitor's chair down to the table and then tiptoed back into my office to think. Having considered things, I shut the office door silently and dialled my father's number.

He answered, sounding preoccupied.

'Dido? Ah! I was working. How is Ben? How are you both?'

I reassured him twice about his grandson and once, less confidently, about myself, and then enquired about his own state of health and welfare. With our daily ritual completed, we both paused. I sensed that his mind was beginning to focus on my call.

'And how is the new computer?' he demanded after a moment. He knew the story.

I offered some details about the machine and expressed the belief that it was nearly up and running and that Ernie would be able to install the finishing touches when he arrived for work the next afternoon.

Barnabas said, 'Mmn. But something is worrying you.'

I said tentatively that I could use some baby-sitting, if he felt up to it.

'This evening?'

'If you could.'

He paused to give me a chance to elaborate. When I didn't, he said, 'Six o'clock? Earlier?'

I told him that six would be fine, and Barnabas said, 'Mmn' for the second time. He had something on his mind. I hadn't told him about the cash, but I'd better, as soon as I saw him, or his cynical 'Mmns' would overwhelm me when eventually he found out the truth.

I hung up and poked my head around the door, discovering my customer deeply engrossed and happy in his work. I trilled, 'If you want anything, just let me know,' and retreated.

My next phone call reached Chris Kennedy's voice mail one more time. I hung up without leaving yet another message for him to ignore and rang the switchboard of his newspaper, where the operator transferred me to another line, and a brisk woman said that Mr Kennedy was taking a week's leave and invited me either to leave a message or ring again next Monday. I snarled silently. Then I folded my arms on the desk, put my head down, closed my eyes, and tried to make sense of it all. It seemed that my brain had seized up. I decided to loosen it by stages.

Somebody had just pushed a significant amount of cash through my letterbox, with a note saying it was payment for a book which was, in fact, still in my possession. I'd had only the briefest glimpse of the person who had brought it, but he – or 'she', I thought – had looked, or (I shifted into Barnabas-speak) had an appearance consistent with, the description of Tim Curwen's sister which my father had heard from somebody in Lavender Way, but dismissed. It certainly hadn't been Dona Helmer, the only other woman involved in this business as far as I knew. *So far*, I reminded myself hastily.

Then, that sum corresponded precisely to the price of my Dickens, and was offered in payment for the book which was now sitting in my desk. Why somebody should have decided to do this remained unclear. I played frivolously with the idea that I'd just received an entirely new order for *The Haunted Man* with payment in advance. No. Or maybe some honest anonymous murderer had recalled that Tim had failed to pay up for his latest purchase, and had thoughtfully sent me the money in case I was upset. No.

Say there had been two murderers, if Timmy – no, that was Daniel, of course, and I suddenly found myself worrying because nobody I met these days was who he was supposed to be – if Daniel Thompson could be believed; and they had been speaking in a style not much used in polite society. I could assume that such people wouldn't give a toss for any books, much less my legal ownership of that particular volume. Perhaps I had a secret admirer in low places?

This line of thought was becoming more and more blatantly silly when a gentle knock on the door reminded me that I was not alone.

I said, 'Sorry! Yes?' and my customer's beard poked itself around the edge of the door.

'It's past noon. I'm going out to eat, Ms Hoare. I'll be back at one, if that's okay with you.'

American lunch hours. I pulled myself together, assured him that I would be here when he got back and that his lap-top would be safe if he wanted to leave it, and pointed him towards the restaurants on the main road. Then I locked up and retreated upstairs, where Mr Spock was pacing stiffly back and forth in the corridor, waiting to complain that he had been on his own for several hours, that it was too wet for him to enjoy his usual rooftop, wall-top, back-yard morning hunt, and that I might wish to pay him a little more attention at the very least and probably also some milk. Since my less than inspired thinking had left me with a headache, the two of us spent the hour stroking and being stroked. I, at least, felt better afterwards.

At five minutes to one, having remarked to Spock that I needed a lot more information about certain faceless people before I could expect to make any sense of this business, I went downstairs, phoned Paul Grant's office again in sheer desperation, and got no reply. Chris Kennedy's voice mail provided the same message as before. At one o'clock, Mr Teran rang the bell, paused for a moment to discuss the books he had set aside, helped me to carry them in and pile them on the packing table, and then got quietly back to work. I sat at my desk and smiled at his selection – this is my favourite kind of customer: polite, quiet, knowledgeable, businesslike and loaded. If only everybody . . .

Just after four o'clock, as the daylight was starting to fade, I heard a car stop outside. The door was locked and the new arrival had to ring the bell. I lowered the auction catalogue I was reading and looked down the aisle. Paul had turned up.

That is, Criminal Intelligence, I reminded myself firmly, edging past Teran to open the door.

'Dido—' He saw that we were not alone.

I introduced them: 'Mr Grant, an old friend; Mr Teran. I'll take Mr Grant into the office to talk. Please don't let us disturb you. Do you need anything?' But my customer had already turned back to the shelves.

We walked between the rows of books and slipped into the office; Paul shut the door firmly, stared hard at my face, contemplated the computer, said vaguely, 'That's new, isn't it? Racing model?' and perched on a corner of the desk. We looked each other over a little warily.

He never changed much. The brown eyes watched me out of the same tanned, wedge-shaped face. His hair was a little shorter and the grey suit a little more expensive than in the spring. He was still spending time in the gym. I asked myself cautiously how I felt about him now and answered myself: All right. I had not suddenly become immune, but a part of me was happy to keep some distance between us.

'Dido, what's going on? How did you know Tim Curwen?' He had lowered his voice to a rumble calculated to be inaudible through the closed door.

I said, 'He was a customer. How do *you* know him?'

At first I thought he was going to refuse to say anything. Our history is filled with my asking Paul Grant questions and him refusing to answer. This time, he gave me a reluctant grin. 'Business. I don't know how much . . . ?'

I said, 'He was a drug dealer. I assume that's it?'

I'd shocked him. He raised his eyebrows, lowered them into a scowl, stared at me fiercely and stammered, 'You . . . ? How do you know that?'

'Marylebone CID mentioned there were traces of cocaine in his flat,' I said with exaggerated patience. 'Then somebody else told me he was a dealer. Then a CID person I spoke to said that you people had "taken over" the investigation. He kept saying it was very nice of you to help out, although I think he may resent it. That's just an impression, he didn't say so. I assumed that hard drugs were probably at the bottom of this, so I phoned you about it, and obviously I was right.'

He shook his head impatiently. 'I *haven't* been personally involved with this project to date, but I'd heard about it. I don't understand what you're doing, wandering around talking to CID. Did they get in touch with you? Why? What have you been up to?'

I looked at him and could feel myself starting to glower; but I still needed information, so I compromised by telling him politely about my good customer and how he had, probably unintentionally, given me a worthless cheque to cover his final purchase, which had led to my working for his executors. For some reason or other, that last scrap of information seemed to interest Paul. He started to say something, stopped himself, and threw me a sideways glance.

'I thought,' I said sweetly, 'that you could probably straighten out a few problems for me. You see, the last thing that Mr Waites told—'

A polite knock on the door notified us that time was up already. I opened it. Teran was standing on the other side with his laptop case in his hand and his raincoat on. Looking past him, I could see several more piles of books waiting on my display table. He announced, 'I'm finished here, Ms Hoare. Thank you very much indeed. Will you ship them over and bill us? You've got my card?' I had. I reassured him, thanked him, wished him a most successful trip, and saw him out. Then I made sure that the street door was locked and picked up the nearest stack of books. Paul appeared at my elbow suddenly to carry the rest of them. We placed them gently beside the first lot on the packing table. Teran had selected two boxes' worth of quality stock, and I'd done a remarkably nice day's business.

'What did Waites tell you?' Paul asked, and I realised with a start that for him our conversation had never even been interrupted.

'He said I should be careful. So did you, this morning, if not in so many words. What are you both warning me about? Why?'

Paul looked down at me thoughtfully. Brown eyes . . . I shook myself mentally and looked back at him coolly.

'You know what we do.'

It was a statement, and he was right – I did. He had got his transfer to SO 11 the previous winter: the branch of the Met which deals in long-term intelligence gathering. I just nodded.

'We knew about Curwen because of a project we've been working on for the past year. You're right; he's – was – involved in Category A drugs, and working for an outfit we're trying to close down. When news of his death came up, we let Marylebone know that his friends may have killed him, and when their local intelligence officer asked for input, a couple of the central departments got involved. But that isn't the point: the point is that we know quite enough for me to be able to warn you not to get mixed up in this. Forget about him.' He hesitated. 'Are you still working for . . . who was it? Price Rankin Burke?'

I shook my head. 'I resigned.' I stopped to wonder whether this was the right time to ask him how the appearance of a £200 cash payment could possibly fit with what he had been outlining, and in the silence I heard the bell of St Mary's Church, just south of the shop. Five o'clock already. I said, 'I have to go and get Ben from nursery,' and made a grab for my jacket.

'I'll drive you.'

I accepted the offer, partly because I was late and mostly because I hadn't finished with him, not nearly. My mind scurried around the problem until it came up with an answer. Two birds with one stone, maybe. I said, 'Are you busy this evening? There's something I need to talk to you about, and it happens that I've arranged some baby-sitting.'

I switched off the lights and armed the security system.

He said, 'I just have to make a phone call.' At the time, I assumed he was back with his wife again. That was a habit of his. Afterwards I guessed that it was business.

23

Nice Disguise

We stopped under the streetlamp. I knew perfectly well that Paul had been staring at me all the way down the stairs. I glanced up furtively at my windows. As I'd expected, Barnabas and Ben were standing at one to watch our departure. So far as I could tell Paul hadn't noticed them. He was looking me over with what was, I slowly realised, appreciation rather than well-based horror.

'Nice disguise,' he observed. 'Can you walk in those shoes?'

I said, 'Of course I can. A reasonable distance. I'll take them off if I need to run.'

'I don't suppose it will come to that.' He laughed and continued to survey the landscape.

I would have liked to think this behaviour indicated lust, but the reference to a disguise had given him away. I'd dug through my bottom drawers to find the black top with metallic bead embroidery around a neckline which was just high enough that, although they might still arrest me for indecency, they couldn't make the charge stick. I'd bought it in a charity shop in Upper Street in a moment of madness and hadn't had many chances to wear it. My bottom half was lovingly shrink-wrapped in black stretch trousers, and I was tottering on my favourite old pair of strappy shoes with three-inch heels. I'd even found the matching handbag, because there was nowhere in this outfit for me to keep my keys and money and mobile phone. Then I'd brushed my short, dark hair the wrong way until it stood out in a mad, curly bush all over my head, and applied more than enough eye make-up. I felt seventeen again, and I looked like a tart; I was still surprised that Barnabas hadn't lost control and tried to tell me I was grounded.

Inspection finished, I made my way to the passenger door of the big silver Rover which Paul was driving this evening: a change from the old banger he used to run. It reminded me that he had got his promotion six months ago and was climbing on up the ranks.

'Talking about disguises,' I said, sliding voluptuously into the passenger seat, 'you do look respectable.'

He slammed my door and walked around the back of the car. The lid of the boot went up and remained that way for a minute, blocking my view behind. When it slammed down, and he reappeared at the driver's door, he was wearing a manky-looking black windcheater and his tie had disappeared. Well, perhaps it made him a slightly more plausible escort for me, at least in a dim light, after a few drinks, and if you assumed that my taste in men matched the clothes I was wearing. That was good.

'I'll head towards Homerton,' he said. 'I want to look at the house you mentioned. Then we'll find the nearest pub and I'll buy you a drink and we'll talk about it. Frankly, I'd say there's something funny about this sister story; but it won't hurt to spend an hour looking over the ground.'

I had finally got around to confessing about the cash when he had turned up at six. Paul had thought about that for a while and then shut himself into the sitting room and started making phone calls; but he seemed to have dismissed it by now as some kind of inexplicable red herring. However, I had interested him in my plan of wandering through Lavender Way and its environs. I might enquire after my old mate, Theresa Clark; and if Paul would play along, he could stand around and look out for familiar faces. I hadn't said anything to Barnabas. He was supposed to believe that we were going out for a meal. I'd probably have to cut my way out of this tangled web as soon as I got back.

We pulled up around the corner from the dead house in Lavender Way, left the car parked under a streetlamp to deter thieves, and walked back. Nothing had changed. When I hesitated by the front path, Paul placed a possessive hand on the nape of my neck and pushed gently.

'That's it? Keep going. We can't do anything here.' We kept going. After a moment, he said, 'I'm going to have somebody contact Hackney and come over to make sure the place really is empty, so I don't want us to be too conspicuous just now.'

I said, 'I thought you told me that you weren't on this case?'

'That was true,' he muttered after a moment. 'I made a phone call.'

I didn't have to ask any more.

'We'll cross here,' he said at the next corner, 'and walk back to the car. Let's drive around and check things out.'

There were three pubs within half a mile of the house, and not much else by way of entertainment unless you counted two video hire shops, a curry house and a chippie. Two of the pubs were in Clapton Road and one in the High Street. We left the car tucked away in a narrow lane behind a parade of shops and headed into the first of them, ordered drinks in the front bar and sat with our heads together, smirking at each other self-consciously.

It wasn't until the Anchor – the third of the pubs – that we hit pay dirt of a kind I hadn't anticipated. We went in through double doors set into the corner of the building and found a large, noisy saloon bar. All the cramped tables were taken, and the space around the bar was crowded. A huge television screen was blasting out rap music, which made conversations difficult though a lot were going on anyway. Paul leaned over to shout into my ear, 'Grab those two seats. I'll get the drinks.'

I flung myself into one of two momentarily empty chairs and dumped my jacket on the other. When I looked up, Paul was still struggling towards the bar. I let my eyes wander.

Chris Kennedy was backed into a corner four tables away, with a pint in front of him, eyes half closed, and a baseball cap tipped over his forehead which almost hid the red hair. He looked either sleepy or drunk; but I noticed that he was awake enough not to glance my way. I went on staring; after a minute he got up and headed past, pushing through a door marked 'Toilets'. I nearly went after him, though perhaps in the circumstances . . . Then in a momentary pause between music tracks, I heard a muffled trilling inside my bag. I kept my eyes on the door where Kennedy had disappeared while I was feeling for the phone in a nest of tissues.

'Dido, what are you doing here with that copper in tow?'

I took a deep breath. 'Mr Kennedy! How sweet of you to return my phone calls at last.'

There was the sound of flushing; I withdrew the phone from my ear for a few seconds. When I returned it, he was just saying, '. . . do they always think that normal people wear naff windcheaters?'

I guessed what I'd missed and enquired sweetly, 'What are *you* doing here under a naff baseball cap?'

I heard him snort, but when he spoke his voice was serious. 'Dido, just get him out of here. Finish your drinks and go away.'

'Why? Does he know you?'

'No, I don't think so. Who is it?'

'Somebody I've known for years. He used to be in Islington CID. He's with a depart—'

'We can't talk now.'

I was watching Paul's head. He had been standing at the bar for a while, and I thought he was paying now, so, no, we couldn't talk. 'I've been leaving messages on your voice mail for the past two days,' I said icily, 'and you've been ignoring me. Why should I do anything you say?'

'Because you must. Look—'

'You look,' I interrupted. 'I'm here looking for somebody else, not you. If you want anything from me, you'd better stop ignoring my phone calls. Ring me on this number between twelve and twelve thirty tonight. I should be at home by then. We'll discuss it.'

'Nice outfit,' he said, and I was fairly sure that he had picked up the basic message before he switched off.

In a moment, he was back. I watched him marking time at the door until Paul had reached me; then he passed behind my copper's unconscious back and sank into his own seat, rounding his shoulders and slumping like a drunk, putting his face into shadow. He was still there when I'd finished my vodka.

'Nobody with ash-blond hair and purple jackets here, either. Shall we go?' Paul asked. He had barely touched his beer. I got the idea it was his second time of asking, though only the first time I'd heard him.

'This will take some doing,' I admitted gloomily.

'It would need a lot of manpower to operate a surveillance on the whole area,' he said flatly, 'and you'd need beginner's luck to get your lady anyway without more specific leads. We're not even sure what we're looking for. We need to know where she's based. If she exists.'

I said humbly that he was probably right. But the sight of Chris Kennedy, still slumped in his seat across the room and looking carefully – I was sure of it by now – at every newcomer, suggested that I was not mistaken. I got languidly to my feet, grabbed my things and swayed sexily towards the door. Outside, I took a deep breath of damp air, struggled into my jacket, and used the moment to decide that I should find out what Kennedy thought he was doing there, before I shopped him to Paul.

'Food?' Paul was suggesting from behind me. 'A curry? That Indian back there looked reasonable.'

My stomach gurgled: for the moment I couldn't remember whether or not today's lunch had ever happened. Besides, it would give me more time in these littered streets to look for the invisible woman.

I heel-and-toed my shoes off, stretched my legs, wriggled my toes, leaned back against the cushions and closed my eyes. I didn't open them when a furry body landed on my lap, slipped, and anchored itself with a claw in my thigh.

Just ten minutes earlier, I had been standing at the down-stairs door listening to Paul Grant's car moving off down George Street. A minute after that, I had entered the sitting room to find my father dozing over a book and waiting to ask pertinent questions. Two minutes later, I was trying to explain everything by the arrival of a lot of anonymous cash, a story which Barnabas had made me repeat in detail and which had reduced him, though only temporarily, to speechlessness. Now I listened to the sound of water running in the bathroom and stroked Mr Spock dreamily. A door opened and closed. My eyes remained firmly shut.

My father's voice said gravely, 'No.'

I clamped my jaw on a yawn, gulped a breath, and said, 'What do you mean, "no"?'

'I mean, no, something isn't right. Think about it. I suppose you can't remember any other customer who might owe you two hundred pounds?'

I opened one eye, looked at him, closed it again and said, 'You know we don't operate that way. Don't wake me up.'

He sat down with a thud on the other end of the settee. 'You aren't thinking this through. Tell me one thing: who could have known the price of the Dickens or the fact that Curwen's cheque had bounced?'

I yawned again, thought about it briefly, and said, 'Police, lawyers, journalists, you, Ernie . . .'

'You aren't attending,' he said loudly. 'I repeat: who could have known the precise sum *and* wanted to cover Curwen's cheque?'

Mr Spock departed in a huff as I sat up. 'I see what you're saying: whoever sent the money knew the book hadn't been paid for. They must have heard that from Curwen before he died. It's as though somebody's trying to complete his purchase.'

Barnabas muttered, 'Exactly. But I ask you: why? It puts the book into Curwen's estate. Again: why?'

I said, 'His sister, obviously.'

'But you did maintain that *she* could have known nothing about this?'

I thought about that. No, I couldn't maintain anything of the kind, not any more. Who else could have benefited from this deal? Well – Kennedy knew the story. Or it might have been somebody like Dona Helmer – the solicitors knew about the book and I'd told them I'd found it. I'd mentioned it to the police at Marylebone, and they might have included something in their notes – Waites or one of his men could even be involved, though I couldn't imagine why they would have paid over that cash. Anyway, I'd seen the person who brought it. I said, 'The more I think about this, the more I'm sure it *was* a woman who delivered that envelope. I'm keeping an open mind about who she is, though I don't suppose there's really any doubt.'

'I was merely pointing out to you that she is not the only possibility.'

'I know that,' I said, sitting up straighter, 'but why would *anybody* do this? I've told the solicitors that I got the book back.

If his sister knows about it, why should she care? She's under no obligation. The interesting question is whether she was in touch with her brother during the fourteen hours or so between when he emptied his bank account and when he died, because then she might know something about the murder. But why would Curwen have told her about the book, and why would she bother?'

I waited and stared at Barnabas, who stared back. When no inspiration struck either of us, I told him about finding Kennedy in the pub. 'He made a fuss. He guessed that Paul was a policeman. At least, he said he was guessing.' I told him about the call to my mobile, which amused Barnabas briefly.

'He was perhaps hoping you wouldn't acknowledge him in public while you were wearing your glad rags,' my father suggested. His eyes trailed across my disguise, and he shuddered slightly. 'I shouldn't draw too many conclusions.'

I said that Kennedy had been wearing a baseball cap, and could not therefore complain about *my* taste in clothing. Then I made my point: 'He knew Curwen personally, they were close I think; and I found him hanging around over there when he's supposed to be on holiday. Doesn't that mean he believes Curwen's sister lives around there somewhere, and that she knows something about this mess? You know, I keep thinking that he might be mixed up with that money himself.'

'If he is in the habit of "hanging around" there, he may well be up to his sharp nose in everything that has happened. I shouldn't trust him. You've seen the car – you should never trust a man with cream leather seats in his car.'

He was trying to make me smile. I responded by saying dramatically that at the moment I didn't trust anybody except Ben and perhaps Mr Spock, and my mobile rang. We exchanged a look.

'Talk of the devil?' Barnabas enquired.

I retrieved my phone and listened to a voice saying, 'At your command.'

I twitched my eyebrows affirmatively at Barnabas. 'Where are you?'

'I'm parked round the corner. I wanted to make sure you were alone.'

'I'm not alone,' I said, 'but my policeman has left. Barnabas is still here.'

The voice sighed. 'If you offered me a coffee I'd probably tell you anything . . . I mean, everything.'

I said loudly, 'I think you used the right word the first time round, but I'll risk it. And don't ring the bloody bell, because I don't want Ben woken up.'

He sighed. 'Don't throw a hissy fit; I'll whistle outside your windows when I get there, all right?'

A hissy fit? The man was getting familiar. I said to Barnabas, 'He's patronising me.'

My father smiled.

24

Black

Kennedy was just slightly drunk. He sat on my sofa taking his coffee black and stiffened with a lot of sugar. He thought about what Barnabas had been saying, shook his head, and answered, 'He never said a word to me about his childhood or his immediate family. A bit about aunts and uncles, ancestors . . . I assumed he was an orphan.'

'So why were you over there this evening, if she doesn't exist?'

He looked at me slowly. His eyes were amused. 'I don't say she doesn't exist, I just said he never mentioned her, and so obviously I know nothing about her. I think he once told me he was an only child, but that doesn't mean she doesn't exist. Tim was a congenital liar, you know. If she exists, I want to talk to her. Why were you over there this evening yourself?'

I said, 'Nobody ever told me she doesn't exist, so I was looking for her too. Didn't I say, she's named in his will?'

'Who was the cop with you? Not out of Marylebone?'

I said that Paul was somebody working at the Yard for Central Criminal Intelligence, and that I'd known him for a while.

Kennedy looked at me hard, then looked down at his coffee. 'Did this geezer explain why he got in touch with you?'

I controlled myself. 'I got in touch with him. I want to know what's going on, and even if he didn't already know about Curwen's death, I was sure he'd know who to ask. I just need a few answers. He hasn't given me any, but I still have my hopes. I did confirm that his department is involved in the case now. There was a point this evening when he phoned somebody and got the authority to poke around. So we went looking for Theresa Clark.'

Kennedy frowned at me. 'Excuse me? You've already said that at least once before, but I think I'm missing something. *Why* are you doing all this?'

He was still dancing around me, and it made me angry. I could have explained about the money then, but instead I said, 'Why are *you*?'

He hesitated and muttered, 'Research.'

'For your book or your article or whatever it is?'

'Exactly.'

Oh yes? I told him about the delivery anyway.

He woke up. 'Are you sure? Sorry, scrap that, you are. It was brought here? By a woman? Why didn't you let me know? No, scrap that too. Why didn't you at least give me a hint why you wanted me to ring you back?'

'Why didn't you just risk it and ask me?'

He shrugged, looked away, and drank his coffee. 'I didn't see why you should get involved.'

'You mean I should mind my own business?' I suggested very sweetly.

He hesitated briefly and said, 'Dangerous.' He put his mug down on the coffee table slowly but slightly clumsily. 'Sorry. I couldn't . . . ?'

I said, 'I think you'd better,' and refilled the mug hurriedly with what was left in the pot.

He shovelled some more sugar in, stirred it clumsily, drank it off, and said, 'I've been over in Hackney for days, keeping an eye on that house and poking around the neighbourhood; but either the place really is empty or else somebody flies in down the chimney whenever I look away. Joke. This morning, I tried knocking on doors and asking after "a woman I used to know who lives around here". Nobody knew the name. I did find out that somebody else has been asking. A couple of people said that on Sunday morning there was an old man . . .' He broke off and stared at Barnabas. Then he looked back at me. 'I should have answered your calls.'

'It might have saved trouble,' Barnabas mused. 'Dido is extremely persistent, and rather a loose cannon. If you don't mind my asking: you say this is dangerous. I assume we are talking about drugs, guns, criminal gangs and suchlike excitements? May I also enquire why, in these uncertain circumstances, a law-abiding journalist should wish to be so closely involved?'

Kennedy's face seemed to close up. He said, 'I've already said: it's my job – crime reporting. I know that something big is going on somewhere, though the Met are keeping it very close to their chests. What you've just said about SO11 getting involved, and Waites turning up to talk to you, all says I'm right and that it could involve police corruption as well as drugs and murder.' He hesitated; there was a moment when I could see him deciding that cynicism was the best defence. 'It's a great mixture: the public have become very interested, these last couple of years, in reading about corruption investigations in the Met and the South-east Regional Squad. In a nutshell, this has all the signs of being a great big story, and I want to break it in my paper. I'm pushing for the "Journalist of the Year" award. All right?'

Barnabas and I exchanged looks. This was getting silly.

Kennedy noticed the atmosphere and mumbled something about getting some sleep.

I said, 'Wait a minute – I haven't finished yet. What would happen if I told my copper friend about you?'

He looked at me hard. 'He'd ask questions. Depending on my answers, he might make trouble with my editor. Unless he himself is involved in some kind of cover-up, in which case he might make *big* trouble with my editor. At best, he could make my life a little more complicated. At worst, they might all get together and string me up by my thumbs and then ask me lots of questions about Tim Curwen. Is this blackmail?'

I smiled sweetly. 'Might be.'

'What do you want?'

'I want you to help me find Theresa Clark: I want to talk to her. That's all. For the moment. You see, our interests are identical. It seems to me we should help each other.'

He looked at me for a few seconds. Then he glanced at Barnabas, which I took as evidence of sharp intelligence. He said, 'I'm open to negotiation.'

'All right,' I said; 'we could even start this way: you call me back when I leave a message on your voice mail.'

He narrowed his eyes at me, half smiled, and said, 'Done. Just tell me one thing that makes any kind of sense: what are you really up to?'

I'd been asking myself that same thing for days now, so I had an answer ready. 'I've bowed out of this situation several times over, but for reasons that I don't understand, everybody keeps coaxing me back in. I want to find out what's going on before anything serious happens, and everything you say, or Paul Grant, tells me I'm right to be worried.'

We exchanged long and not altogether trusting stares. He broke first. 'I have to go home, but I'll either phone you tomorrow morning or drop in to the shop. All right?' When I nodded, he added, 'Mr Hoare, can I give you a lift somewhere?'

Barnabas said, 'I live on Crouch Hill, but I was going to phone for a minicab . . .'

'It's on my way home,' Kennedy said, 'and I don't think I'm over the limit, if you were worried about my driving. If you're ready?'

Barnabas was apparently in a mood to live dangerously and

even put up with the cream-coloured leather. I chained the door behind them, poked my head into the bedroom, where I found Ben sleeping extravagantly, then pulled the door shut to muffle the noise while I ran a deep, hot bath, into which I poured the remains of two bottles of bath foam and my own tired body. I sank down under the bubbles and lay with my eyes closed until suddenly I found myself focusing on one single thing: I was going to find Theresa Clark, with or without anybody's help, ask her about her brother and his books and his recent actions and above all why she had given me £200, and then decide whether or not to believe her. If I could do this I would probably learn why my doorstep had been crowded, of late, with self-important liars who all wanted something from me without bothering to explain what. Put that way, my intentions seemed almost rational.

Next morning, returning from nursery, I stopped in at the shop to check my answering machine and deal with the first postal delivery. The pile waiting under the letterbox was all the usual, plus one long envelope with the return address of certain tenacious solicitors. Finding it there made me aware that I hadn't yet had enough sleep, coffee or aspirin. I flung the rest of the mail on to the desk, ripped the envelope open, tipped it upside down and shook it. Two things fell out: a long slip of stiff paper which was a company cheque made out to Dido Hoare for the sum of £200, and a letter which I read slowly, three times.

> *Dear Ms Hoare,*
>
> *Mr Burke has authorised me to inform you that our investigation of Timothy Curwen's estate has revealed enough net value to allow us to pay out the money he owed you. In the light of your kind assistance to the firm, Mr Burke is anxious that you should not suffer financial loss because of the damage to your book. Our cheque for the sum of £200 is enclosed.*

Please send the Dickens here by registered post, marked for my
attention. Thank you.
Yours sincerely,
Dona Helmer

I flattened out the folds in the paper, placed it flat on the
desk, put the cheque down on top of it, stared in disbelief, and
started worrying again. This was the final straw, and I certainly
hadn't expected it. I was now, very definitely, back in the
black on this deal. With all these nice people making £200
donations, you'd think it was my birthday.

25

What If?

A fresh pot of coffee produced the glimmerings of a desperate plan. I took my third cup of the morning to the little writing desk in my sitting room, where I searched the drawers for an old greetings card. The one I found showed a bunch of red roses under a waving banner inscribed: 'Thank you!' It was only slightly grubby around the edges. I opened it up, stared at the blank interior, and wondered how to put this. A plea? A threat? Reassurance? In the end I printed: WE'D BETTER TALK. D Hoare. If anybody ever got around to reading it, they could make up their own mind about its tone. I sealed the card in its bright pink envelope, addressed it to 'T. Clark' at 253 Lavender Way, and dug out a first-class stamp. Then I folded up Lloyd Burke's cheque, scrawled the words 'Thank you, but I have already sold the book to somebody else' on a sheet of old notepaper, addressed another envelope to the solicitors, sealed it, and found another stamp. Then I took both envelopes across the main road to the postbox to catch the 12.30 collection, which should ensure that they would reach their destinations by the first delivery in the morning.

By the time I was back in George Street, the old blue Jag was in the parking bay and Chris Kennedy and his hangover were hovering on the pavement outside my door.

I asked him, 'Coffee? Bicarbonate?'

'If that's a bribe, I'll take it.' Oh, this man was sharp.

Upstairs, I poured the remains of the breakfast coffee into two mugs and left the machine brewing again while I carried

them into the sitting room. Kennedy had settled in the
armchair, looking battered. I plonked the coffee down beside
him and paused as I was moving over to the settee to make
sure I'd left nothing in sight on top of the desk which might
incriminate me. I could hear the rain blowing against the
windows behind me all the time I was telling him about my
thank-you card.

He sipped gingerly at his coffee and asked, 'What's your
plan?'

'Well, maybe she'll get in touch with me because she wants
to pick up the book. That would make my life easier.'

'There is nobody living in that house.'

I shrugged. 'If you say so. I'll phone Paul Grant at lunch-
time and find out what the council told him. He was sending
somebody over.'

'I've been watching the place,' he snapped.

I smirked. 'They'll get the council to let them in. I don't
suppose *you* . . . ?'

He glanced at me and shrugged. 'All right. If I'm wrong,
that will be something. But if I'm right, then what?'

I said, 'I'm working on a scheme. I don't suppose that you
know what time the mail is delivered at Lavender Way?'

He shrugged again. 'I've seen a postman doing the walk . . .
let's think . . . not too early . . . ten? As late as eleven some
days? There's sometimes a second round at about one, not
always. Why?'

'Have you ever seen the postman going up to the door of
that house?'

'What would be the point? You think he pushes the mail
under the boarding?'

I said patiently, 'Don't be so superior. What happens to mail
when somebody moves away and doesn't leave a forwarding
address?'

He looked at me as though I were gibbering. 'I suppose the

junk mail is binned and the rest is "Return to Sender". Why?'

It was my turn to shrug. 'That's what ought to happen, but I was wondering whether it always does. The card I've just mailed doesn't have a return address, and it's in a cerise-coloured envelope, pretty conspicuous. I was hoping that somebody might remember if it's delivered to another house over there. I know this is an outside chance, but if Mrs Clark really does live somewhere around there, maybe she has a way of getting mail delivered. Perhaps she caught the postman one morning and said, "Hey, babe, I've moved from my old place, and could you drop my stuff in around the corner?" What if I drive over there in the morning and hang around to see what happens?'

'You could just ask the postman.'

'Don't be so enthusiastic. There's no harm if it doesn't work, and I can still ask the postman later. If I drive Ben to nursery and keep on going I'll get there in good time.'

'Ask your copper about it,' Chris said suddenly. I'm starting to think that address is just a red herring, but it would be nice to know. When you talk to him, ask him whether there's a redirection notice in force at the sorting office. Can you do that without getting up his nose? I don't know . . . you say you've known him for a while. Will he slap you down?'

'Probably.' I may have spoken a little acidly, because Kennedy looked but had the sense not to comment. I changed the subject. 'Can I ask you a question?' He nodded unenthusiastically. Blow him. 'Do you know anything about a law firm called Price Rankin Burke, in Mayfair? They were his solicitors.'

He looked at me blankly. 'Tim's solicitors?'

I started to feel uneasy. 'Yes. They told me that they dealt with his lease, his will . . . things like that.'

'All right, if you say so.'

'What's wrong? I have a solicitor. Don't you? Why wouldn't Curwen have one?'

'Yes, but then you are a nice, well-organised, middle-class lady with a business and a small child, and I'm . . . respectable. Whereas Tim . . .'

'Thank you,' I said, 'for assuming that I'm well organised. "Whereas Tim" what? Wasn't organised? Wasn't middle class? Barnabas called him "semi-literate".'

He squinted at the window. 'He might be right. Though believe me, that doesn't matter much to some people. Look, I can make a phone call if you like. I have a contact who works at the Law Society and I can find out what kind of reputation the firm has. Is that what you want?'

I pointed to the phone on the sideboard, said, 'Let's do it,' and prepared to eavesdrop on what turned out to be a long and slightly complicated conversation.

At the end of it, he thanked his informant, hung up, and looked at me quizzically. 'You got that?'

'Not all of it,' I admitted. 'I had the impression there's a question mark?'

'Not a big one. It's a stodgy old firm of family solicitors. Price and Rankin are dead and retired, respectively; the third partner runs it more or less on his own these days with junior staff, some of them trainees. There have been no formal complaints, and nothing is known against them, though the word in professional circles is that they are a little slow at processing things nowadays and that Burke may be getting past it.'

I said, 'I've met him; he was rushed off his feet, and I'd have said not at all past it.'

'You wouldn't like to let me in on this?'

'It's a little complicated.'

'Did I hear you grinding coffee beans a little while ago? Is there some more . . .'

I said that there probably was by now, and he followed me into the kitchen, carrying the empty mugs, and watched me pour out a double caffeine overload. I explained about the missing book and how it had led to my doing a probate valuation for the firm, as a result of which they had provided Theresa Clark's address when I said I needed to talk to her. We leaned against the door jamb and the counter top and considered this sequence.

'So that's how you got the address. I must have missed that.'

I said, 'There's more,' and explained about my ineffectual attempts to stop working for the firm. Then I told him about the cheque which had just arrived and been returned, and had to add: 'Maybe Mr Burke is getting senile after all.' My visitor did a little more frowning and whistling through the teeth, which roughly echoed my own feelings. I said, 'I've sent the cheque back politely and told them I sold the book to somebody else. I won't hear from them again.'

He hesitated. 'I suppose so. Sorry . . . I need some more sleep. Your father invited me in last night to talk about Philip Sidney's poetry, and I got to bed late.'

I said, 'He did?'

Kennedy snorted. 'Don't look so shocked. Your father is all right.'

'I know that,' I said crossly.

'He was warning me off.'

I whimpered, 'Off . . . ?'

'You. Getting you involved in my sordid business. He says that you are incapable of backing down even when you know that you should. There's somebody else who is going to string me up by my thumbs. Don't apologise, you don't have to. I'm going over to Lavender Way now to waste another day. I'll see if I can catch the postman, shall I? If your copper softens enough to tell you anything useful, will you ring me? I'll give you the number of my mobile, which I do always answer. If I see anything over there, I'll let you know. Are you . . . ? Your father told me that you're likely to be getting into some kind of trouble; do you have any immediate plans and if so can I do anything about it?'

I said slowly, 'I see that Barnabas made a strong impression. No, I'm going to do some work now. Ernie is coming in after lunch, and we'll be busy downstairs setting up the new computer.'

He said, 'Have a look out for my car if you do go over to Homerton in the morning. I'll be there before you.'

Maybe. 'If I see you, I don't know you,' I said, 'and vice versa, of course.'

He replied, 'I'm the soul of discretion, unlikely as that may seem,' and went away.

26

Surveillance

The clock on my dashboard said it was 9.23 when I pulled in on the far side of Lavender Way about thirty yards past the empty house, and sat with my engine running.

The pavements were almost deserted: people had left for work and school about an hour ago. Of course, a stream of cars and vans was still using the road as a rat-run. I'd caught sight of the Jaguar as I drove past the side road; it had looked empty, but at least its presence there showed that Kennedy was keeping his word. There was no sign of the postman yet. Of course. But it looked as though the situation was covered. I shifted into gear, turned the van around in a gap in the traffic, and drove back westward.

I'd just turned into the main road when my phone rang. I picked it up and heard Kennedy's voice saying, 'Dido? Was that you just now?'

At least he was awake. I admitted it, wondering whether I should hire a less conspicuously purple vehicle.

'Where are you now?'

'On my way home.'

'Checking up?' He was apparently both telepathic and amused.

'Just can't keep away from the party,' I growled. 'I didn't see you. Are you hiding in your car?'

'No. I'm sitting on the step at the side door, wishing I wasn't. Dido – did you notice?'

'What?'

'Dark grey saloon car parked in the side street, just south of Lavender Way, with a direct view across to the house. Two men sitting in it. I'd say the police are here.'

'What makes you think that?'

'Just believe me. They arrived about eight thirty and they haven't budged. I may have to climb over the fence if I want to leave without them noticing me.'

'Do you mean you've been there since *before* eight thirty?'

'Let's not think of it,' he said. 'Look, I just wanted to know whether you've spoken to your copper yet.'

'He's out. I left a message.'

'All right.' There was a silence, but the line was still open. 'He probably knows about the surveillance. I'm curious to hear what happened to get this approved: their budgets don't allow for much of this sort of thing nowadays. If they're looking so hard for Sis, I'd really like to know why.'

I would too. I'd give Paul another hour to sort himself out and get in touch. Then I'd start getting persistent with the office phone.

'You'll be at home?'

'I'll be in the shop. We open at ten thirty. Theoretically. Or as soon as I get back.'

'I'll ring you if I see your pink envelope,' he said. 'See you later.'

I needn't have worried. When I slid the van into the residents' bay and started across the road, I noticed that the sign on the door had been reversed and the lights were on inside: the shop had opened without my help.

I found Barnabas absorbed in the title page of a Merriman with Rackham illustrations. He focused on my arrival and said, 'Do you realise it's October already?'

I said, 'I do. How are you?'

'Busy. The Christmas catalogue. Illustrated books and fancy bindings? You realise that it should be ready for the printers a fortnight from now? We'll need a few photographs.'

I thought about it and said, 'Three weeks will do. Ernie got all the systems up and running yesterday, you know, so our database is back. Shall I show you?'

Barnabas threw what I could only think of as a nervous glance at the new machine. 'In a minute. You weren't here when I phoned earlier.'

I didn't ask about his intended subject matter because I thought I could guess. 'Errand,' I said, 'and now I need to go upstairs for a few minutes. Do you want anything?'

He glared at me. Then he laughed. 'Go on, then. If you attempt to escape—'

I sighed. 'I know: resistance is futile. Coffee? A cup of tea?'

'I think I could risk another small coffee,' he conceded. 'By the way, take a look at the residents' bay across the road when you go out there.'

I stared at him. 'Why? I've just parked in it.'

'There's an old black Vauxhall without a permit or, for that matter, I believe, a valid tax disc; it was sitting there when I arrived and was still there five minutes ago. The driver is at the wheel. He appears to be reading a newspaper and waiting for somebody. When I came up to this door, he looked at me . . .'

I couldn't resist: 'A cat may look at a king, you know.'

'. . . and then looked away rather ostentatiously when I caught his eye. I thought he knew me. I don't believe I know him. A "G" registration. I didn't care to stare long enough to memorise the number. Is this anybody we know?'

'I'll look,' I promised, and left a little faster than I'd intended.

The car wasn't familiar, nor was the driver, whose head was bowed over his newspaper, but who could have been watching me out of the corner of his eye. I hesitated just long enough to

catch the licence number and then got myself indoors and up
the stairs to the flat. Barnabas was probably jumping to
conclusions; though perhaps Paul Grant had decided that I
needed a watchman? But that made no sense. Neither did
anything else I could think of. I wrote down the registration
number on my pad before I forgot it.

The red light on my answering machine was flashing
rapidly. The first message was from my father, enquiring
where I'd got myself to and saying that he was about to turn
up and get some work done.

The second was from Paul. 'Dido? Sorry I've missed you.
I wanted to tell you that I did send somebody around to
Hackney, and she's rung in to let me know the house is shut
up tight, and there are no signs of squatters and no records of
anybody called "Clark" who's anything to do with the place.
It's a dead end. Look, Dido—' He broke off. I could hear
somebody speaking in the background. 'Dido, I want to ask a
favour, but I have a meeting right now. I'll ring as soon as I'm
free. Take care.'

I wiped them both and headed towards the kitchen, speculating about favours.

The joint proprietors of *Dido Hoare ~ Antiquarian Books and
Prints* were in the middle of their own meeting on the subject
of the Christmas list and its contents when my mobile rang. I
grabbed for it.

'Dido?'

'Chris? What is it?'

'The postman's just been. He walked straight past the
house.'

Well – it was what you'd expect. I opened my mouth to
thank him, but he went on, 'On the other hand, I think that he
had something bright and pink in his hand. I couldn't see what
it was.'

'Where are you now?'

'Back at the car, wondering what to do. Have you heard from your copper?'

I said impatiently, 'He isn't mine, his name is Paul Grant – that's "Superintendent Grant" to you. He had the place checked out by one of his people. The message is that it really is empty and the council don't know about any Theresa Clark.'

I could hear him whistling tunelessly through his teeth again. Eventually he said, 'Could he be lying?'

'What?'

'If what you say is right, what is he doing sending a surveillance team over here to sit and sulk?'

I had an idea. 'Should I ask him?'

Kennedy snorted with laughter. 'Good one,' he said. 'One more thing. Are you busy this lunch-time?'

I threw a look at Barnabas. 'Not necessarily.'

'I picked up a message on my voice mail a few minutes ago: an invitation. Bob Waites was wondering if I could meet him for a sandwich and a pint in Wood Green at about one fifteen. Would you like to come?'

I repeated, '*Waites?*' in a tone which struck me even in that moment as being a little shrill.

'Yes. We sometimes talk about this and that, and we've spent the odd hour in pubs before. Only usually I call him when I have a question – he doesn't ring me up out of the blue and issue urgent invitations. In the circumstances, I think I might need a minder. I rang back and said that you and I already had a lunch date. I think he likes you. Are you coming?'

I breathed hard through my nose.

He said, 'I could pick you up.'

I snorted. 'I wouldn't miss it.'

I came to and found Barnabas watching me from under his eyebrows. When he saw that he had my full attention, he said,

'What did the unreliable journalist say to make you squeak that way?'

I told him that the unreliable journalist had been reporting the failure of my pink-envelope scheme and the arrival of an invitation to lunch from a possibly-alcoholic policeman. As stories go, this one sounded thin. He put down his fountain pen and the pad of lined paper on which he had been making notes and regarded me gravely. 'I appear to be behind with the news. I spent yesterday, just one single day, in the peace and intellectual clarity of the British Library, and here—'

I came to a decision and interrupted. 'I think we need to put our heads together. I told you how people keep trying to give me money – maybe you can suggest what's going on, because I'm walking through quicksand and I can't even work out why I'm here.'

My father looked at me. He picked up his fountain pen and a fresh sheet of paper and said, 'Start at the beginning.'

I told him that I didn't know what the beginning was, unless you went all the way back to Tim Curwen's first appearance.

He nodded ironically. 'What a good idea.'

It probably was, though not right now; I'd just remembered something else. I held up an apologetic hand, got out of my chair, and went to look through the display window. The Vauxhall was still there. I returned to the desk and punched Kennedy's number into my mobile. Once again, he actually answered.

'It's me again. I want to change our arrangement. Don't come here. Can you meet me at a quarter to one in the pub around the corner? The Crown. Will that be early enough?'

'If you'd rather.'

I told him carefully that I would.

'Just in case,' I said to Barnabas when I'd switched off. 'I'm wondering whether the man out there really is police. If he is,

I'm not sure I want him seeing that Kennedy and I are in cahoots. But perhaps he's only a burglar, casing the houses down the road.'

'That would be a relief,' Barnabas pretended to agree. He looked at me, hesitated, and repeated, '"In cahoots"? Really?' I ignored that. He said abruptly, 'Well then: if you are quite ready?'

I looked at my watch. We had nearly an hour before I needed to leave, and I'd be happy to spend it bringing Barnabas up to speed and being forced to put my ideas into something like order. It was time I had a fresh perspective on where this was going.

I leaned back and started with, 'Tim Curwen came in for the first time about a year and a half ago . . .' It was a long journey before I arrived at: 'When he phoned me just now, Kennedy said that my note hadn't been delivered to the house but it might have been left with a neighbour, and that Waites, the CID man I told you about, has asked to meet him this lunch-time, which is another thing I don't understand, but he was joking about my coming along as bodyguard.'

Barnabas had stopped writing. 'This gun for hire?' His tone was acid.

'It makes no sense.'

But that wasn't true. Some things were just starting to edge into view out of the fog. It would be nice if I found a pattern. I looked at my watch, which said it was time to go. If the man in the Vauxhall started his engine when I appeared at the door, I'd need to take a couple of extra minutes to walk around through the churchyard and shake him off. Barnabas was smiling faintly, looking at the ceiling above my head.

'Will you be all right?' I asked him.

'I shall be thinking,' he informed me, 'probably upstairs for much of the time. You do have tea bags there? And some fresh milk? I may nap. Will you be back in time to get Ben?'

I said, 'Good. Yes, some, but I'll bring more. Good. I think so. Is that . . . ?'

'You have missed nothing out,' he said. 'Dido, just keep your eyes open.'

I said seriously, 'Barnabas, I am only going for a drink in a public place with a real policeman and a man who writes for a reputable broadsheet newspaper.'

He said, 'Maybe. But you might want to consider the fact that neither of them can possibly be acting *ex officio*. The policeman might be operating from a personal resentment that his "case" has been taken over by others, or his motives may be much more sinister. As for Mr Kennedy . . .'

'As for him?' I cooed.

My father looked at me closely. 'As for Mr Kennedy, he is not just researching a newspaper article, whatever he may claim. As far as I can see, his motivation is both personal and eccentric, and Lord knows what he's really up to. Still . . . as you say, you will be in a public place: I think you should make sure to remain in one. Please keep your eyes peeled.'

I told him I would watch for anything that moved and aim between the eyes; and I meant that at the time.

27

Personal, Eccentric and Messy

Down at the southern end of the High Road, Kennedy swung his car into Turnpike Lane and parked on a yellow line in front of a dry cleaner's. I could see the Lord Nelson's sign about twenty yards ahead.

'Why here?' I wondered aloud.

'We've met here before,' Chris muttered. 'He lives up in Enfield. This is halfway from Seymour Street, and it's outside my own stamping grounds.'

He was saying that they were unlikely to be recognised.

'Sorry,' he added. 'I'm afraid it's not really your kind of pub.'

It wasn't, but then the Curwen business had been taking me to these places. Passing a grimy window, I caught a glimpse of a small room with a pool table and a lot of men and lager. Inside, we turned the other way and entered a larger and slightly less crowded bar dominated by the usual huge satellite television set. The place looked as though it had last been decorated some time before I was born, although somebody had cleared the empties and wiped the tables probably no longer ago than yesterday afternoon. The clientèle seemed local; they were male, and the racial mix was typical of the area: English, Turkish-Cypriot and black in fairly equal proportions – not a fashionable crowd. Waites was already sitting at a tiny table halfway down the room, and, except for the fact that he was on his own, he blended in with the rest.

'You go over,' Chris said in my ear. 'I'll get them.'

I said, 'Vodka and tonic,' edged down the room, and was moving Waites's raincoat from one of the chairs he had been keeping for us before he noticed my arrival.

'Miss Hoare. All right?'

'Fine,' I said. 'You? Mr Kennedy has gone for drinks.'

Waites seemed to have exhausted his conversational powers. He nodded and fixed his eyes on his nearly empty glass. I leaned back. Between the television that was broadcasting MTV and the bellowing voices around us, our silence had no chance of becoming oppressive. Even so, I was glad when Kennedy arrived with a couple of pints and my vodka. We said, 'Cheers' to one another, and Waites lightened up and found his voice.

They started talking about the cock-up that Spurs had made of their game on Saturday. Tottenham was the local team. Probably everybody else in the bar was having exactly the same conversation. I shifted from buttock to buttock and found it easy to switch off, and hard to imagine what I was doing at this party.

I woke up to Waites saying, 'I'll get these. Was it gin?'

'Vodka,' I said. I said, 'Thank you.' He went away. Looking sideways, I could have sworn that Kennedy was trying to keep a straight face. 'I might get very drunk if you go on talking football.'

'Anything you like, so long as you aren't sick,' he muttered intimately into my ear. 'It's going very well. By now he's checked out everybody in the room and made sure there are no faces he recognises, and that nobody's paying any attention to our arrival. Bear up.'

I was just saying that I wished I smoked when Waites came back. He picked up his fresh pint and said, 'Cheers.' We both answered, 'Cheers.'

I suspected Kennedy of taking pity on me when he reopened the conversation with, 'Day off?'

Waites grunted. After a moment he said, 'New rosters again. Spreading us thin. Reorganisations every month, making do.'

'The Met is badly understaffed,' Kennedy agreed. 'I saw that report yesterday, and I gather—'

'Saw it,' Waites interrupted. 'Surprise. Ignorant bloody MPs and the tabloids bleating about street crime . . .' His voice trailed away. After a few moments he said, 'I don't think I care. I'm just about decided – keep my head down and go through the motions. I can get out in another eighteen months. Thirty years is enough. Then they'll have one more to replace.'

'You'd miss it.'

'Would I?'

I half switched off. This might be going somewhere, but at a snail's pace. If I'd been here on my own, I would have thought I'd only been invited to listen to a grumpy detective going through a well-rehearsed moan. But I didn't know the man and Kennedy did; and Kennedy had been sure something would happen.

I snapped back at the sound of Tim Curwen's name.

Kennedy was saying, 'What's going on? Why no progress reports, no publicity? There's something about this that I don't understand.'

Waites was silent for a moment. Then he said flatly, 'He was a friend of yours.' Nobody spoke. Waites was staring at Kennedy's face as though he needed to memorise it. His eyes flickered in my direction, and he frowned.

When Kennedy spoke, his voice was so quiet that I barely caught it. 'Would it help if I told you I know about the drugs but that I wasn't involved? I don't know if you'll believe me.'

I held my breath.

After a hesitation, Waites said, 'I think I do. I've known you for a while, and I remember that other business. Anyway . . .'

'Then what is going on behind the scenes?'

'It might not be what you think.'

'Tell me what I think.'

I was watching them both. Waites had certainly been drinking.

He said, 'You think your man was killed by some mates of his. You're wondering whether they robbed him, or just got rid of him because they knew something about him that you and I don't.'

Kennedy wasn't looking at him now. 'More or less. I was thinking about some stories I heard: that those mates may have included some policemen.'

'I heard that story too.' Waites stared at him, then suddenly threw me another calculating glance.

Kennedy said, 'Don't worry. She's involved, but she doesn't even know why. Look, if you do accept that I'm not with the other side, what have you got for me?'

'Nothing. I've got a big nothing. The whole investigation has gone upstairs. They came in last week and took away every scrap we had – all the records, all the notes. I heard they were taking Curwen on because he was part of an on-going investigation. There's nothing wrong with that.'

Kennedy just nodded, but his eyes had narrowed.

'They cleared out the incident room, and we're getting on with other things. Dead right: the last murder we had was a domestic, two months ago, and it took us nearly two weeks to get even *that* one sorted. Bloody clowns.'

'So the evidence has all gone?' Chris said softly. 'And you're out from under? I think you should be relieved.'

'I *am* happy.' Waites laughed. 'But you know, we couldn't even get the files together without cocking up. Would you believe I found one of the scene-of-crime photos on the floor behind a desk just this morning? One of the close-ups they took before they moved the body. Somebody dropped it. I'm going to have to send it in to the people in charge now, with my humble bloody apologies.'

He reached into his raincoat pocket, pulled out a manila envelope and threw it down on the table in disgust. I could see a typed address label and the scrawl 'Please Do Not Bend'. The flap of the envelope was unsealed. 'I only just remembered I was carrying this. See what I mean? Time for me to go and grow roses before I forget my own name. Well, it's been nice talking, but I'd better get on. I need a pee. I'll mail this thing on my way home. P for photo. Bloody mess.'

He was pushing himself to his feet; he was more drunk than I'd realised, and he staggered slightly as he straightened and moved unhurriedly towards a door at the back. Chris slid his hand into the open envelope and pulled out a folded sheet of paper – a letter – and an eight-by-ten black-and-white photo.

He looked at the picture with a blank face. When I reached over, he twitched it away. Maybe he thought that I was too ladylike to grab. I disillusioned him. He watched without expression as I turned it around, pushing my chair away from him, and saw Waites's bloody mess.

Not much blood.

The photographer had focused on the head and shoulders of the victim from a distance of two or three feet. The body was lying on its back, the head turned slightly away from the camera. The man's jaw had dropped, and he lay with his mouth open, astonished. The throat under the left ear was a mangled mess, which made the absence of blood on the ground even more noticeable. I couldn't see any straight cuts, any clean damage, so I assumed that I was seeing the fatal bullet wound. The left cheek and forehead were swollen, blackened masses of bruises and little cuts running from above the staring, half-open eye all the way across the temple and into the short, almost shaved dark hair. It was a nasty mess.

'Put it back in the envelope.'

Kennedy's voice sounded like a stranger's.

'But . . . this . . .'

'*Put it away.*' His voice grated. 'He'll be back in a second. He doesn't want to find us looking – that's the deal. Don't you understand anything?'

He slid the photograph out of my hand, looked at it for a second with eyes that had become as blank as the dead man's, replaced it and the letter in the envelope, and positioned that exactly as Waites had left it. You wouldn't have to notice it had been moved.

Then he sat staring at the table while I stared at him. Finally he blinked, glanced over my shoulder, then at me; and Waites reappeared. The two men exchanged some sentences. The tone was casual, but I couldn't have said what they were talking about. I don't know what I said to Waites. 'Goodbye,' probably.

When we were alone, Kennedy touched my hand. 'I'm sorry. I should have warned you – those things are ugly when you aren't used to them. Do you want another drink?'

I pulled my hand away. He was barking up the wrong tree; I have seen dead men in the flesh, although he couldn't know about that. What had hit me was just the knowledge that the man who had died in Tim Curwen's flat was somebody I had never seen before. And if this was the deal, as Kennedy had maintained, then no, I did *not* understand. I didn't understand anything – with one exception: I'd just understood that Chris Kennedy had not been entirely surprised by what he had seen.

28

How It Turns Out

I asked carefully, 'Do they know?'

'That it's not Tim? If they were half awake, they'd have identified the body within hours. Something tells me that this corpse had his fingerprints on file. In the context.'

'Then what was going on back there? Was he playing some kind of game?'

After a moment Kennedy said, 'I suppose you could say that. Waites is a good man, full of decent instincts, and he'd prefer to play things straight. He doesn't necessarily like himself for talking to me about police business. He isn't sure he knows what's going on, but if it has anything to do with police corruption, he hopes I'll be able to bring that out into the open, because a detective sergeant can't. He persuades himself that he isn't saying anything that I couldn't find out anyway. Sometimes I think he tells himself that I'm useful to him, and there's some truth in that – I try. He's happier pretending, so we pretend. He's not bent – I want that clear. He wouldn't talk to me if he didn't trust me not to misuse information.'

I had three more questions. 'Do you pay him?'

'I pay for the drinks. I've sent his wife some chocolates.'

Nothing in this was ever simple. I found myself wondering cynically whether today's information had been worth a pound of chocolates, or maybe even five, in a round box with a big gold ribbon.

'Does he always tell you the truth?'

He barely hesitated. 'So far, yes. Not necessarily the whole truth.'

We were driving straight up Hornsey High Street, looking for a turning that would take us back to Islington. It was raining hard, the traffic was heavy and the road narrow, and we weren't making much progress. I fixed my eyes on the back of the double-decker bus blocking our way and said, 'Do you know who it was? The dead man?' When he remained silent, I twisted around in the bucket seat and stared at him. The traffic lights changed at the junction ahead, and we swept forward. He seemed to be giving all his attention to his driving. I waited.

Eventually, he glanced my way and said, 'I've been trying to place him. I have the feeling that I've seen the face, but I can't remember where. One of the clubs? I assume he's one of Tim's so-called "mates". It must have been a while ago. It will come to me.'

My next question had just turned into two. 'Did Tim Curwen kill him, and where is *he* now?'

His hands clenched on the wheel, and he turned the car clumsily at the next junction. The nerve was jumping under his eye again. It had been an abrupt process which confirmed Curwen as possible murderer rather than victim, and I didn't think I was going to get any answers.

But I decided to try. 'Why weren't you more surprised, back there? Why do I get the idea that you already knew Tim was alive? Was it because there was no cocaine under the ivy?'

The silence that met my question didn't surprise me. What was astonishing was that he finally answered: 'Partly that. Partly the way that the case seemed to drop out of sight so quickly: no public statements, no appeals for witnesses. But partly . . . I've been getting some silent phone calls on my voice mail. Four in the past seven days. And once, when I answered,

I just got silence and a hang-up. They were all made from a phone booth in the Hackney area.'

Ghosts. I sat and felt my skin creep. And told myself to get it together.

All right, then. Say I could trust little Daniel Thompson's ears, and there had been three men in the flat that night: Tim Curwen, the man who had wound up dead, and the kind of unidentified third person traditionally known as 'X'. 'X' must have been a friend of Curwen's, since it was the other man, not Curwen, who had died. Logically, when three people are together and one is murdered, then the others are both guilty, aren't they? Unless the delay in throwing the body off the balcony simply showed that one of them did the killing and then had to deal with the other before he could dispose of the original corpse? No – that was unrealistic. It was most likely that Curwen and the third man had acted together.

Second: though Curwen hadn't struck me as the violent type, being kind to little blind boys and polite to female antiquarian book dealers, he hadn't particularly struck me as a criminal, either. Maybe I'm naive. Kennedy had known about it, though. I found myself wondering what else Kennedy knew, at what point he had discovered it, and why he hadn't done anything about it. Also whether this might be 'X' himself who was driving me home. I'm not quite naive enough to think that murderers walk the streets of London talking Cockney rhyming slang, with smoking gun in bloodstained hand, so maybe I should just suspect the worst of everybody.

I asked faintly, 'What are you going to do?'

'Drive you home. Then I'm going home myself. I need to think about this. Dido—'

'What?'

'I'm sorry. I shouldn't have dragged you into this. It really wasn't what I was expecting. But that's it.'

I took a deep breath. '"It"?'

He said, 'You know. I would have enjoyed taking you out to lunch, but you don't want to know me. I'll give you a ring when things are settled: locked away in some filing cabinet at Scotland Yard, probably – I think I can read the signs. But maybe we'll all be lucky and this thing really will be resolved, and you'll read about it in a newspaper article one morning. Maybe my article. I'm not going to contact you for a while, because I've started to think that this situation is a lot too ambiguous.'

'You mean dangerous.'

'Yes.'

It seemed he was being straight with me now; and there was nothing I could think of to say to him.

As I see it, a problem always arises when you get to the point where you have to make this kind of choice. The rational thing, then and always, would have been for me to give up on the whole business and forget that it ever happened. This was what my unreliable acquaintance was advising, and I'd been saying the same thing to myself on and off for days. I couldn't evade it – I had no responsibility for problems like this one, no standing at all; and any idiot could see that there were nasty and incomprehensible things happening all around: dead men still walking the streets. Every wise coward, also every rational person – Barnabas primarily – would say it was past time for me to back off; but all I could think of was that I wanted to know the truth. The only problem is what you do with the truth if you get it. Here, nothing and nobody had turned out to be what they pretended, and I tried telling myself that I couldn't do any good by interfering, that I might easily harm myself and others.

And so I knew that I should forget that I'd ever even sold Tim Curwen a single book. Only I'd never be able to stop thinking about it. Truth is a good thing. People need some kind of resolution.

'I promise,' he said distantly, reading my mind again, 'that I'll let you know what happens.'

When I remained silent, he focused on the road ahead.

I climbed out of the car on the corner of Upper Street, remembered to stop at the newsagent's for milk, and turned the corner into George Street trying to look thoughtless and carefree, like a woman who has just had a man buy her a good lunch *and* has also remembered to do her essential shopping. However, the Vauxhall had gone. I checked the door of the shop and saw that our sign had been changed from 'Back in 10 minutes' to 'Open', which meant that Barnabas was now downstairs again. I was tempted to creep up to the flat and pull myself together while I put the milk in the fridge. I wanted a cup of coffee and a sandwich – since nobody had bought me any lunch either nice or otherwise – and maybe another stiff vodka and some serious inspiration. But the part of me that needed to talk to somebody won out.

When I walked in, my father was standing halfway down one aisle with both hands resting on a shelf. At first I thought he was examining the spine of a book; but then I saw he wasn't looking. The tinkle of the little Nepalese bell on the door caught his attention; he glanced up and nodded more to himself than to me.

'Dido – I'm glad you're back. I've been thinking.' He hesitated, frowned slightly at the innocent shelves, and nodded again: he had re-examined an idea and approved it. 'I know this seems improbable, but I have come to think that Mr Curwen is still alive.'

I stared.

Barnabas held up a warning hand. 'Don't say anything yet! Just listen.'

I shut the door behind me and leaned on it. 'Go ahead.'

He half smiled. 'Good! I've been thinking very hard about all that you've told me and . . . I'm bothered by that money.

Well, that in connection with the vanishing sister, the attitudes of the police and the empty flat you describe. And then Miss Helmer complained that somebody had broken into the flat and disturbed the books there? Who but Curwen himself, looking for his book? Incidentally, we must find out why he needs it. In a nutshell, I have concluded that there is nobody who could possibly have any reason to send you two hundred anonymous pounds except Mr Curwen. *Not* his sister. Precisely why is another question.'

I said simply, 'Well, let's say he realises that I must have got the Dickens back, and he wants it. Otherwise, he miscalculated – if he wanted to stop me asking questions, it was certainly the wrong way to go.'

'Of course, we should ask how he—' He stopped and stared at me. 'What?'

'I've just been shown a photograph of the man who was killed in Tim Curwen's flat,' I said, and told him.

He heard me out. When I had finished, he asked sharply, 'You believe that Mr Kennedy was not taken by surprise?'

'He had reasons to suspect Curwen might still be alive.' I left it at that.

'And yet so far as the police have ever stated publicly, the dead man is assumed to be Curwen? No wonder there's been no inquest! Did this detective suggest any reason for such irregular behaviour?'

'He might not know the reason. By the time the corpse was identified, some other people had turned up and taken over the investigation and all the evidence, and I think Marylebone were probably told just to keep quiet.'

After a while, Barnabas said, 'Now: is their true interest in the dead man, or in Curwen?'

'Both,' I said. 'It has to be both. They're part of the same case. Curwen probably killed him. It must be about drugs – the cocaine.'

My father's face folded into an expression of sour mistrust. 'What about Mr Kennedy?'

I snapped, 'I don't know! Mr Kennedy has gone home to think, and he will kindly let me know how it all turns out.'

Then at last Barnabas smiled faintly and said, 'Good! Do you know something? I have just read in today's newspaper that seventy per cent of all criminal convictions nowadays are drugs related. If I were only a little older, I should probably be asking what the world is coming to.'

I just managed to mutter that I hadn't had any lunch yet and would be back in twenty minutes to debate the matter, and then I turned and put my hand on the door and saw a big, bronze-coloured Mercedes pulling up at the kerb. It was a car that shouted 'Money!' so loudly that I was still standing there, hoping that it had brought us a new customer, when Lloyd Burke stepped out, slammed his door and walked towards me. I opened our door in turn, smiled at him as warmly as I could manage in the circumstances, and welcomed him in.

'Miss Hoare.'

'Mr Burke.' I caught sight of Barnabas from the corner of my eye and introduced them: 'My father, Barnabas Hoare. Lloyd Burke – I think I mentioned him, Tim Curwen's solicitor? I did the probate listing for him.'

My father said coolly, 'You did,' and the men shook hands.

Burke was running his eyes up and down the aisles. I watched one of those greedy, happy collector's expressions start to form. 'I was driving along Upper Street,' he said, 'and I thought I should take a look at you. Did I tell you I collect early travel? Do you . . . ?'

Barnabas pounced. 'Would you be interested in the four-volume 1784 Cook and King? It's the octavo abridgment, but it's in nice condition.'

Burke consulted some mental list and said, 'I have the 1777 quarto, but if the price is right—'

'This is the travel section,' Barnabas said, and ushered our new customer towards the back of the shop. In a moment, the two men were juggling the four volumes and checking for the presence of half-titles. I lurked in the background, uncomfortably aware that there were many remarks my father might drop which I would prefer not even Mr Burke to hear; but I relaxed when I realised that they were deep in a discussion of the number of charts called for, and slid past into the back room to pretend to read a catalogue while I eavesdropped and ignored my gurgling stomach. It was forty minutes before they were finished; Burke had taken the Cook, added the 1776 Dublin edition of *Journal of the Resolution's Voyage*, and said he would think about our first English edition of Bougainville's *Voyage Round the World*. After a little gentle haggling he handed over his cheque for £2,800. While Barnabas was enveloping the volumes in bubble-wrap, I moved myself into the shop to say goodbye.

His finds had made Burke happy. He beamed at me knowingly. 'Well, Miss Hoare, so you're taking a cheque from me after all! I hope you've made your profit out of this deal.'

I half smiled. 'I'm not *against* making money,' I assured him.

'But you prefer to earn it?' He laughed. 'That's not a bad thing. I don't suppose the lady we were looking for has turned up?'

I shook my head. 'I told you – the address you gave me is a council house that's been shut up for a couple of years. If she ever lived there, she's long gone. Actually . . .' He looked at me sharply when I hesitated; I said, 'Did you tell me that it was Mr Curwen who gave you that address? Frankly, I think he invented it.'

Burke gave a mirthless bark. 'The more I learn about that person, the more sure I am he was a con man, short and sweet.'

He was standing with his back to the packing room, so he didn't see Barnabas stop in the doorway with the books he had been wrapping. I shrugged and said lightly that I had no idea, really, because the bounced cheque might just have been an oversight. I saw Barnabas give the ghost of a smile.

'So . . .' Burke said, and stopped. When he continued, it was with something else: 'Miss Hoare, we are giving a little party for clients and friends at the Wellington Hotel tomorrow evening, from seven thirty. Just drinks and a buffet. If you'd care to join us, I'd be happy to see you, and so would Miss Helmer, I'm sure.' He dipped into a breast pocket and handed me a white envelope addressed to 'Miss Dido Hoare and friend'.

If I'd been expecting anything, this was not it. I muttered something about baby-sitting in a voice that cracked with surprise. Then Barnabas came to the rescue by handing over the purchases. Burke switched his gaze to my father and said, 'It's been a pleasure meeting you, Professor Hoare.' He nodded courteously to us both in turn, and we watched him walk out of the shop and to his car. When he looked back across its roof, I nodded courteously in return. We watched the big car depart.

'Well,' I said feebly, clutching the envelope, 'another day, another dollar. And an invitation for drinks. Barnabas, I'm starving, I have to eat something before I go and get Ben.'

My father said, 'He called me *Professor* Hoare.'

'Well,' I began. Oh. 'Didn't I introduce . . . ?'

'You introduced me as "my father, Barnabas Hoare".'

I shrugged wildly. 'I must have mentioned you to him some time.' But I hadn't. He must have been checking up.

By the time I was pushing a slice of cold chicken into a split bagel in my kitchen, another idea had popped into my head – one that would explain the solicitor's persistence. What if he also had guessed or found out that the late Tim Curwen was unexpectedly alive and kicking? With one eye on the clock and one on the engraved invitation that I'd pulled out of its envelope only to drop it into a smear of mayonnaise on the kitchen table, I began to invent scenarios in which Price Rankin Burke had started asking questions either at Seymour Street or elsewhere and discovered the truth about their client. They were an old and prestigious law firm, and Burke seemed perfectly capable of pulling strings and asking blunt questions throughout the old boys' network of London solicitors. Exactly what his attitude to Curwen might be, I couldn't imagine.

A ginger movement caught my eye: Mr Spock crouching at my feet, eyes fixed on the table edge and his rear end lowered and twitching, ready to spring.

I said, 'Woof!' and he stood up to groom his right shoulder with an embarrassed, casual air. 'You don't eat until after Ben and I get back,' I reminded him.

I threw the remains of the chicken into the fridge out of his reach, grabbed the bagel and the invitation, and wandered into the sitting room. When I had propped the card up on the mantel I stood looking at it and chewing. Burke's suspicion or knowledge, if I was right, could explain his persistence. It might even explain this invitation: I had known Tim Curwen personally, and maybe I interested Burke for that reason.

I was busy stirring it all around in my head when the sound of the church bell intruded faintly. My watch agreed that it was five o'clock, so I flung my jacket on and clattered down the stairs carrying my half-eaten bagel in one hand and an umbrella in the other, because it was still raining. It had been raining now for days.

29

The Favour

As I opened the door from the street, I could hear the phone in the sitting room ringing. It stopped and the answering machine cut in.

'Phone!' Ben shrieked.

'Coat! Shoes!' I said equally urgently. We had walked the last two hundred yards through the kind of hard downpour that causes small children to jump into puddles and shriek at the raindrops bouncing back up off the pavement; and I have certain priorities. When things had calmed down and been mopped up, I wandered barefoot into the sitting room and discovered that I'd received eleven phone calls up there that day, though I'd been too absorbed by my own worries even to notice the light flashing on the machine. That brought all my preoccupations back in a rush. I pressed the 'Play' button hastily.

Number one: 'Dido? Paul. Hello. It's ten thirty. I'll try your mobile.'

Number two: the sound of somebody hanging up. Also three and four. I hate it when people do that.

Number five had also been recorded that morning: it was Barnabas saying, 'I've arrived – I'm downstairs. Dido . . . ?'

Number six was Paul Grant again, sounding exasperated. 'Dido, why aren't you answering your mobile?'

Seven through nine were clicks. Ten was no more than half an hour old: Barnabas saying, 'Mr Grant seems to want to speak to you. He says he needs you to do him a favour and will

you ring him back.' My father's voice oozed doubt. 'Let me
know when you get in.' Eleven was Paul saying without
preamble, 'I'll drop by.' He sounded fed up. I went slowly to
brush my hair, put on some dry shoes and wonder what was
going on, stopping *en route* to discover that the battery in my
mobile was flat, look for the charger, remember that
yesterday's message from Paul had also spoken of a 'favour',
and wonder whether I might somehow be vulnerable until my
mobile was recharged.

This was all very bad.

I was still in the bedroom when the doorbell rang. I made a
detour past Ben, who was doing something conspiratorial with
Mr Spock, to a window in the sitting room from where any
caller would be in my line of sight. The new silver car was at
the kerb, and I noticed Paul Grant keeping as dry as possible
by standing close up against my door. Despite this, he was
damp by the time I got downstairs.

He brightened slightly when his eyes fell on me, though
there was a kind of fading annoyance around the edges of his
smile. I stepped back and made room for him.

'I've only just picked up your messages. What's wrong?'

'Can we—?' He glanced over my head cautiously, as though
he expected someone to be lurking on the landing.

'Come up; I'll make a pot of tea,' I suggested, and heard my
voice sound grudging. Never mind.

Paul had chosen to turn his chair sideways to the kitchen
table in order to face me while I fussed. Hemmed in by the
table, he looked oddly as though he had his back to the wall.
He obviously wouldn't push past me and walk out without his
tea, so it was time to move things forward.

'Your message said "a favour". Problem?'

'Yes. This is complicated. I don't know where to start.'

I realised with a shock that I was about to make a Barnabas-
style recommendation to start at the beginning, caught

myself, and substituted, 'This is about Tim Curwen?'

'Of course it's about Tim bloody Curwen!'

'When I asked about him, you said you weren't working on the case.'

'I wasn't. Obviously I'd heard things because word gets around, but lately I've been working on a conspiracy to bring in illegal immigrants—' He broke off and flashed a glance at me. 'Maybe I'd better get to the point. When you originally mentioned Curwen, the name was familiar. I spoke to a friend who was part of a team investigating the firm that Tim Curwen was mixed up with. They specialise in importing, processing and retailing drugs, mostly cocaine these days, although they aren't fussy. They operate in London and East Anglia, and we've been looking at them for nearly a year. You don't need the details.'

'Curwen was a member of this gang?' I asked innocently.

'Ye-e-es.'

I blinked. 'That's a "Yes, but". But what?'

He grimaced. 'I need to ask you to promise that you won't talk about this to anybody for the time being, not even Barnabas.'

I nodded quickly.

'He'd turned. He made contact with the Yard almost a year ago through one of our minor informants, said he wanted to get out, and made a deal. Information for protection.'

The kettle had boiled, so I used that as an excuse to turn around and do something while I digested this news. It fitted. It might explain everything Kennedy had told me about Curwen's behaviour. I plonked the teapot, a couple of mugs and the milk down on the kitchen table and leaned on the sink, ready to ask, 'What went wrong?'

'That's what's worrying everyone. The powers that be have decided to push this one now, before the whole thing goes pear shaped and we lose months of work – if that hasn't

happened already. I've been asked to help out for the time
being; a bunch of us have been reassigned to beef up the
operational unit.'

His eyes were fixed longingly on the teapot, so I gave the
brew a stir, poured out a couple of healthy-looking cups of tea,
splashed in some milk, and by then had identified a problem
with this story.

'If Tim Curwen was an informant for so long, what's
wrong? With an insider in your pocket, why hasn't the gang
been rounded up by now? He can't have been just a minor
figure, surely?'

Paul looked unhappy. 'There were two problems. We
wanted it all, for one thing. Standard practice – there's no
point moving before you're ready to grab everyone involved,
from the muscle right up to the gaffer. If you're not careful,
you'll lose most of them and they'll simply start up all over
again the next week. That goes without saying. Also there was
still a question about the head of the firm.'

I said delicately, 'I heard that it might be somebody very big,
possibly a policeman?'

He barely twitched, and I knew that my offering was going
to be ignored. Apparently there were strict limits to what I
needed to know.

'The second thing?'

'The second thing was that it was becoming difficult to get
Curwen to keep his promises. He blew hot and cold. At the
beginning, it seemed as though he'd co-operate on the usual
basis: protection and an agreement either not to prosecute, or
at the worst to recommend a short sentence with maximum
remission in an open prison, followed by a new identity. After
a while, people started to wonder whether he was having
second thoughts. He kept claiming that he was in danger,
that we couldn't offer him enough protection. Of course,
informants always take a risk, but the team began to wonder

who had been pointing that out to him. Maybe somebody had got to him. They decided that he wasn't solid enough, and they began looking for more corroboration, more unshakeable evidence of everything he'd told us, before they would risk making a move. It meant going on with surveillance and evidence-gathering, with Curwen's co-operation as much as possible.'

'And did he go on co-operating?'

'To some extent. He knew that they weren't going to let him off the hook; but as I said, there were some big question marks. This kind of thing happens all the time.'

I could imagine. More to the point, I was starting to think that I understood what had happened in Abbey House that night.

'Get to the favour that you want,' I suggested, pouring him a second cup to lubricate his confiding mood.

'The sister. Mrs Clark?'

Of course. I thought about it and remembered. 'The other night, you said you didn't think she existed.'

'But *you* said she delivered some money to you, that you'd seen her.'

'And ever since,' I remarked with saintly patience, 'you've been sending police officers over there looking for her.'

'We sent *one* detective constable to check it out with the council. It's a genuinely empty house with ex-tenants who have been traced and who knew nothing about this when we spoke to them.'

'I was wondering whether somebody had broken in to squat there,' I admitted. 'Did your constable actually go inside the house?'

'She checked the boarding on the doors and windows and reported that it's all secure.'

'Then why have you sent some men over to sit outside in a car and watch the place?' I asked reasonably.

'What do you mean? Don't be daft; why would we watch an empty house?'

'Are you seriously telling me it's not you over there?'

He skewered me with the kind of stare I remembered from other occasions like this one. 'Is this some kind of joke?'

I told him that a grey car with two men in it had been noticed hanging around in the street there only that morning, and saw his frown deepen. 'Nothing to do with us. Have we missed something?'

'What about the Vauxhall that's been parked outside here today?'

'What?'

I said sweetly, 'Somebody turned up before ten o'clock this morning and sat outside my door until lunch-time. I made a note of the registration number.'

He said, 'Get it,' sharply enough to start me wondering all over again.

I remembered putting it on my writing desk and went for it, with him at my heels. As soon as I passed it over, he pulled out his mobile phone and punched a button. I pretended to be distracted by Ben while I listened to him ask for someone to run the number for him. There was barely a pause before he switched off. 'Reported stolen last week,' he said. 'I don't think you should worry about it, but if you do see it here again—'

'I will phone you,' I interrupted sourly.

Why wasn't I surprised? I would even have preferred to have been under surveillance by a police car. Although, as I'd said to Barnabas, it might be nothing to do with us. I tried to convince myself.

'Dido . . . ?'

'You still haven't got to the favour,' I said nervously. 'Look, I have to make some food for Ben and get him ready for bed. Come into the kitchen again.'

'I need to find the sister, if she exists: Theresa Clark. There's no evidence that she has anything to do with that house, or anything else, but then I wonder where the address came from in the first place, and what she knows about her brother's friends.'

'What if it was just a mail drop?'

'What?'

'A mail drop. The house. A postal address.'

'I told you, the place is empty.'

'But there are people living all around it,' I said quietly, and told him all about my card.

Paul scowled. 'Yes. Well . . . And the sister does exist, because she's already made contact – with you. Damn it, I wish I knew what's going on here! I wonder if I can get to her faster with your help?'

I said carelessly, but not at all accidentally, 'You're hoping that she knows where Curwen is hiding.' Just for once, Paul seemed involuntarily speechless. Striking while I had the advantage, I swept Ben up into my arms and asked quickly, 'Who was the man who was killed in Curwen's flat?'

He moved abruptly to stand between me and the door. 'What's going on?'

I thought about Kennedy, and then I thought about Waites, and then I made my choice. 'I was curious,' was all that I told him. 'I've been thinking hard about this whole business. So incidentally has Barnabas. Now you're asking me for help, and I want to know exactly what I'd be getting into.'

After a moment he said, 'Dido, please don't play games. Who told you that the dead man wasn't Curwen?'

'Nobody told me.' That was the literal truth, and of course I found myself modifying it immediately. 'Well, Barnabas worked it out too, but isn't it obvious? Aside from the fact that there's been no publicity, no inquest and no date set for one, and that the police are all acting dumb, there's the money

that Theresa Clark brought me, the payment for the book.
I can't imagine why Tim Curwen would have asked his
sister to deliver it, but it's impossible that it came from her
on her own initiative. Why would she know about the book
business unless he'd told her? Barnabas and I both worked this
out. You aren't going to try to tell me the corpse *is* Tim
Curwen?'

I walked around him and led the way down the passage and
into the kitchen, where Ben and I consulted on the beans-
versus-burger option and Mr Spock joined in with interest.
Paul leaned in the doorway and contemplated this scene of
frenzied domesticity while I used the tin opener. In the middle
of it all, I heard him say, 'McKane. DC William McKane. One
of ours.'

Oh. Curwen's minder, then. I turned down the heat on the
grill and speculated that Curwen might not be very eager to
be found.

'What are you thinking?' Paul asked after a while.

'That this doesn't get any clearer.'

He made a noise almost like a laugh.

'What do you want?'

'In the first instance, for you to promise to let me know if
Theresa Clark, or anybody else, makes any further contact.
I've given you the number of my mobile. If you see so much
as a shadow that looks like the person who brought you that
cash, ring the number. If it's four in the morning, that doesn't
matter: just ring me.'

That seemed harmless. A safety measure, even.

I nodded. 'What else?'

My question made him uneasy. 'Nothing, I hope. But as
you've just pointed out, neither Clark nor Curwen has any
reason to be afraid of you. You're an outsider. Possibly, and
only at the last resort, I might have to try to get in touch with
them through you.'

'More evenings with us hanging around the pubs over there?'

'Something along those lines. They don't know my face, and Curwen seems more or less well disposed towards you. Besides, you have something he wants. If you're willing in principle to help us I'll think some more about this.'

My first thought was that I wouldn't mind, and my second was that I'd need to organise more baby-sitting. Then something else struck me. 'You know how I first heard of her? Curwen's solicitors told me her name and gave me that address. I have an invitation from them for drinks tomorrow. If you'd like to come with me, I could introduce you to Dona Helmer, who's one of the juniors. Maybe we could find out some more from her. It would be a chance to just . . . establish a link, chat. It will be a bit formal though.'

'I wouldn't miss it.' Paul grinned. 'Formal? So you won't be wearing that outfit you had on the other night?'

I looked up at him and said heatedly, 'Whyever wouldn't I? That's my party gear!'

He smiled a little smile, but his thoughts were somewhere else already.

30

Various Parties

Price Rankin Burke had hired the hotel's Marlborough Suite and arranged for it to be filled with long, damask-covered tables, urns with formal arrangements of fresh flowers, waiters carrying trays, and a grand piano on which somebody was playing Cole Porter, or maybe Irving Berlin. By the time that we arrived it was already full of noise, cigarette smoke, thin women in black dresses chatting to ponderous men in dark suits, and a diminishing buffet of sushi. Pausing just inside the door, we ran our eyes over the assembly and discovered (at least in my case) only two familiar faces. Dona Helmer was circulating, stopping beside one group or another, smiling the same smile and saying little. She looked stunning in a little black dress. More to the point . . .

I hissed, 'Big man in evening dress – over by the buffet' at Paul, who said, 'Burke – I see him. Let's wander over there gradually and see if we can make friends. Come on.'

He grasped my elbow and moved us casually towards the far side of the room. When a waiter stepped in front of us, we took glasses of bubbly from his tray. I tasted it: probably real champagne. That didn't concern me as much as the thought that Paul had recognised Lloyd Burke across a crowded room. He must have been doing his homework. I fixed a vivacious smile on my face and stared up at him adoringly, which allowed me to notice that he was scanning the room with a purposeful air. When we were close enough to the piano that its music would mask our voices, I reached a gentle hand across to the one that was gripping my arm painfully and started to bend his little finger back. I had his attention.

'Paul, what are you doing?'

He growled, 'What the fuck do you think *you're* doing?' Interested by his outburst, I stopped what I was doing and watched him regain control of himself. He said, 'I'm looking for familiar faces. By the way, have I complimented you yet? Red suits you.'

It was a bit obvious. Despite that, I felt a little surge of pleasure, modified when I noticed that his attention was once more on everybody but me.

'Who are you looking for?' I murmured adoringly.

'Always a policeman,' he retorted. 'Consider this an undercover operation. Don't you? Why else did you suggest we should come?'

And why did you agree?

'All right, Dido: let's wander over and say hello to our host now and get some food.'

I smiled and fluttered my eyelashes and we drifted onward.

Burke saw us from a little distance, said something to an old couple to whom he had been listening, and advanced.

'Miss Hoare! Good to see you here.' He picked up my free hand, gave it fleeting squeeze, and turned his gaze on Paul.

I said demurely, 'Mr Grant, my fiancé: Mr Burke,' and watched Burke smile.

'Mr Grant – happy to meet you. Are you a bookseller too?'

Paul opened his mouth, and I heard myself saying, 'No, he's a dentist.'

Burke blinked and his smile faded. He said, 'Well . . . enjoy yourselves,' and turned towards the people behind us.

So much for the friendly chat. We smiled and nodded and continued on our way towards some smoked salmon.

At the table, Paul dropped my arm, grabbed two plates, and

started to stack them with canapés and sushi. He was shaking with silent laughter. 'You cow! I wanted you to talk to him. You know everybody hates dentists! Now we'll probably have to bump into him again later on.'

I pointed out very reasonably that he had just told me this was an undercover operation, and that I couldn't think of anybody more undercover than a dentist. He snorted and observed that at least I hadn't told the truth. And his mobile rang. It took me a moment to identify the faint single tone: it was one of the most discreet mobile rings I had ever heard.

'Dido—'

I grabbed the plates from his hands and followed him past the piano as he dug the phone out of a pocket and said, 'Go.' I turned my back to indicate that I wasn't interested and edged closer, but if I'd hoped to hear anything, I was disappointed. During a long silence, I caught Helmer's eye. She had been working her way in our direction, but she hesitated when she saw me. There was something tentative about her smile. Then she seemed to make up her mind and started to drift towards us again. At my back, Paul muttered, 'I'm on my way. I'll be there in half an hour.' I turned.

He switched off and looked at me silently.

'Look, I have to get to Heathrow.'

'Broken denture?'

'They might have got your former customer there. He's catching a plane to Frankfurt – if it is him.'

'You have alerts out for him?'

'Ports and airports. I have to go now. I'm really sorry.'

I said thoughtfully, 'A dentist's life is not a happy one. If you're going, I think I'll leave too. This isn't really my kind of party – almost everybody's twice my age, and rich.'

'You might as well,' he said shortly, which had the immediate effect of making me regret the decision.

I left our plates balancing on the edge of a plant stand, threw

Dona Helmer an eye-rolling 'Oh, men!' grimace, and took my fleeing escort's arm in order to avoid being outrun. Our exit probably looked normal, though we covered the distance to the cloakroom at speed and were going through the glass doors in the front lobby before I'd had a chance to put my coat on. A line of taxis was waiting on the forecourt. Paul yanked open a door and more or less pushed me in. By the time I had sat down, he had thrust £20 at the driver and given him my address. I was tempted to shout, 'Follow that policeman!' but it would have been useless, because he had disappeared in the direction of his parked car before the taxi managed to get out into the stream of traffic heading north. I gave up, wriggled into my coat, and sat back defeated. And hungry. And reminding myself again that getting mixed up with policemen in general and Paul Grant in particular was, and always remains, a bad idea.

I leaned forward, opened the sliding glass panel between myself and the driver, and shouted at the back of his neck, 'I want to get out in Upper Street – I'll tell you when we get there.'

At home, I unlocked my front door and stepped inside, listening for sounds. Some faint chamber music was coming from my CD player, but there was nothing else. I sighed, climbed the stairs and put down the food I had just bought. Before I had got out of my coat, Barnabas was standing in the doorway.

'You're early,' he observed unnecessarily. 'Bored with high legal society?'

'We may have a solution, with luck,' I said. 'Is Ben asleep? I've brought some takeaway from the Chinese. Enough for two. You haven't eaten, have you?'

Perhaps it was the pork in sweet chilli sauce, but at some time past midnight I was still wide awake. I got up in the dark, listened for a moment to Ben's undisturbed breathing, and then crept out to the sitting room. This was a bad idea, because it was already Saturday, always a busy day in the shop and – as Barnabas had felt forced to remind me just before he left – this Saturday was worse than normal because it was the day for packing ten boxes of stock to take to the monthly book fair in Russell Square which started on Sunday morning. I'd actually managed to forget about that until he reminded me.

I drifted over to the nearest window and looked out. The rain had stopped for the moment, and I crossed my fingers that it would stay dry until I got the books and shelves out to the van. I hadn't heard a forecast, but the road was full of fresh puddles. My van was, as usual, in the residents' bay just down the street; I'd better remember to move it on to the yellow line outside the door at midday when the parking restrictions lapsed. I looked along to where it was parked; the Vauxhall was back.

My recharged mobile was in my shoulder bag. I slipped back to the window to use it, imagining the discreet little noise his phone was making and wondering whether it could possibly be loud enough to wake him up. It was certainly a fair time before it was answered by a kind of wordless grunt.

'Paul?'

'Uh . . . Dido? What's wrong?'

'It's back. It's outside again – the stolen Vauxhall. You wanted to know.'

There was a second's pause, during which I heard a voice asking a question in the background . . . a woman. Ah. Then there were a few seconds of the dead silence that you get when a hand is placed firmly over a mouthpiece.

'Dido? Is there anybody inside it?'

'I can't see from here,' I told him. 'I could—'

'Don't move! I'll send a car over.'

I said quickly, 'At Heathrow – did—?'

'False alarm – not even close. I'll get a car sent over from Islington. You stay where you are until I ring you back.'

I settled myself at the side of the window, leaning against the frame and looking around the edge of the curtain.

It was late. The streets were as quiet as they ever get in Islington, with the traffic out in Upper Street hushed to a murmur, and only the occasional car gliding past the junction of my road and the cross-street to my right, sounding twice as loud as usual. I was just starting to wonder whether I'd made a fool of myself when I noticed a single flash of blue light. I paid no attention until it was answered by a fainter flash from the far end of the street, and even then it took me a moment to understand what was happening. I focused on the shadowy Vauxhall. In the second or two before anything started, I inched my window up and leaned out.

Two cars were turning into the road simultaneously, one from each end. I could only see the headlights of one vehicle, but the nearer one was a marked police car. I caught a movement out of the corner of my eye. A dark shape had emerged from the parked car and run into the shadows along the brick wall of the old auto repair workshop which has stood empty on the far side of my road all the time I've lived here. The patrol cars advanced, met, and stopped alongside the Vauxhall. Dark figures emerged from each. One of them shone a light on the licence plate, and a second directed a torch inside; but the party was already over and there was nobody left for them to find. I watched them realising this fact and discussing it. After a few minutes I lowered my window and went back to bed. It had been a long and unsatisfactory evening. Paul didn't ring back. I fell asleep.

31

Talks about Nothing

Usually when I pack for a book fair I think of a theme before I start to choose my stock: nineteenth-century literature, or modern firsts, or natural history, for example. Today, the theme appeared to be 'miscellaneous', or 'she isn't keeping her mind on business'. By ten o'clock, when my father's black umbrella came bobbing along in front of the window, I had filled seven cardboard boxes with whatever was to hand and stacked them in front of the packing table.

Barnabas had unlocked the door, snibbed the catch, lowered his umbrella and stepped inside, flipping the sign to read 'Open', before I could move.

He looked me over. 'Is something wrong? Where is Ben?'

I told him that I had delivered Ben just after breakfast to the house of a friend from nursery, where he had a social engagement for morning play followed by lunch, and had decided to use my free time instead of giving way to my natural desires and going back to bed.

Barnabas looked at me. 'I get,' he said heavily, 'the impression of a candle burning at both ends.'

I admitted that my sleep had been disturbed and told him about the return of the Vauxhall and the disappearing act performed by its driver. 'And when I came downstairs this morning, there was no sign of the car. They must have towed it away during the night.'

Barnabas sniffed and said that he hoped and presumed that forensic investigators were even at this moment swarming

over it collecting fingerprints, hairs and hypodermic needles.
I almost said I wouldn't be surprised, but decided not to labour
the point in case he drew the same conclusions that I had. The
police had displayed unusual speed and determination in
getting over here, so presumably the situation was worrying
somebody in authority. Barnabas could only draw the worst
possible conclusions and fuss even more than he normally
does about what I was doing and what might be done to me.
Whereas I suspected that this had very little to do with any
danger to me, more with the murder of a policeman and the
disappearance of a useful informant, along with police hopes
of winding up an important case.

And in the meantime, Paul had still not rung. I assumed he
was still in bed with the female voice. It was fortunate that I
hadn't been standing by the upstairs window, as suggested, for
the past seven or eight hours.

Barnabas hung his mac and umbrella on the old coatstand
and turned with a glint in his eye. Luckily, the door of the shop
opened to admit our first customer of the day before he could
open his mouth.

I said quickly, 'I'm going to get one more box packed before
things get too busy, and leave it at that.'

'And I shall sit at the desk and think and receive money.' He
managed to make it sound like a threat, but then the postman
arrived and gave him something to think about. The next
time I looked, he was reading a catalogue of early English
books and taking notes. I breathed a sigh of relief and raised a
prayer that nothing else unconnected with business would
happen for an hour or two at least.

Customers drifted in, bought the occasional book, and
drifted away again; and I started to relax into the routine. Wet
weather seems to discourage serious book-buying; people do
come in to browse, or maybe just dry off for a while, but they
seem to feel it may be risky if they leave the shop with a serious

purchase, even one protected by our plastic carrier bags. I dealt with the few who were still buying. Ernie turned up only a little late: after a long Friday evening which he would have spent on the door of a club up the Holloway Road, it was really wonderfully early. He and Barnabas negotiated a desk-share. At some point the phone rang, and I wondered fleetingly whether Paul had just remembered me waiting around, but it was a wrong number, and the caller broke the connection when Barnabas answered. I finished packing an eighth box of books. I started a ninth.

Paul Grant arrived. I slid around one of our customers, who had been turning the pages of a foxed copy of *The Englishman's House* so slowly that it was clear she was reading it, and joined him at the front of the shop.

'Hi.'

I agreed, 'Hi,' and added that the Vauxhall had vanished before I got up.

He nodded. 'It's sitting over in the carpark at Islington until we can transporter it down to the lab. They say it looks clean – I don't suppose we're going to find much.'

'At least you can give it back to its sorrowing owner,' I reminded him brightly. Out of the corner of my eye I saw Barnabas notice us and said quickly, 'Coffee. Upstairs.' I pointed a finger overhead for my father's benefit and got us both out of his sight.

Waiting for the coffee machine to finish spluttering, Paul said, 'Look, on Monday—'

I said, 'Book fair. What about tonight? Saturday night is a night to make whoopee in E9. You could buy me drinks and meals again. That is, if I can get somebody to baby-sit. I don't suppose the departmental budget runs to paying a sitter?'

'The departmental budget doesn't even run to buying your vodkas.' He thought about it and apparently decided that the sacrifice was worthwhile. 'All right, then. Wear something dark and not too in-your-face, and we'll have a quiet look-round, if you like.' If *I* liked? 'But on Tuesday, can you get away for the morning?'

I tried to remember whether there were any customers booked in and decided that, if so, I would get Barnabas to deal with them. I asked what we were doing on Tuesday.

He said, 'Meeting some of my people and going over to Lavender Way. Let's say it's to make up to you for last night. I'm curious about that address after all, and whether it's really as empty as it's supposed to be. I'll arrange for some council workmen to meet us there and let us inside. You can look for your pink envelope, and identify any cache of valuable old books we find there – unless we get a break before then, in which case we'll just go out for lunch. I wanted to say I'm sorry about running out on you last night.'

I said I could live with it, but I took care not to say it so cheerfully as to let him off the hook. Seeing the inside of the house in Lavender Way would at least satisfy my nagging suspicion that there was something important waiting to be found there, if only because there had to be a reason why that address had come up. We finished our coffee, talking about nothing, and I went out to the kitchen for refills. Returning, I found Paul standing over my writing desk reading Chris Kennedy's article on Curwen's death, which was spread out on top of the mess. I pushed Paul's mug at him and waited. When he had finished, we shook our heads disbelievingly at one another.

I asked tentatively, 'Do you know the writer of that piece?'

'What – Christopher Kennedy?' I caught a distinct hesitation. 'I know the name. I understand that he and Curwen moved in the same circles.'

I jumped in cautiously and offered, 'I've met him. Is he mixed up in the drugs thing?'

'No.'

There was no hesitation, but I know Paul Grant and said carefully, 'How can you be sure?'

'We've looked. They say that Kennedy had a younger brother, John. Heroin addict. He dropped out of university and then died of an overdose about five years ago. Kennedy dug into his life, talked to his friends, and wrote a big, angry exposé. He named names, and he nearly got himself killed doing it. That's how he got into investigative journalism. He used to do international affairs.'

'But he and Curwen were friends – isn't that odd? You must have looked at him hard?'

'According to the notes I've read, the team were thinking about him at one time, but they couldn't find anything wrong – this was long before I had anything to do with this business. They decided that the relationship with Curwen was purely personal. When the news came that Curwen had been murdered, somebody brought up Kennedy's name again. They thought for about half a day that they might have something. Then we found out who the victim really was.'

I said slowly, 'There was a third man in Curwen's flat in Abbey House when your . . . when McKane was killed. You don't think he—?'

'Kennedy was at the newspaper that evening. We checked.'

I nodded and turned away to put my mug down on the side table and find myself light with relief.

When he had gone, I checked my answering machine and found that I'd had two phone calls while I was out. The first had been from Paul, warning me of his visit. The second, which had come while I was downstairs packing books, was another of those hang-ups. When I checked, the usual electronic voice gave me a number. I dialled and let it go on ringing.

After about a minute, the receiver was picked up. Silence.

I said tentatively, 'Hello?'

A voice answered, 'Hello?' It sounded like a girl.

I said, 'Somebody was trying to phone me from there . . .'

'It's a phone box.'

I said, 'Oh. Where?' but the connection was broken. When I rang back, nobody answered. I put the dirty mugs in the sink with the breakfast things and went back downstairs.

In my absence, the shop had filled up nicely. Barnabas was circulating and seemed to be in control; I stopped by the door to see whether anybody needed my personal help, and I missed her at first: Dona Helmer, wearing some unlikely-looking old jeans and a long black raincoat and staring at a shelf of children's books without actually touching any of them.

I made my way over and said hello.

She jumped. 'Oh! I didn't see you! I was just . . . I thought I'd look for a book.'

'Of course,' I said. 'What kind of book? By the way, I'm sorry I rushed off last night before we could say hello to you, but my . . . fiancé got a phone call – something urgent. Anyway, he thought it was at the time. How are you?'

'All right,' she said, and her voice trailed off. 'Busy.'

'The Curwen business still taking up your time?' I asked sneakily.

She hesitated. 'Not really. There's nothing much happening there. I think Mr Burke's trying to find out about those books in America.'

I said, 'Um. Good notion. Well, what kind of book are *you* looking for?'

'I'm not sure. My aunt has a sixtieth birthday next week. I was thinking – she used to tell us that when she was little she loved fairy stories, and she had some books with lovely illustrations. I was wondering whether she might like something like that now, and Mr Burke said he was sure you could help. He bought some books here himself just this week, he said.'

I told her that she was standing right in front of a little bunch of Langs, which were probably the books her aunt remembered, and showed her the *Lilac Fairy Tales* to prove my point. She smiled faintly and nodded, looking relieved. 'It's very pretty,' she said. 'I'll take it.' Her voice was happier, and I guessed that the old aunt was not an easy person to buy presents for.

She followed me towards the office and waited in the doorway, silently watching while I made out an invoice, took her credit card, and placed the book carefully in one of my blue plastic carrier bags with the drawing of the shopfront in gold, looking picturesque and leaving out the litter on the pavement.

I handed everything over and smiled.

She smiled back and showed no sign of leaving, which made me ask, 'Is there anything else you'd like?'

She glanced at Ernie, who was deeply engaged in catching up with website alterations. 'Perhaps we could meet some time for coffee?' she said tentatively.

I said that would be nice and then she smiled and turned towards the door.

A voice at my elbow asked, 'What's your best price on this?' and a copy of Charlotte Mew's *Collected Poems* appeared in front of my face, leaving me without any time to wonder whether I ought to be wondering about Helmer's unexpected visit; but Saturdays are like that.

32

The Ladies

By eight o'clock, there were a lot of little parties going on in the Anchor. Paul and I had managed to find a free half-table just inside the front door, and settled there beside a couple of local seventeen-year-olds who were so absorbed in one another that static electricity was forming around their bodies. Behind the screen provided, we sat close and murmured quietly. Paul was doing his covert survey thing. I followed his example and, like him presumably, saw no familiar faces. It was a mixed crowd, but none of the women was wearing a purple jacket. Nobody was hiding under a baseball cap.

Paul leaned close. 'We aren't going to find her.'

'Of course not,' I agreed. 'I expect surveillance is just nothing happening all the time.'

'You expect right,' he said, 'except that usually you're not sitting in a nice warm pub. Which reminds me . . .'

I said, 'I'll get them,' and went and ordered.

Two rounds later, we were both growing restless and decided, in one exchange of glances, that the time had come to escape from the hot action on the other side of the table. I got to my feet, gathered up my jacket and my bag, and said, 'Give me a minute.'

I followed the arrows pointing to the door marked 'Toilets', and went through it into a dim, dank passage. I passed the door of the gents' and located the ladies' toilets just beyond it. Its door was pulled inward, away from my hand, and I found myself facing a skinny woman in a black leather jacket. She caught my attention, not just because she nearly flattened me as she was leaving, but because of her make-up – under a shock of black hair was a clown-like face covered in white foundation, with bright red lips and what seemed at first to be no eyebrows, though at second glance I saw a thin line of blond hairs above each eye. Her gaze slid across my face – hazel eyes behind the lenses of a pair of trendy wire-framed specs – and then she sidestepped me and headed out towards the bar.

I froze. You always know when somebody recognises you: as you exchange a casual glance you see their eyes flicker and turn away too quickly. This woman had just recognised me. I stared after her retreating back. There was something oddly familiar about her gait. And the set of her shoulders. Something that reminded me . . .

I yelled, '*Wait! Theresa Clark?*' just as the door to the bar closed behind her. Then I ran, ploughing into someone who was just coming out of the gents', disentangling myself, gasping an apology and flinging myself away without even looking at my victim. By the time I had reached the door to the bar, Black Hair was walking out into the street. Paul saw me come bursting out and rose to his feet. I pointed and mouthed at him the length of the room, and he turned and sprinted after her.

I was starting to follow when something happened that stopped me in my tracks. A big man sitting at one of the side tables stood up so fast that he spilled his beer. He hesitated, staring towards the door. There was an empty chair beside him – she must have been sitting there, but she had run straight past him and out into the street. I turned and pretended to look at a poster on the wall, but I needn't have bothered. The fat man shoved her chair out of his path, stumbled over somebody's feet, and was pushing through a group of boys and heading after Paul and the woman. He wasn't going to notice me. I joined the race.

Out in the dark street I stopped to look for them. The man I had followed was hesitating under a lamppost, staring down the road: so they must have gone that way. I put my jacket on while I watched him think about it. Finally, he gave himself a little shake and turned in the opposite direction, passing me without a glance. He was heading in the direction of Lavender Way. The others were out of sight, so I waited until he was a block ahead and then set out to follow.

When he turned into the empty stretches of the familiar street, his pace quickened. I let him get well ahead at first; but as he reached the side road nearest to the empty house, I speeded up again. By now there was no reason for him to connect me with the pub – if he noticed me at all. I was crossing that road as he passed 253 and saw him turn abruptly towards one of the houses just beyond it. I found him again by the side of the unit at the far end of the terrace, and slowed to a stroll so I could make sure he had reached his final destination. When the door of the house banged behind him, I realised that I'd seen him before tonight, and right there: this was the fat man with whom Barnabas had discussed Theresa Clark.

A light came on in one of the downstairs windows. I kept on walking, watching the shadows, but somehow not really expecting that Curwen's sister was going to reappear so conveniently.

My mobile rang as I was crossing the road.

'Dido?'

I asked, 'Where are you? You'd vanished before I got outside.'

'That woman turned out to be an Olympic sprinter. I take it that was Mrs Clark?'

'Must be. I didn't recognise her at first – she's dyed her hair.'

'Where are you?'

I said, 'Lavender Way. I followed the man she was drinking with.'

'*What man?*'

I said reasonably, 'I don't know what man. A tallish, fattish man. I think she was with him. I noticed him because he got up in a rush and followed the two of you out. I came after him, but you were out of sight by this time, so he turned around and walked back here. He's just gone into one of the houses.'

'Any sign of . . . ?'

'No. He went in alone and switched on the lights. She may not even be coming back here, but if she is, she hasn't arrived yet.'

He thought about that. 'Just so long as they don't realise we've found them. I need to make another phone call. Give me the address. I'm going to organise surveillance now, because I don't want to talk to this man until she's back. Which house number?'

I was just opening my mouth when I heard the sound of a door slamming across the street and the lights went out in the house. Something was moving on the path. I said, 'It's two five nine, but he's just come out again. Wait a minute: I can see him. He's turning east. I'll fol—'

'No! If you don't stay back, I'm going to take you into protective custody.'

I opened my mouth to say that he'd have to catch me first, but decided that a loud attack of bad temper would make me too conspicuous. I stored it for later. The man was a dark bulk moving unhurriedly along the far side of the street. He stopped by a car. I heard a tiny scrape and knew what it meant. I whispered, 'You're right, I'm not going to follow. He's getting into a car.'

'If you can do it without him seeing you, get his number.'

I heard the engine start and expected him to shoot off without lights, but nothing so dramatic happened: the side-lights blinked on, the car pulled out slowly, and I read the registration number aloud into the phone as it came into my view. He drove off unhurriedly and made a right somewhere ahead.

'He's turned south.'

'All right. I'm going to make that call. Walk back this way, but don't go into the pub. I'll pick you up at the southbound bus stop nearest to the Anchor as soon as I've—'

But I was fed up with it, and when I noticed what was coming my way, I stepped out to the kerb and waved and said, 'Paul, I've caught a taxi. I have an early start in the morning. I'll see you on Tuesday.'

I climbed in, was tempted for just a second to tell the driver to make a big circuit through the surrounding streets, but got hold of myself and said instead to take me home. Maybe Paul and his lot really would get all this cleared up tonight. I sat back, feeling impatient, hungry, dissatisfied, curious and cross.

As the taxi finally turned into George Street, I caught myself looking for the Vauxhall in the parking bay. Only of course it wasn't there because the police had it. The windows of the flat were dark. I wondered about that for a moment, but my watch warned me that it was nearly eleven. I paid the driver, let myself in, and climbed the stairs as silently as I could. The little hallway was darker than normal – the door of the sitting room was closed, cutting out the light that usually shone in from the streetlamp outside its windows.

Something moved silently at my feet. I leaned down to pick Spock up. He burbled a greeting.

When I switched the hall light on, I saw the sheet of paper taped to the sitting-room door. In Barnabas's florid print it read: 'Wake me up at once'. I opened the door an inch and located a long mound on the settee under the windows. It was wrapped in my duvet and snoring fiercely. I pulled the door to and crept away.

In the bedroom, Ben was not quite asleep. When I hung

over his cot, he looked up and said something unintelligible before his eyelids started to droop. I reached down and stroked his cheek, and he sighed and slept again. There was a spare blanket on the top shelf of the wardrobe. I found it by touch, kicked off my shoes, rolled myself in it, and fell on to the bed. Spock was there already, settling on to one of my pillows. I put my head down on the other one for a few minutes' hard thinking.

The sun was shining. Hot sand under blue sky. Glare on the water. An invisible seagull screamed. Just beside this beach I could see the only building for miles around: a high-rise glass-and-concrete hotel, with a swimming pool and a jungly garden full of flowering trees which I knew were jacaranda. The sign on a gate read simply 'HOTEL'. I'd thought that I was alone, but then behind me a voice spoke: 'What do you think of my hotel? Wouldn't you like a holiday? I'll let you stay free for the first fortnight.' I whirled around. It was a blond man who had spoken, and he was smiling charmingly; I knew I'd never seen him before and yet at the same time he looked familiar.

I said, 'You're Chris Kennedy's brother! I know about you: they think you're dead.'

He looked at me and grinned and vanished in the glare bouncing off the waves.

When I woke, the duvet had been spread over me and I could hear the street door shutting quietly. Then before I fell asleep again I started to worry that I'd been forgetting about something.

33

Deals and Conversations

I stood on the pavement by the side door of the hotel on Russell Square, waving and watching Ben and Ernie wander off hand in hand towards the Tube station. The two of them had been helping me to unload my folding shelves and boxes and get my stand set up. Now they were on their way back to the flat for a morning of male bonding and watching cartoons on the box, leaving me to earn a living. Oh well. I turned, made my way up the steps to the entrance, paused while one of my fellow exhibitors struggled to disentangle his laden trolley from the doorpost, and plunged into the maelstrom.

In theory, these fairs do not open until one o'clock. In practice, that means two or three hours of frantic unpacking, positioning of stock, greeting friends, and trying to find disregarded bargains on other people's stands while at the same time getting the best possible prices for anything of one's own that any other exhibitor offers to buy. It would be a hectic and absorbing couple of hours and would leave me no time to worry about Theresa Clark's abrupt appearance and equally startling departure.

I had phoned Paul earlier and left him a message to contact me; the fact that he hadn't probably meant that nothing had happened last night. I could also assume that the phone call from Barnabas, which came at eight o'clock as I was rushing to make breakfast for Ben, Spock and myself, and during which he had announced that we were eating together that evening, meant that he wanted to get at least a full account of yesterday's events and very likely more. For two or three days past, my father had taken on the character of a semi-active volcano, ruminating, rumbling, taking notes, and waiting for a chance to let off steam.

It was almost a relief to join the pushing throngs – antiquarian book dealers can become modestly aggressive on these occasions. I managed to find a signed copy of Logue's *Wand and Quadrant* for £10 and sell it on immediately for £70 to a dealer from Liverpool who had a customer lined up, which meant that at a pinch I could even pay for this dinner I'd been threatened with. And yes, I do enjoy my work.

I got home just on seven. The air in the stairwell was filled with smoke and an attractive smell which I identified, as I was climbing towards its source, as roasting potatoes. The only meal that my father ever cooks consists of large grilled rump steaks with potatoes, fried mushrooms, and a token grilled tomato for vitamins. I had skipped lunch, and after a day's hard labour it all smelled wonderful.

The atmosphere inside the flat was blue with smoke; but I could hear Ben chattering in the sitting room, so I assumed that there was no immediate threat of fire. To my left, I could see Barnabas with a bath towel tied around his waist, bending over and closely examining my smoking grill; to the right, I could hear Ben deep in conversation with someone who sounded like Paul Grant.

Barnabas heard my arrival and straightened up. 'You're late.'

I found myself looking guiltily at my watch. It wasn't true. I pointed to the sitting room and made an enquiring face.

'He said he would stay and eat with us. Luckily, I brought plenty.'

Luckily. I asked myself where four people were going to find the space in this flat to sit down together and eat, and answered my own question by wandering into the living room and discovering that the furniture there had been pushed back and the kitchen table moved in. Paul and Ben glanced up from their chairs when I appeared, expressing satisfaction, and the smell of grilling beef wafted in behind me along with Barnabas's voice calling, 'Medium, you said?'

Paul shouted, 'Thanks!' and managed to find enough space on the table to put down his glass of wine.

I went and washed my hands in the kitchen, but Barnabas was too absorbed in his grilling to talk, so I decided to play this by ear and left him to it.

At the table I sipped from my glass, which turned out to hold some of my father's 1990 Fleurie, and asked, 'What happened?'

'Nothing. No sign of either of them. I've got people sitting outside but there's been no movement all day.'

'But you traced the car?'

'Curiously enough,' Paul said in what I realised was a carefully controlled voice, 'it turns out to be another stolen vehicle.'

'That's a coincidence.' I looked at him. 'Or not?'

'It's professional,' he answered sourly. 'You'd be surprised how many worthless old bangers are being nicked these days just because they're more insecure than later models. If they aren't burned out by teenagers within twelve hours, then there's a good chance they've been taken for a one-off job by professional criminals.'

'You think that the fat man and Theresa Clark are . . . ?'

'They aren't teenage joy-riders,' Paul said shortly. His expression brightened when Barnabas arrived with a large serving dish in each hand. He must have spent a week's pension on the steaks.

'Who aren't teenage joy-riders?' he enquired.

I said, 'I'll bring in the plates,' and left Paul to explain. He continued doing this throughout the serving and into the cutting-some-steak-up-small-for-Ben process. By the time that I'd tasted my first mouthful, Barnabas had been brought up to date and was scowling at his unoffending wine.

'These steaks are *very* good,' I said quickly. 'So is the wine.'

Paul joined in with a congratulatory mumble and put a large enough piece of beef into his own mouth to avoid having to say anything more for a whole minute.

'It occurs to me,' my father said, throwing our chewing guest a glance, 'that there are still a few unanswered questions. Who is this man with whom Curwen's sister appears to be living in domestic bliss? Or is she? Have some mustard.'

Paul hesitated; I watched him calculating that there couldn't be any harm in telling us. 'According to the council, the tenants are a black married couple called Williams, with two children; they both work at Homerton hospital. According to the neighbours, the house has been sublet. The tenants are a couple who keep to themselves. I'll get somebody over to the hospital tomorrow when the personnel office opens and see about having a word with Mr Williams and finding out what's going on.'

Barnabas said, 'Hm,' and sank into a thoughtful silence.

Paul looked at me. 'It would be very useful if the pair we're looking for just came home, so I'll give it until Tuesday morning, but if they haven't turned up by then I'll get the council to let us into both places. There won't be any problem with Hackney: Williams isn't allowed to sublet. Anyway, I'll have a search warrant by then just in case your fat man is back.'

'It wasn't Mr Curwen in disguise?' my father enquired.

He and Paul both turned and looked at me.

'Not unless he's gained two inches and four stone since he died,' I told them both.

Barnabas said, 'Hmph.' After a moment's silence, he added, 'Then where exactly *is* he now?'

Paul said, 'Anywhere.'

I said, 'Abroad. He's gone to a tropical island—'

I was talking about the fairy story he had told Daniel Thompson, but my words recalled last night's dream. I'd forgotten it until this.

'Not without a passport he hasn't,' Paul snapped.

Barnabas and I fixed our eyes on him, and I said, 'What makes you think he doesn't have a passport? Just because Marylebone confiscated his passport when they searched the flat?'

Paul contemplated his plate. 'He doesn't,' was all he said. His tone said that there was no argument; but his eyes said that my question made him uneasy.

Of course there was an argument. How difficult can it be to get a false passport? Even I know how to do it. I pointed this out.

Paul shrugged. 'Forget it. It's lucky that this is a slow season for travel right now, because we've been able to arrange for all new passport applications from men aged between thirty-two and fifty to be handled in London and double-checked.'

'Then why,' I demanded, 'do you have people watching for him? "Ports and airports", you told me.'

'Just a precaution,' he lied. 'Look . . . this has been a great meal, Professor Hoare, but I've been working all week, and if I don't get to bed . . .'

'I have bought some kind of lemon meringue thing—'

'I couldn't,' Paul said. 'Dido – I'll pick you up on Tuesday morning. A quarter past nine?'

'A quarter past nine,' I agreed, and let him see himself out while I finished my mushrooms.

Barnabas also sat unmoving, talking to Ben with his eyes fixed, disconcertingly, on me.

'I've been waiting to point something out,' he said when an opening permitted. 'Where is Mr Curwen at this minute? His sister's behaviour certainly suggests that they are in touch, and therefore I would question whether he has gone very far – yet. But in that case – why not? As you say, it can't be impossible to obtain a false passport, despite all precautions. Furthermore, the disappearance of his books abroad does suggest that he specifically intended to follow them.'

I positioned my knife and fork neatly parallel on the side of my plate, the way I had been taught when I was a little girl, and said, 'Something stopped him.'

'I suppose he just might be dead after all,' Barnabas suggested tentatively, 'although then . . . ?'

He *might* be. My 'X' – that third man who was in the flat when the police detective was killed – must know. Mrs Clark presumably did too. This evening, it had sounded as though even Paul Grant might have an answer, though if he did he considered it none of our business. Which, to be fair, was true.

At the back of my mind was the idea that I had heard something just recently – something about this. I started to stack plates and gather the used cutlery together while I poked through my memory. When I heard Barnabas talking, I guessed and said, 'I'll have some of your meringue thing, but Ben will have an orange. I'll peel it. You stay here and finish your wine.'

By the time I had scraped the plates, stacked them in the sink, and was attacking an orange with a sharp knife, the answer had swum grudgingly to the surface. Since the police had checked Chris Kennedy's alibi, he could not be our presumably murderous third man. Kennedy did not necessarily know where Curwen was, but he would have a better idea than anybody else, and it would be safe enough to ask him. Ever since I'd bumped into Theresa Clark, I'd been meaning to talk to him.

I left the water running loudly into the sink while I crept out into the hallway and retrieved my mobile. I could hear Ben's voice asking questions and Barnabas explaining everything. Sneaking back, I pulled the kitchen door to and rang Chris Kennedy's mobile. When I got his voice mail, I said, 'I found Theresa Clark,' and switched off.

That should get his attention.

In the immediate present, however, Ben was late for bed, and there were various preliminary matters to attend to, like his bath and his bedtime story. Tomorrow was the second day of the book fair. It wasn't going to be an easy day for getting books in and out of the MPV safe and dry, because outside I could hear the rain falling on the slate roofs and overflowing the gutters, and the forecasts had been promising something like Noah's flood.

Barnabas stayed until Ben was asleep. At 9.30 he phoned for a minicab, and had to wait for half an hour before the doorbell rang. Then I saw him downstairs and chained the outside door carefully after him. There was no special reason to wash up. I was tired, not sleepy, and in these circumstances a hot bath . . .

I was submerged in aromatherapy bubbles when the phone rang. Barnabas, saying he'd got home safely? Barnabas, saying Crouch Hill was under water and his building had floated down to Finsbury Park? I sank lower into the water and closed my eyes, listening to the answering machine cut out halfway through the outgoing message. I reached for the shampoo.

Some time later, wrapped in a bath sheet and with my eyes starting to close, I wandered into the sitting room with my portable hairdryer, plugged it in, and sat down at the desk. Five minutes more, and I'd be asleep.

The phone rang again. I switched the dryer off, picked up the receiver and said, 'Hello? B—?'

'Dido Hoare.' It was a husky voice, almost a whisper. 'You don't never answer your phone, do you, love? Well, I know it's late, but we fuckin' need ta talk.' This was a stranger, speaking estuarine English: the London dialect that drops every third consonant and turns a soft 'th' into 'f' and 'well' into 'weh-oo'; I couldn't place the voice. On the other hand . . .

I took the gamble. 'You could've left a message instead of just hanging up all the time.'

My midnight caller snorted into the mouthpiece. 'Leave my messages recorded for any cozzer to hear? That's no way for a good girl to keep outa trouble.'

I was sure now. I said, 'And you didn't exactly have to run away from me when we bumped into each other last night, either.' That brought a short silence. I took advantage of it to say, 'Mrs Clark, if you want to talk to me, you'd better do it right now. I'm just off to bed.'

Another pause. 'You got Tim's money, then?'

I yawned. ''Course I got the money. Thanks for bringing it round. How did you know I'd got the book back?' I crossed some fingers on my free hand and waited for her to make up her mind.

Eventually, she said, 'Tim saw you on his balcony one day. When he found out his book was gone, he guessed it was you. He said you were probably pissed off with him for giving you that cheque. He really wants the book. He didn't mean ta do you.'

I said casually, 'Well, I accept cash. He only had to come to the shop and ask for the book.'

'He's gone away for a while. He wants me ta get it off you.'

I didn't hesitate. 'All right. I'm out at a fair tomorrow—'

'What about in the morning?'

'I guess I could,' I said coolly. 'I'll be free at nine thirty. Shall I come over to your place in Lavender Way?'

Another of those little pauses. 'What place?'

I said carefully, 'Two five three Lavender Way – that's the address your brother's solicitors gave me. I mailed you a card over there to thank you for the money – didn't you get that?'

I hoped that I hadn't gone too far, because this time her pause was longer. Awkward. Eventually then she said, 'I moved. See you over your way? You know a place on Islington Green called Aldo's?'

'The coffee shop?'

'That's it. Nine thirty? Make sure you come on your own. Leave the filth out of this. Tim doesn't need the hassle – and nor I don't. See you later.'

I was opening my mouth just as she broke the connection. When I dialled 1471, the electronic voice gave me the same number as last time. From which I was able to deduce that it was Theresa Clark who had been phoning from a call-box over the past three days, rather than (as I'd assumed) a cold caller trying to sell me double glazing.

I went into the bedroom, stopped as always to look at Ben and straighten his duvet, and set my alarm. If I did any dreaming, I didn't remember it in the morning.

34

Silences

I kept on hoping for forty minutes. I'd got to Aldo's early, and by 10.15 I was awash with cappuccino and the waitress was showing by her sympathetic looks that she thought I'd been stood up by someone much more important than Tim Curwen's sister, or any other woman.

When my mobile rang, my first thought was to wonder how she had managed to get my number. But the voice that greeted me belonged to Dona Helmer. I settled with one shoulder against the wall, keeping my eyes peeled on the door, and asked her how things were going.

'Thanks.' But she sounded mournful. 'You?'

I found it difficult to decide the answer to that question, and settled on, 'So-so.' I pulled myself together. 'I hope you still like that book?'

'Oh, yes. Fine.' But there was something wrong: she obviously hadn't been thinking about the Lang. I started to listen hard when she said, 'I don't suppose . . . Could you possibly meet me for lunch?'

I removed the phone from my ear and looked at it stupidly. Then I replaced it and said, 'I'd love to. It would have to be an early lunch, though: I have to be at Russell Square by two. Would that be all right?'

'No problem, Dido. Why don't we eat over near there somewhere?'

Russell Square? I was starting to wonder whether she might have lost her job, because Russell Square seemed too far from

Price Rankin Burke's offices for a casual lunch date. I suggested the smart Chinese place just down the road from the hotel, and she laughed and agreed, sounding relieved. Twelve thirty, we agreed.

In the meantime, it was clear that nothing was happening in Aldo's. I left £7 on the table, waved at the waitress, and made my way the length of the empty room to the door. The streets were jammed with southbound traffic, left over from the rush hour and slowed to a crawl by the rain. I turned north. Just as I was approaching the cinema, I wondered whether I'd been lured out so that Tim Curwen could break into my shop for his book. I tried to remember when I had last checked the security system. I was almost positive that I'd noticed the red light blinking above the big window when I got home last night, but despite that I hailed a taxi which was just overtaking me with its light on and was dropped off in George Street about ninety seconds later, where the security system was armed and operating normally and everything was quiet. I let myself in, picked up a slew of letters from the floor, and went to the desk to check the answering machine. There were two messages: another hang-up – Clark again, presumably – and one from this morning, from a customer.

If I left now, I'd get to the book fair just after it opened and would have the whole time between now and 12.30 for free-range worrying, since there's never much going on the morning of the second day. It wasn't very tempting. Alternatively, I could go and show myself in Lavender Way. I told myself that maybe somebody would be so annoyed by my presence that they would condescend to communicate.

I abandoned the mail and looked up the number of Jeff Dylan's mobile. Jeff is an old friend who runs a second-hand book shop in Swansea; this weekend, he was exhibiting at the book fair and staying with an adult daughter in Peckham.

When he answered, he sounded a little blurry. I'd obviously missed a good party at the hotel last night.

'Dido? What's up?'

'Why should something be up?' I asked innocently.

I heard a snort. 'Isn't there always something up, with you?'

I agreed, and arranged for him to keep an eye on my stall as well as his own until I arrived.

Then I tried to pick up the messages on my voice mail, discovered that there were none, phoned Kennedy again with no more success than the last time, and finally rang his paper. Somebody in Features said he had called in ill, and I spent a minute or two wondering why I seemed to be the most unpopular girl in the school.

The phone rang while I was still debating the subject, but it was only Barnabas. 'What's wrong?' he demanded almost as soon as I'd wished him a good morning.

I said, 'I think it's getting to me. Mrs Clark phoned last night after you'd gone.'

He listened without interruption to how I'd been stood up. 'She will be in touch again,' he said then, 'most certainly. You are quite sure that she wasn't sitting there in some dark corner, observing you to make sure that you hadn't been sensible enough to have brought a police escort? She and her brother may be worried that the police are anticipating they will make contact.'

'Well, she didn't have to suggest the meeting!' I snapped illogically. 'And if she was there in a corner, why *didn't* she say something?'

'Testing?' Barnabas suggested, sounding interested.

'Well, she's lost her chance,' I said sourly. 'I'm leaving here now. I'll be back by seven. Are you still all right to pick Ben up from nursery?'

My father said, 'Of course I am.' He seemed offended.

I said, 'Good. I'll see you both later.'

Then I pushed myself back out into the rain, setting the burglar alarm and double-locking the door as I went, and, with my programme decided for the day, set out for Balls Pond Road and Lavender Way. This time I parked my big purple van directly opposite number 259, which still showed no signs of life, and settled to watch the street for a little while and be seen doing it. If Theresa Clark was hiding somewhere here, she might just appear. My plans were thrown into confusion briefly when I noticed that the second vehicle ahead was an unmarked blue Transit van with something like an aerial attached. Its windows were darkened glass, which made the thing look sinister and suspicious. Or like a genuine police vehicle undertaking electronic surveillance. The realisation depressed me: I might just be out of my league. Also – unless she was feeling suicidally reckless – Clark was unlikely to come tripping across the road for a little visit while we had these observers. I hung on for half an hour, mostly because I had nothing better to do; but I might as well have stayed in bed.

I turned towards Russell Square. I'd have lots of time to get the van into one of the parking garages near the hotel and then stroll over towards Holborn for my next weird engagement. I just hoped she would turn up. So far, I wasn't having a very good Monday.

But when I walked into Hoon's, Dona Helmer was already sitting at a table at the back behind two menus, a bottle of mineral water and a pot of China tea. I could see, from her black cashmere suit and the briefcase parked on a spare chair, that my speculations about her unemployment had been unfounded. Closer, I noticed that her mood was no brighter than when she had phoned. A forced smile flitted across her face, but she greeted me warmly. I sat down. We talked about the weather. She seemed to need to discuss the news reports of flooded rivers along the south coast: apparently they had warned that the town of Lewes was going to be under water by the evening.

It was almost a shock, somewhere during the dim sum, when she made her characteristic gesture of smoothing the side of her hair and cleared her throat. 'I'm hoping you can help me with a problem.'

I indicated that she had my attention.

'Mr Burke has assigned me to find Mr Curwen's sister, Mrs Clark. We really do need to liaise with her. I've driven over to that address we have.'

I nodded and said that I also had gone there.

'Nobody's lived there for a long time.'

I nodded my agreement and waited.

'When I told Mr Burke, he said to have a word with you because you'd looked for her too. Find out whether you had any suggestions.'

I was just wishing that he'd leave me alone. What made the man think that I was interested in Sis? I sighed. 'I've had no luck either. I asked around, but there's nothing to go on. She must have moved away a long time ago. Look, why don't you just go to the police? Mr Burke gave me the name of a man called Waites, at Marylebone. That's in Seymour Street. He seemed like . . .' I heard myself hesitating and plunged on. '. . . quite a helpful officer. The police must be trying to trace Mr Curwen's relatives too, don't you think?'

One of the important things about lying is remembering exactly what you are supposed to know. I'd crossed my fingers under the table to remind myself to think before I spoke, and I seemed to have got it about right.

She shook her head impatiently and speared a prawn ball. 'I've already been there. They said that they hadn't been able to trace any relatives.' She popped the ball into her mouth and chewed. I followed her example appreciatively – Hoon's prawn balls are particularly sweet and fishy. When her mouth was free again for alternative use she added, 'My boss wondered whether you might have heard something since you were last in touch with him.'

I looked at her and widened my eyes and said, 'Really? Why would he think that? What a weird idea!' Especially when I had made the situation perfectly clear to him just a couple of days earlier.

She laughed. 'He gets these bees in his bonnet! Well, I was sort of hoping I could impress him with my efficiency, but it looks as though I'll have to go back and tell him I'm foxed.'

I said wonderingly, 'Mr Burke seems awfully . . . I don't know . . . rigid in his thinking. Why doesn't *he* just go and wave his umbrella at the CID and demand their help? I'd have thought he carries some weight.'

She shrugged. 'It doesn't work that way. The juniors do the errands. Well . . .'

We talked about the weather again.

Walking to the book fair afterwards, I examined our conversation and found myself confused. Maybe she'd only wanted to bend a sympathetic ear and complain about the pressures on women in a masculine culture? Or was this lunch actually another errand she had undertaken for the firm? She had insisted on paying for us both, which implied that it was business. I even briefly considered the possibility that I was being stalked, by proxy, by a middle-aged Yorkshireman with some spare employee-time and a big ego. It was one of those fruitless speculations I'm so good at.

35

Police Procedures

We zigzagged through the network of bleak streets behind the hospital and approached 253 from the east. Paul, silent and preoccupied at the wheel, edged his Rover in to the kerb just short of our goal, switched off his engine and glanced at his watch.

'The people from the council are meeting us here at ten. They'll open up 253 and 259, and we'll go in and look around. The unit I've had over here say that there's been nobody around either place for the past two days. The phone has rung in 259 a few times, but nobody's answering it. This shouldn't take long. You wait here. I'll send somebody for you when I know it's clear.'

I hadn't really expected to be at the head of a task force storming the terrace, but there was something about his instructions that got up my nose the way, let's face it, they usually do. I said, 'Will you look and see whether my card is in either of those houses? The one with the bright pink envelope?'

He nodded vaguely and got out of the car, already fixed on the scene ahead, and marched off. I made my own survey.

It would make anybody laugh. Although there wasn't really any need for discretion by now. Even so, this covert operation had managed to attract a lot of interest and a little audience had started to gather. Its nucleus was a gang of teenage boys, who should have been in school but instead were lounging against a wall, smoking. Three or four women with toddlers in pushchairs formed a second section of audience and, as I watched, an older woman hurried along the street to join them. Judging by the way they were chatting, these people all knew each other. There was also a growing interest inside the houses opposite. Something about the way that people were lounging at their windows made them look as though they were expecting the lions and martyrs to appear. I could see their point.

Yesterday's big blue van had gone, but a white one was parked in the same place today, and I could see a twelve-seater coach just beyond it, with some people inside. You didn't need to be especially sharp to understand what kind of entertainment was scheduled.

When I looked down towards the main road, I noticed a little van coming towards us. When it swept up in front of the terrace, I could see the council's name on the side. Somebody emerged from the driver's seat and looked over at the spectators. Paul moved towards him. A second man started to unload a toolkit. Passing drivers were slowing down now, looking for a space to stop so they could watch the show.

I grabbed my shoulder bag, raised my umbrella and walked up the other side of the street to join the women. As I'd expected, they were too interested in what was happening to notice me.

'Whassup?' I muttered.

One of them shrugged without looking my way. I held my umbrella lower, peered out from underneath, and slouched and watched with them, listening to their talk. We were in broad agreement that what was going on over there so far was a little disappointing.

We watched the man from the council lead the way to the door of 259, unlock it, and stand back. Somebody spoke, and then two officers vanished inside. At the same time, the man with the toolkit started unscrewing the sheet of board from the door of 253. He leaned it up against the wall of the house, and the man with the keys did his part and then stood back. Paul and two others went inside.

I perched on a low wall and sheltered under my umbrella.

It took just a minute. Then one of the men burst out of 259. We spectators tensed expectantly. He put his hand against the wall of the house and appeared to be leaning on it and examining the footpath. It took me a moment to understand. Then he sprinted along the front of the terrace and plunged into the abandoned house at the other end.

I looped back in the direction of the Rover, where I was supposed to be waiting patiently. From beneath my umbrella, I watched the terrace and saw them all rushing out of 253. One of them stopped in the doorway. Paul led the rest of them at a trot to the Clarks' house. I could see that he was talking to the others before he disappeared inside. One of his companions remained outside this door, too, and a second one went over to speak to the driver of the van. When he stared toward me, I knew he was looking for Paul's Rover. I was standing on the pavement beside the car when he reached it. I realised that it was the same man who had emerged so abruptly from 259 a few minutes ago, and his face was still white and sweaty. He said shrilly, 'Are you Dido Hoare?'

I nodded.

'Mr Grant asks if you'd come and look at something. We've found a body.' I knew how bad it was when he paused for a moment to remember what he had seen. 'Mr Grant would be grateful if you could come with me.'

I nodded and said, 'Just a second.' I folded up the umbrella and threw it into the car. Then I indicated that I was ready.

Paul was waiting. He beckoned me in past the detective standing guard on the door, grabbed me by the arm, and backed me up against a hall mirror. His expression was fierce.

'Dido – I need your help.'

'You've found a body.'

'That's the point. He's a mess. I'm sorry. He's been dead for a little while. The thing is, he's a big, plump man and I think he must be the one that you followed here from the pub on Saturday night. I need to know right now. Do you think you can?'

It made no sense. 'When did he get back here? I thought your people had been watching this place ever since Saturday night?'

Paul hesitated. He looked uneasy, and evaded my question. 'Look – I didn't notice this man the other night, or I wouldn't ask you to do it. You're the only one who saw his face in the pub. You *did* see his face?'

I nodded.

'All right. Will you just look at him and tell me whether it's the man who was with Theresa Clark? That's all you have to do. I'd better warn you—'

'I know,' I said. 'All right.'

He looked at my face, took my arm, and moved me a few feet along an entrance hall to an open doorway. He stopped me there before I could step across the threshold. 'From here,' he said. 'Can't go in there until the forensic team have been. Can you see his face from here? Just take a quick look.'

I had been prepared by the way they were all acting, so I told myself to imagine that there was a thick glass window between me and the world, and then I looked through it. An old armchair sat there to my right, its back to the arched opening leading to the dining room, its seat facing the front window. The curtains on the window were drawn, but enough light seeped in to let me see all that I needed to. The man sprawled lazily in the chair, legs stretched out in front of him and head tilted back, eyes staring at the ceiling. There was a hole in his forehead. I tried to keep myself from staring at the bloody wound, but it was hard to look away. He looked outraged. The room smelled of rotting meat and urine.

'It's him,' I said. My voice cracked. I had just realised that the whole chair was blackened by his dried blood. I let Paul pull me away.

'Dido? All right?'

I said steadily, 'Wait a minute. I'm just trying to work this out. Yes, I'm all right. Who was this man? When did he get back here?'

'You actually watched him drive away?'

I opened my mouth and heard myself saying again, 'Wait a minute: I watched him let himself in, and I heard him shut the door. He turned on the lights. He'd only been here for a minute when the lights went out again. I heard a bang, I thought it was the door again, and afterwards I saw him . . . no, I just saw a shape, because the streetlight's out, but I thought he came down the path and got into that car you said was stolen. Only . . . the person I saw could have been somebody else. His killer. Right? Was it a shot that I'd heard?'

'We'll have to find out. I think there's not much doubt that this is a small-time crook called Frankie Clark. But I had somebody sitting outside this place by about ten minutes after you left, and we've been here ever since, so . . . You didn't see enough of the man who came out to recognise him again?'

'Just that he was so close to this one in size and shape that I didn't realise it wasn't him. It was too dark in that side path to see faces. Was that the killer? I don't think that an interior light came on when he opened the car door. No, I'm sure it didn't.'

'Could it have been Theresa Clark you saw?'

I called up my remembered image and said, 'No way. Aside from the fact that she couldn't have got back here before him, it was somebody much bigger. She's quite scrawny.'

'All right.' He looked down at me. 'I'm going to get one of

my people to drive you home. We'll need a short statement about the other night, but it can wait. Are you sure you're all right?' I nodded. He hesitated. 'Then I'll see you later.'

I had almost reached the door when I remembered.

'Paul?'

He turned back to me.

'My pink envelope – remember? Was it over there?'

'No sign of it,' he said vaguely. He had other things to worry about. 'Sorry, I have to . . .'

I said, 'Of course,' and went to look for my lift.

36

Numbers

When the squeamish young detective dropped me off in George Street, I found the shop door locked. Peering through the display window, I could just make out that Barnabas was standing by the desk, looking down at something. He appeared to be alone, but I felt for my keys without taking my eyes off him. He finally looked up when I opened the door.

'You appear flustered. Is everything all right?'

I repressed the impulse to kick something and said mildly that nothing was all right.

He had been looking through *The Haunted Man*, the task I'd been meaning to get around to for days. Now he closed it and demanded to know exactly what had happened. I told him about the corpse. He demanded to know where Paul Grant was, and why he hadn't escorted me home.

'He's on duty,' I pointed out, 'running a murder investigation and ordering a lot of underlings about. I got a lift from one of them.'

'And you are sure . . . ?'

'It was the man I saw at the pub with Theresa Clark – the same one who talked to you about her when we went over there that Sunday, and he certainly did know her all right. I'm wondering where *she* is now. I wonder whether she's all right, and also I wonder whether she could have somehow got back there to kill him – or perhaps her brother did. I can't think straight.'

'You are shaken up; you need a cup of tea,' my father said

decisively. 'By the by, Miss Helmer phoned here a little while ago. She was asking about the book – whether I could tell her who had bought it. I said, quite truthfully as I assumed, that I had no idea. As soon as she rang off, of course, I remembered your old habit and found it in the drawer. We might go upstairs now.'

The shop with its big window did seem much too public for this discussion, despite the fact that our notice of opening times would tell any passer-by that we were closed. I watched as my father dropped the Dickens casually into his half-closed umbrella and waved me down the aisle to the door. I was thinking that he was displaying all the secretive behaviour of . . . of a very careful, worried man.

'Don't forget to set the security alarm,' was all that he said. 'I believe that we need to get to the bottom of this as quickly as possible.' Then, as I started up the staircase to the flat, he slammed the door behind us. When I heard him putting the chain up, I turned around. He glared. Well, it couldn't do any harm. Once upstairs, he turned his umbrella upside down, caught the little book as it fell out, and leaned the umbrella up against the wall. Mr Spock came to inspect it. I slung my raincoat on a hook.

'Go in and sit down,' he ordered. 'I shall put the kettle on. Here – hold on to it.'

He thrust *The Haunted Man* at me. I received it and tossed the book on to the growing pile of papers that was starting to overwhelm the top of my writing desk. They all had something to do with Tim Curwen and his business, and there were far too many of them.

When Barnabas brought in the tea I sipped mine cautiously. It was horrible. In theory my father understands that tea is made with boiling water, but as usual he had been impatient. Also it was sweet enough to rot my back teeth.

'Drink it!' my father ordered. 'You've had a shock – you

need sugar.' I took a mouthful and put the mug down near at hand; to do him justice, my father made a face at his own when he tasted it. It joined mine on the table.

'Tell me exactly what happened,' he said.

I said, 'That can wait. You explain what was going on here! Dona Helmer just rang to ask about the book *again*? They're crazy at that place.'

'There was a message on the answering machine – she had already rung at eight thirty. So, by the way, did the unreliable journalist. He said he would ring back. But about Miss Helmer, who seems to be acting as the office errand-girl and is a little cross about it: she informed me that Mr Burke had left a note on her desk overnight, instructing her to trace the Dickens. For reasons that Miss Helmer finds unclear, it seems to be urgently needed.'

'You stalled her.'

'I suppose I did,' my father admitted with satisfaction.

We both turned and looked at the little volume.

'Why?' I asked.

Barnabas turned back. 'Remind me: you found this secreted in a padded bag amid Curwen's paperbacks? There can be no doubt that he hid it there? He may be somewhat illiterate and entirely criminal, but he does display a certain practical, low cunning.'

I agreed.

'Presumably he was unable to retrieve it when he left the flat that night, possibly under duress. You say you were told that the books were disarranged at some time *after* you were last there? Did someone get in to look for this, do you think?'

'Curwen had a spare set of keys,' I told him thoughtfully, 'but he obviously had a problem about being seen. I'd already taken it away before he had the chance to get in. I told Price Rankin Burke that I got it back and the estate no longer owed me anything. However . . .'

It struck me, not for the first time, though maybe more forcibly than ever, that subsequent events were more than a little tangled in my mind. Under her brother's instructions, Mrs Clark had delivered a cash payment for this book. As a result, I would have to accept that the Dickens was no longer my property, since it had been paid for (despite the delay). Then Sis had arranged to meet me for a coffee; and she must have planned to pick up the merchandise on that visit, though only after she had made sure it was safe. The fact that none of this had actually happened indicated a last-minute change of plans; she must have found out about the killing and decided that it was too dangerous to come out of hiding. I was beginning to wonder whether I had worked out what business the mysterious Vauxhall had had in my street.

I put these details to Barnabas, who nodded agreement.

'But where do the solicitors come in? Curwen couldn't have got in touch with them and asked them to get it from me, because they think he's dead! And he couldn't just come here and ask me for it – he didn't know I already knew he was alive. That's why he used his sister.'

'He would have anticipated your contacting the police to notify them of his resurrection.'

'But he must have known that they know he's alive.'

Barnabas was smiling thoughtfully. 'Ah, yes – and, no doubt, that they would be more than happy to lay hands on him. Curwen is a young man with a number of good reasons for wishing to remain in hiding. He hid the book (and incidentally, we have no idea why he did so), as he has hidden himself. The man who died in his flat was a policeman. His "minder", you said? His reasons for wishing to remain in obscurity are multiplying.'

'I have a feeling that it does hang together,' I said dreamily, 'and that I might just be on the point of seeing how.'

'I have a feeling,' my father echoed my words a great deal

less dreamily, 'that you should make a concentrated effort to determine the nature of the fit. A sense of urgency wouldn't come amiss! You have here in your possession a humble and inoffensive nineteenth-century literary work which is actually and legally owned by a criminal associated (I put it objectively) with drugs traffic and several murders, and which is being sought by himself and also perhaps by others. While Miss Helmer does not, as it were, bear a sign on her forehead reading "Crooked Solicitor – Beware", perhaps she should? At least, we mustn't forget that she is involved.'

'Or her boss is,' I snarled.

'Possibly, although she could simply have been lying to me.'

Why not? Everybody else was. There was nothing to guarantee that Theresa Clark, for instance, wasn't acting for herself rather than her delinquent brother.

I said, 'I'd better get on to Paul and tell him about this. I'll try ringing his emergency number in an hour; he's going to be too busy until then. In the meantime, you might look at what I found in that book. Did you see where Curwen pencilled some notes in it?'

My father looked impatient but resigned. 'I shall take it away with me. I shall have an hour or two to spare.'

I wished him luck. I had done some scrutinising of my own when I bought this book; then I'd had it in the shop for months, and checked through it when I sold it on to my good customer; and I knew perfectly well that it was a completely normal copy except for Curwen's annotations. It would somehow have been more comforting to have found something sinister there.

It was hard to settle when he had gone. I grabbed Mr Spock and scratched his chin for a while, trying to work out what to do. I could have gone downstairs to deal with the morning's post, wrap a parcel or two, or even dust a few upper shelves. Here in the flat there were unmade beds, a sink piled with dirty dishes, and even worse. Violent physical activity might take my mind off what I had seen in Lavender Way. I allowed my cat to go back to his slumbers and went looking for the bucket and mop. Eventually, when I realised that I was hungry, I poked into my newly spotless refrigerator for the leftover, half-eaten lasagne to blast in the microwave: a lunch appropriate for a woman whose mind was on other things.

I was washing my hands in the well-scrubbed bathroom when the phone rang, and I ran to answer it.

'Dido?'

Damn it! I'd forgotten about the unreliable journalist. I said, 'Yes, sorry, I was meaning to call you back. I *did* phone you a couple of days ago; didn't you get my message?'

'You said that Terry Clark has been in touch?'

For a moment, I'd forgotten that I'd told him that. 'She arranged to meet me – yesterday morning, in fact – but she didn't turn up.'

'All right.' He was silent for a minute, and I pictured him pondering the information. 'All right,' he said again. 'Look – would it be all right to drop by there?'

I asked, 'When?' What I really meant was 'Why?'

'About three?'

I glanced at the clock above the fireplace and found it had stopped. 'I'll probably be upstairs. Just ring the bell.'

He was silent. I waited. He said, 'You haven't asked me.'

'Then I will: what made you change your mind about this?'

'Partly the fact that they know about you anyway, and mostly because an envelope arrived at my flat yesterday, addressed to Terry Clark, who obviously thought my address would be safer to use than her own. Naturally I opened it. It's a brand-new passport.'

Then they were going to try to leave the country together. Find one, find both. I said, 'Listen: something has happened. Somebody else has been killed.'

'What? Who? I haven't heard a whisper of anything!'

'Somebody who lived in that same row of houses in Lavender Way. He knew Terry Clark. I saw him with her. They only found him this morning, but it happened on Saturday night.'

He was silent for so long that I thought he had hung up. 'Three o'clock,' he said finally. I couldn't interpret his tone. I went away to make proper use of the bathtub I had just scrubbed – that's why I resent housework. For once, even aromatherapy bubbles had no effect on my mood.

I was still wrapped in my terry-towel bathrobe, drying my hair, when the doorbell blipped. I ran into the sitting room thinking, *Already?* The clock was still stopped. By the time I got to the window to check on the identity of my visitor, however, I heard the downstairs door open and slam. Barnabas was back. I tensed slightly and opened the door of the flat when he was halfway up the stairs to ask, 'What's wrong?'

He stepped inside, stood his umbrella up to drain, said, 'You really ought to have an umbrella stand here,' and then, 'Nothing is wrong. Unfortunately, I might add. I have examined this book most scrupulously, and the only oddities I can find are, as you say, those random page numbers. You noticed that they are written down in no particular order, are repeated, and do not seem to refer to any common element on the pages listed. I even looked over the paper with a magnifying glass. If there is anything else here, I confess I cannot find it.' He produced the Dickens from his briefcase and placed it in my hand, adding magnanimously, 'I brought it back because I knew you would wish to look for yourself. I thought I'd pop over to the British Library for an hour; I need to order some books and see about a manuscript. After that, I'll come back and we can discuss it if need be. Will you be all right?' He looked around vaguely. 'You've been doing the chores?'

'It's time I caught up,' I said defensively. 'I'll probably spend

the afternoon up here. Chris Kennedy is supposed to be dropping by. I'll give him tea and talk to him.'

Barnabas hesitated visibly. I fixed him with a cold stare. He
coughed and said that he'd see me later. Not too much later,
I suspected. But I believed now that Kennedy was, if not
exactly innocent, at any rate safe. Not in the to-be-met-only-
in-public-places category. Which, now that I thought of it, was
so much better than almost everybody else involved that it
placed him fairly firmly on the side of the angels.

Barnabas retrieved his umbrella and went back out into the
rain. I left Curwen's little book on the desk and went to dress.
When I was ready to face the world, I went back and picked it
up. *The Haunted Man and The Ghost's Bargain.* The book
seemed to be haunting me. On the whole, I would be happy
to see the back of it. For the time being, I decided to hide it
among the ten thousand other volumes downstairs. I put it out
of sight in my shoulder bag, ran down the stairs, let myself into
the shop, and hesitated. Then I thought of the box under the
packing table in which I'd been gathering a number of books
that I was meaning to send away to my binder. That was the
place for this volume. In fact, if I actually owned it again when
this was all over, I'd send it to her and ask her to clean up the
scribbles. I flipped through the book again. When I located the
numbers, I looked through them more carefully. Barnabas was
right, as always: the page numbers were listed in no obvious
order. I started to chase up the references. It wasn't until I
noticed that one of the pages which had been listed was a
blank, and that one was referred to four times over, that my
instincts began to scream.

The numbers were written down in four distinct groups,
almost like paragraphs. I counted the digits and found that
each group had been recorded in a recurring pattern: first four
pairs of numerals, followed by a single number; then two pairs
and a single; then two pairs; then a singleton. It was exactly

the same in each group – my eye had recognised a pattern
without my having any idea about it. I tore a sheet of paper off
my telephone pad and wrote the numbers down in four lines
across: nine digits, five digits, four digits, one. Each of the four
lines was exactly like the others, so I had four identical-looking
columns.

I folded the paper into quarters and slid it into the pocket of
my jeans. Then I buried Curwen's book among all the other
volumes, and pushed the box which held them right out of
sight under the table, set my security system, locked up, and
got the hell out of there.

37

The Haunted Man

I knew that it was nearly a quarter past three because I was just resetting the clock on the mantelshelf when the doorbell rang. I went over to the window. The XJS was sitting at the kerb. I hurried downstairs, opened the door on its chain, and after a quick inspection took the chain off and stepped up on to the second stair to give the unreliable journalist enough room to come inside. When I turned around, he had shut the door behind him and was watching me. Like this, we were almost the same height and I was blocking his way.

'What do you want? What are you after?'

He stared at me. That nerve was jumping again. He slowly raised both arms, his fists clenched, and rested them lightly on my shoulders. I could feel the tension.

'Dido, I think I need help. I'm sorry.'

I took a breath right down into my abdomen and said again, 'Why are you here? What do you want?' I was watching his eyes.

'This man – the one who's been killed. Do they have a name?'

'Paul mentioned a "Frankie Clark". He was living at the other end of the terrace, at 259, and he was in the Anchor with Terry on Saturday night. She's using his name, so I assume they're married or something? I don't believe that she ever lived at 253, I think that was just a drop they used when they needed to, because it was close enough to be under her eye and it had been empty for a long time. You remember my card? You told me the postman was carrying it in his hand. Well, Paul Grant's people will find it if it was left there. Or they'll find out what the postman was doing.' I said it again, slowly: 'What are you up to? Why do you want my help?'

'Do we have to stand here? You may not have noticed it, but I'm not in great shape. I didn't sleep last night, or the night before much. You might have to hold me up.'

'I've noticed,' I assured him. 'You're quite heavy.'

He nearly smiled. He let his arms fall at his sides and waited.

I said, 'I guess I want your confession. I'm tired of being lied to and kept in the dark and made use of.'

'I see your point,' he admitted. 'All I wanted was to get a friend out of the country, alive and in one piece, not being pushed around by eager coppers, not in jail, not dead. If he doesn't get away soon, he probably will be killed, you know. He can't go on hiding in London for much longer – it's a battleground, and they're looking for him, I don't know how he's kept ahead of them for so long. They're the people who caught up with his . . . Theresa's friend. The police won't have the same priorities as I do.'

'Their priority is to round up and shut down a drugs gang. I don't have a quarrel with that.'

'Neither do I. Please believe that.'

I remembered. 'You had a brother.'

He looked at me. 'Your copper told you? Yes, I had a little brother. His name was John. Despite all that, despite having lost sleep over this, I have told you exactly what I want.'

'But Curwen must have had a hand in the killing of that policeman in his flat. McKane.'

'I know. It is quite possible he'd panic if they pushed him too far. He's been scared half out of his mind all summer. If the firm had any idea what he was up to with McKane—

These people kill informers without blinking. I hope it was just that he couldn't stop it happening. I don't believe he had a reason to murder anybody. The man who was there with him probably did.'

I said, 'Who was he – the third one? Would you rather have tea, or coffee?'

He said politely, 'Whatever's convenient. I don't know.'

Then I turned and led him upstairs.

There were two small cups' worth of stale coffee left in the machine. They would do to start with. I poured them out, set a new pot brewing, and pointed him towards the sitting room. We sat at opposite ends of the settee. The clock over the fireplace stood at 3.32.

I said, 'Now: how should I help you? Why?'

'Terry made contact with you: what did she want?'

I thought about that question very carefully and for the hundredth time. 'I can't be sure, but probably it was the book. I think she was trying to phone me for the past couple of days. I didn't know who kept phoning because she never left a message, but then I finally answered when she called on . . .' I had to stop and work it out. Days and events were starting to run together in my head. '. . . Sunday night. That was twenty-four hours after I bumped into her in the pub and she ran for it. She arranged for us to meet at a café near here, but she didn't say what she wanted and she never arrived.' I stopped. 'This doesn't make sense. When we bumped into each other at the door of the toilets, she recognised me. How could she recognise me? I knew *her* because she's so much like her brother; but how could *she* have known *me*?' I could hear my voice rising in something like panic.

'You really don't know?'

I looked at him. 'She's seen me somewhere?'

Wordlessly he reached into an inside pocket of his leather jacket, pulled out a stiff manila envelope and handed it over.

The label on it read 'Mrs Theresa Clark', with an address in Camden Town; the return address was the Passport Office. 'This was delivered to my flat. My address must have seemed safer. Look at it.'

I pulled out a stiff new passport, looked at Kennedy, and opened it. Theresa Clark's face stared back at me. Seen suddenly, in a colour photo, she looked so much like her brother that I laughed. The hair was different, of course, and she hadn't taken her glasses off for the photo, so that the hazel eyes looked at me coldly through their lenses.

I said, 'If she only had his blue eyes . . .'

He said, 'Coloured contact lenses.'

I looked down at Terry Clark's passport again, and Tim Curwen looked back at me. I started laughing. I laughed so helplessly that Kennedy began to shift in his seat.

'Dido—'

'I'm sorry,' I whimpered. 'Oh—'

'Should I slap your face?' he asked warily.

I gasped, 'Jesus! Um. More coffee?' When he nodded, I fled to the kitchen where the machine had just finished brewing, ran cold water from the tap over my face and hot coffee into two clean mugs, and managed to get hold of myself. By the time I returned, I had convinced myself that the situation wasn't funny, and Kennedy had fallen asleep untidily where he sat. The clock said that it was 3.58. I put the coffee down on the table and tried to work out what I was going to do. And failed. And found myself thinking uneasily of the stolen car that had been sitting outside my shop. And saw that I'd better contact Paul Grant again.

The emergency number he had given me was still working miracles of a sort. He answered instantly with, 'Dido, I can't talk, I'll ring back.'

I babbled, 'Paul, I have to know—'

He repeated, 'I'll ring back,' and cut the connection. *Pompous git!*

I heard a stifled yawn, and saw Kennedy watching me.

He said, 'What?'

'Paul Grant. He says he'll ring back.'

His face froze. 'What are you doing?'

'By now he must know whether Terry-Tim was living in that house.'

'He tells you about these things?'

'No,' I admitted. 'Drink your bloody coffee now. It's fresh.'

The doorbell gave my father's usual blip, and the downstairs door opened and shut. The clock said it was ten past four: my father's visit to the library had been truncated. Then Barnabas more or less came bursting in saying, 'The Jag—' He saw my visitor and broke off. 'I was speculating why your car was downstairs,' he said coolly.

'There's coffee,' I told him.

'I shan't sleep tonight if I do. I shall make myself a cup of tea.'

I said, 'I'd better,' and went to boil the kettle, listening hard and hearing nothing but the sound of voices which started by speaking rapidly and then slowed down. I made tea in a mug with a tea bag, to save time, and the water was pretty close to the boil. When I carried it into the other room, I found the two men sitting opposite one another, leaning across the coffee table in what looked like a reasonably polite conference. I put my father's tea down in front of him and retreated to my old seat. They ignored me.

'There it is,' my father was saying. 'Obviously, Curwen has been trying to retrieve his book from Dido. Can you explain why?'

'It's valuable?' Kennedy speculated.

I said coldly, 'No. Not especially.' I was going to say

something about the numbers which were burning a hole in my pocket, but before I could speak my father said, 'It is a perfectly normal copy of the first edition, nothing rare, pleasant if Victoriana interests you – no more.'

I interrupted: 'He wrote something—'

'He did not,' Barnabas said sharply.

He and I needed to have a private talk. I picked up my mug, drank my coffee, and wondered why he was being so cautious.

My father sighed explosively. 'If you locate Mr Curwen, you may give it to him: he has paid for it. At the same time, you must explain to him that if he so much as rings my daughter to thank her for her care and kindness, I shall *personally* ensure—'

His words were lost in a sudden rushing noise outside, and we all turned to the window. Dusk had fallen, bringing a cloudburst. I knelt on the settee to look out at a minor flood already overflowing the gutters. A car turned in from the side road and rolled past the front of the shop as slowly and cautiously as though the driver were negotiating a river ford. The clock said that it was just past 4.30. Even if I waited for a few minutes longer, I wasn't going to be able to walk Ben home in this.

I finished off my coffee and said I was going to drive over to the nursery.

Barnabas hesitated visibly.

Kennedy didn't. 'I'll come with you.' Riding shotgun was the implication. I just shrugged.

'I shall make a pot of tea,' Barnabas said decisively.

When I opened the downstairs door, there was still a torrent outside. My van was in the residents' bay, fifty feet along the road.

'We'll take mine,' Kennedy suggested. It was just outside.

'Don't bother,' I said. 'I'd rather have him properly strapped in his seat when the roads are so wet. I'm not far away.'

'Wait.' He had grabbed my arm just as I was about to step out into the floods. 'I didn't want to say anything upstairs, but they— I'll follow you. Watch your rear-view mirror and wait for me to catch up if we get separated.'

This was no time to debate the issue, or even to call him melodramatic, so I shrugged and ran for it. My hair was dripping by the time I'd got my door open and dived into shelter. I started the engine and switched on dipped headlights. Kennedy was waiting. We got out into the cross-street and turned east.

Since it was the beginning of rush hour, the XJS had no difficulty keeping close. London traffic is the only thing I know that is thickened by the addition of water. I was afraid that I was going to be late, but we drew up at the nursery just as the dashboard clock flicked over to five. The Jaguar slid in right behind me.

It took longer to get back. To avoid the traffic jams in Upper Street, I guided us around the back route and in at the north end of my road. My place in the residents' parking bay had been taken, but a car pulled out just as I approached, and I swung into the space.

Kennedy rolled past. I caught a wave of his hand, and then he pulled in on the yellow line in front of the shop. Just before he cut the headlights, they hit a figure which had appeared suddenly on the pavement, and I saw the white face of the person who had bumped into me on Saturday night. Terry Clark must have been sheltering in the little triangular niche between my side wall and the back of the building on the corner. I gasped, flung myself out of the van, and rushed around to open the door by Ben's seat. He started to complain. He was tired. I slid him out of his seat, gave him a hug and slammed the door.

The big saloon car which had just vacated my space was rolling forward as Kennedy opened his door and stepped out on to the pavement to face his friend. Brake lights flared, and three men piled out of the saloon so quickly that they left me staring. I thought: police. They surrounded Curwen and Kennedy. I carried Ben to the pavement, put him down, grabbed his hand and set the remote locking. Then he and I started towards the flat, walking fast through the rain. The five men under the lamppost by the shop looked frozen. Something about their stillness made me stop. I could see Clark-Curwen saying something. His teeth flashed in a sharp grin. Kennedy's back was turned to me, his face hidden . . .

I grabbed Ben again, hoisted him up on to my hip and held him still. He whined, '*I want indoors!*' He was getting soaked.

I whispered, 'Shh!' as fiercely and quietly as I could, because there was something about the way they were all standing over there that bothered me – especially the strangers. They were three ordinary men, one taller than the others, one square and heavy, all dressed casually in jeans and dark jackets. It was too dark to see the faces clearly, but what bothered me was their body language. It took a moment to work out that this was because they had all adopted the same posture, each man with his left arm hanging loose at his side and his right arm stretched across his body, his hand hidden inside his jacket opening. There was a kind of stiffness in the stance. I struggled against an instinct that said they were holding guns.

A blip from the waiting car's horn made me jump. Ben fell silent. I saw the heavy one glance across at the car and its invisible driver; he spoke to the others. It looked as though there was a moment's disagreement, and then two of them, like dear friends, grabbed Curwen's arms and ran him across to the car, pushing him in through its rear door. One of them followed him, and the other ran around the car and also disappeared inside. Both doors slammed. I turned my eyes back to the other pair and saw Kennedy moving unhurriedly to his Jaguar. First he walked around it and unlocked the passenger door; the other man came behind him and stood watching him across the roof while Kennedy circled back and paused by the driver's door. The two of them got in at the same instant. Nobody looked my way.

'Want to go *home!*' Ben shrieked into my ear.

'One second!' I hissed, giving him a quick squeeze.

If this was the police, then both men had just been arrested. If this was not the police . . .

I was feeling for my mobile when the Jaguar's headlights sprang on, and I pressed the buttons desperately. I would have had my fingers crossed if I'd had any hands or fingers to spare.

Paul Grant's voice snapped a question.

I took a deep breath and screamed, 'Some men have just come here! They've grabbed Tim Curwen and Chris Kennedy, and they're taking them away *now*. Paul – *they have guns!* You have to help!'

'WHAT?' he was yelling in my right ear. 'What are you talking about? Curwen's over there at your place?'

'GO *IN*!!' Ben screeched into my left ear.

I held him and ran across the road. 'Paul, *listen to me!* Some men just came here and grabbed Curwen and Chris Kennedy. *Just listen!* They're driving off now in two cars. I think—' I cancelled that; this was no time to let him wonder whether it was serious. 'Listen: they are *armed*, Paul! I think they're going to kill them!'

'Dido—'

'*Hurry!*'

'I will, I will, I'll get somebody there from Islington as— *Can you tell me the registration numbers of those cars?*'

I turned in a panic – and then discovered that they were still only ten feet away from me, waiting to get out into the cross-street. The traffic out there was solid and unmoving.

But the police would take for ever to get here when it was like this. I put Ben down on his feet and moved a couple of steps towards the junction, reading the Jaguar's number aloud into the phone and then, just as the lead car managed to bully its way out, I saw its number too. The Jaguar lurched after it.

'*Have you got that?*'

'Stop yelling! Yes! Dido . . . I'll do my best. Which way are they heading?'

East, I told him. I said that there was the granddaddy of all traffic jams here, and that I could still see the rear bumper of the XJS.

He said, 'Christ! All right. They're on their way. I'll ri—'

I switched off before he had finished saying 'ring back'. The police might be on their way, but how could they get here on gridlocked roads in time to do anything? A helicopter – they might just manage something with a helicopter; but it would take at least twenty minutes for anyone, even in a police car, to get here by road, and by that time Kennedy and Curwen would be gone. I ran back to my front door, where Ben stood wailing, and pushed my key into the lock. As the door swung open, I found Barnabas standing at the top of the stairs, probably asking what we were doing down here. I lifted Ben over the threshold and leaned down to his ear. 'See? Grandpa's here! Lovely! You go upstairs and stay with Grandpa.' He stopped crying.

I didn't dare look Barnabas in the eye. I just slammed the door and ran back to my van. At least George Street was still clear. I pulled out and put my foot down. At the corner, I ran the van forward as far as I could and located the Jaguar inching towards the Essex Road. Then I turned my headlights on to high beam, leaned on the horn and rolled steadily onward. Brakes squealed and I scraped in so close to a car that I'm pretty sure I nudged it. Horns blared all around: road rage time. I turned my wipers to high speed. Nobody was going to get out and come picking a fight, not in this downpour, and if they did I couldn't care less.

The seats in my MPV are higher than in a normal car, and I could see over those ahead of me to the light cream top of Kennedy's XJS. I was almost certain that the other car was the one immediately ahead of him. What make of car had it been? What colour? I hadn't noticed. Something ordinary. I felt for my mobile phone in a panic, brought it up to the steering wheel so I could keep my eyes on the traffic, and rang Paul Grant again.

'Dido, I told you—'

I howled, '*Shut up a minute!* I'm following them. We're just coming up to the Essex Road. They're signalling left, they're going to turn north. If you can get a car there, you might be able to stop them at the lights at the Balls Pond Road junction. But don't forget . . .'

'What?'

'Don't forget they have guns.'

'I'd expect it.' Paul was sounding really pissed off. 'All right, Dido, thanks. Now just turn around and go home, will you?'

I said, 'I'll stay well back!' and dropped the phone on to my lap. The traffic thinned momentarily and I was able to get out into the main road. The streetlights were brighter here, and I could see the Jaguar clearly about a block ahead. I pulled into the outside lane without being hit, though there was more honking and braking, and made up a few yards.

My phone trilled. I held it in front of my nose and checked; I was being rung up from the flat. Barnabas. I switched on and said, 'Take care of Ben. Dry him off and give him a drink. If he starts shivering, give him a warm bath. I'll be back as soon as I can. I'm going to switch off now – I'm in touch with the police.' He had been talking, but I'd spoken over his voice because I knew what he was saying.

When we reached the next junction, the roads to left and right were jammed solid, and there were no police cars anywhere. My quarry drove straight over and headed towards Stoke Newington. I caught the last of the green light and followed.

38

The Ghost's Bargain

The line to Paul was open again.

'All right.' My eyes turned to the dashboard clock. 'It's six ten. We're on the big roundabout south of Potters Bar. They're turning east on to the M25. I can see the motorway from here – it's busy, but moving. Where are your people?'

'Three cars are on their way, just leaving Southgate. We've told them to get a move on, but not to use their lights and sirens until they're close: they'd only warn our friends that they're coming. We have one car on the motorway, westbound from the A10. I want you to keep your phone switched on; when it comes into sight, tell me and I'll warn them to give us your exact location.'

'I won't see him,' I said simply. 'The rain is letting up a bit, but there's spray twenty feet high down there, like fog.'

'You wouldn't like to go back home now?' Paul suggested, not for the first time. 'All right, I'll tell him to turn on his flashers. He can scare the westbound idiot speeders while he's at it, and when you see the blue light, just shout and let me know.'

I said I would, put the phone down on the dashboard, and used both hands to manoeuvre the van off the slip road and on to the motorway. I lost sight of the cars at once. Everyone was travelling too fast for the conditions, and the spray they were throwing up was so thick that I could see nothing ahead but shadows and disembodied tail-lights. Time to speed up, then: for all I knew, the people I was following were recklessly blasting up the outside lane and getting farther and farther ahead. I wriggled out to the right and joined the boy racers in the fast lane. We were doing a wild sixty, overtaking the sane drivers to our left, when I suddenly located the Jaguar again. I slowed, signalled, and pulled in behind it. Even if Kennedy's passenger noticed the van, he wouldn't think anything of it now. There were several other cars hanging around just ahead. One of them looked like the vehicle with Tim Curwen in it.

In the wet clouds ahead, I saw a sudden flash.

'Paul, are you there?'

'Yes?'

'I can see a blue flash coming this way.'

'All right, we'll tell everybody where you are. Dido?'

I said suspiciously, 'Yes?'

'We know where they're headed. We've got an address in Hertfordshire. I want them to get there without any trouble – those people you're following are just the hired help, and I don't want to risk stopping armed men on the road if it can be avoided. This is what's going to happen: some of my people in unmarked cars will pick up your two vehicles when they come off the motorway at the A10 roundabout. What I want you to do is this: you come off at the same place, but you turn right. Go home. Do you understand? Barnabas has been ringing us – I've had to tell them to say I'm too busy to talk to him. Call him as soon as you're heading towards town and tell him you're on the way, for Chrissake, before he complains to the Commissioner or the Queen or somebody.'

'I'll tell him it's not your fault,' I promised shortly, and switched to stand-by. I wasn't sure that I was going to do what he said. I was thinking that if they shot Tim Curwen – well, he'd walked into it with his eyes open; but Kennedy had got himself into this mess out of love. Stupid bastard! And I was supposed to drive away. And I wasn't sure that I could. Now who was being stupid?

I checked my speedometer and found it hovering just under fifty. We'd been slowing gradually. It couldn't be much farther. In a moment the advance warning sign for the A10 exit came dimly into view, and I got ready to follow them up the slip road.

They ran under the flyover and kept on going.

I was already reaching for my phone when it rang.

'Dido? Where the hell are you?'

'Still on the motorway. They went straight on!'

'Wait a minute!' I waited instead for a small eternity before his voice returned. 'All right, I can see what's happening. They'll be taking the next exit, a couple of miles ahead. When they do that, you keep straight on. Come off at the M11 and take that route back into central London. Thanks. I'll ring you just as soon as I have any news.'

We ran, one after the other, up the next slip road, past the blue-and-white sign for Waltham Abbey. Halfway up the slope, my engine hiccupped. It recovered after a moment, but the needle on the fuel gauge had been on empty ever since I'd left home. I pounded encouragingly on the steering wheel and put my foot down to the floor. For a moment I had power again. I pulled into the outside lane and passed the XJS. Kennedy didn't look my way, which told me that he knew I was there.

Then the engine faltered again, and the Jaguar started to pull up beside me. I leaned on my horn and swung the wheel. The van banged hard against something and jounced, and I had just enough time to scream, 'Damn it!' and regret this stupid chase and everything else stupid that I'd ever done before a white balloon exploded in my face, there was another bang, and everything skidded sideways and stopped. I leaned my face against the air bag and tried not to cry. I kept my eyes shut even when the door beside me jerked open. I said, 'Did I kill anybody?'

Kennedy's voice in my ear said, 'No, but you'll need some body work doing. What happened?'

I said, 'I was running out of petrol. I was going to have to stop. Are you all right?'

'May you never run out of anything really serious, like coffee beans,' he said solemnly. He sounded all right. 'Would you like to get out of there? I think the police are here. I've got your seat belt unbuckled. Hold on to me.'

I slid and was pulled out and landed on the gravel of the verge. There were flashing blue lights coming up from the motorway.

I caught my breath. 'Where's the man who was with you?'

'Scarpered. Ran down the embankment as soon as we stopped. It's too dark to see where he went, but he's gone. Probably looking for a taxi.'

I said, unnecessarily, 'I hope he can't find one,' and leaned against him, feeling dizzy.

'Dido?'

'What is it?'

'I'm going to put you in the car. You're getting wet. I think you're in shock, and you don't want to get cold.'

I let him lead me like a child around the back of the van to his car, which had stopped diagonally with its nose against a post at the far side of the paved verge. The passenger door was standing open, so I fell inside and lay back with my eyes closed. I'd need a minute to stop feeling sick. But there were blue lights flashing on my eyelids, so I opened them again in time to watch two police cars disappear up the road, while a third pulled in behind us. Then they were all standing in the rain, Kennedy talking fast to a couple of uniformed officers. The three of them disappeared around my van. Then the officers reappeared, climbed into their car, switched off the flasher, veered on to the road and left. It took Chris a little longer to return. He climbed behind the wheel and dropped two things into my lap: my mobile and my house keys.

'What did they say?'

'They said they were glad we were all right and would we please get out of their hair and mind our own business.'

I liked the way he said 'our' – a gentleman at heart.

'I'm going to take you home. The police will send a tow truck as soon as they have a moment. I've locked your doors.'

'My car keys . . .'

'I've pushed them up your exhaust pipe for the recovery people. Nobody is going to steal it, don't worry. Are you all right?'

I told him that I felt numb. As soon as I'd said it, my mobile rang. I lifted it and looked at the caller's number. It was my home phone – Barnabas again – so I switched on and said, 'I'm just on my way back.' Then I switched to stand-by, and on second thoughts off, did up my seat belt and closed my eyes again. I felt cold. I could hear scraping noises just in front of my feet as we started to reverse, but they stopped after a second. Then I switched myself off, too. When I switched on, we were pulling up in front of the shop and I was rational again.

Upstairs, Barnabas had put Ben to bed, and my nose could tell that pizza had been delivered.

'Is there enough for three?' I asked faintly.

'For four or five,' he said. 'Keeping warm in the oven. I'll put everything on the coffee table, it's more comfortable there. Wash your hands and then come and tell me what the *devil* you've done now!'

I whined, 'I'm hungry.'

Kennedy said, 'Before we eat, do you think you could find out what's happened?' His voice was tight.

As always, I was a little surprised when Paul answered his phone. He growled, 'Are you all right?'

I said I was fine but that wasn't the point. 'Have you caught up with them? Have you got Tim Curwen?'

'We're outside that house I told you about. The car arrived twenty minutes ago. Four men got out and went inside – Curwen looked all right. They're holed up in Lloyd Burke's house near Ware, you understand, and nobody's going anywhere. I'm busy here – we'll talk later.'

He switched off. So did I. Barnabas and Kennedy were watching me. They had very similar expressions on their faces.

I said, 'Burke! Of course, it was *bloody Lloyd Burke* all along!'

Barnabas said smoothly, and possibly even truthfully, that he wasn't surprised. He pushed a large triangle of pizza in my direction and then I found that I didn't want to eat after all.

By eleven o'clock it was clear there was no point waiting any longer. My companions both looked half dead. As for me, the world was still disjointed. I said that they could do what they liked, but I was spaced out and had to lie down. I heard Barnabas phoning for his minicab. When the doorbell rang, he leaned over me and said, 'I'll come over early. Tomorrow is Wednesday: Ernie is coming in the afternoon, you remember? Do you? You, I presume, will be occupied all day with trivia and policemen; I shall take charge of the shop.'

We listened to him descending to the street. It struck me that he was moving very slowly, and I hoped that he was only tired. Personally, I couldn't keep my eyes open.

Kennedy stood up with what seemed an effort. 'I'd better go too,' he said tonelessly.

'You can sleep here if you like.' Maybe I didn't want to be left alone.

He hesitated. 'I'd appreciate that,' he said.

I heard my voice going on about blankets and the long settee; he put an arm around my shoulders and headed towards the bedroom.

Ben stirred in his cot. Somebody near by whispered, 'Shhh, it's all right!' as I fell down on to the bed. I could feel him tugging my shoes off and rolling me under the duvet; after a pause he slid in beside me. He had a long, bony body. I stretched out in his warmth, and he dropped a kiss on my right ear and held me while I fell asleep.

At some point later on, I realised that I was hearing something. Beside me, Kennedy stirred.

I whispered, 'Telephone. Paul Grant,' and went to pick it up.

'Dido?'

I was nearly awake. 'Paul? What's happened?'

There was a movement behind me and I turned and saw Kennedy standing in the dark rectangle of the doorway.

'Sorry, did I wake you? I thought you'd want to know that it's all finished.'

I croaked again. 'What happened?'

'When everyone was in place, I rang the house and told Mr Burke we were just outside, waiting to have a word with him. He was explaining what I could do with our word when something happened – we heard a couple of shots, so I sent in an armed response team. Curwen must have had a gun hidden on him and he decided that it was his best chance of getting out of trouble while they were otherwise occupied. Our boy is a crack shot – Burke and one of the others are critical. One of them shot back, but they must have been taken by surprise and Curwen was lucky: he has a hole in him, and bruises, and a couple of burns on his face, but nothing serious. He's in the North Middlesex. If you wanted to visit him later today, that should be all right. That's it.'

'He'll be all right? You aren't going to arrest him?'

'Unfortunately, yes. And no, I don't think I can.'

'Your case . . .'

'Not sure. Up the creek? We're going to try to pick up as

many of them as we can lay our hands on, but I imagine that the word will have gone around already.'

I said, 'I'm sorry. I know that you wanted it to be clean and tidy.'

He paused and then said, 'I have things to do. I'll see you later.'

Kennedy stirred as I replaced the receiver.

'Tim was hurt, but he'll be all right,' I summarised. 'He tried to shoot his way out. It's finished.'

'Maybe,' he said. He made a noise which could have been mistaken for a laugh and said, 'Tim died once already; I hope that's going to be enough.'

So I understood that Kennedy was indeed a romantic man, and just said, 'He's in the North Middlesex. You can probably visit him tomorrow. Today. Later.'

I heard him expel a breath. After a moment, he said, 'We both need some more sleep.'

I hesitated. It must have been a bit obvious. This time, it was certainly a laugh that I heard. I couldn't even remember him laughing before that – at any rate, not for days and days.

Despite his promise, the clock over the fireplace was showing 9.50 when the doorbell blipped and we heard Barnabas coming upstairs fast. It sounded as though his night's sleep had done enough for him to be worried about me again.

Kennedy and Ben and I were in the living room instead of the newspaper offices, the nursery and the shop, respectively. Two of us were still drinking coffee; the third was constructing a tower of interlocking plastic blocks while Mr Spock investigated, wound himself around it, and occasionally tried to knock it over with his shoulder. Barnabas entered and surveyed the domestic scene from the doorway.

I smiled blandly and beat him to it by saying, 'If you'd like to help yourself to coffee, I'll bring you up to speed.'

While he was in the kitchen, Kennedy stood up and looked at me. 'I'd better go.'

I thought of saying that Barnabas's bark was worse than his bite, but instead I walked across to the writing desk, picked up the little book I had brought upstairs from the office, and held it out. 'Give him this. There's something written inside it that I think he needs. I expect he'll tell you: it's what he's been trying to get back – not the book, the notes he wrote in it; but he paid me for the book.'

Kennedy took it, looked at the cover, looked at me and said, 'Dido, I'll see you later.'

Barnabas returned as the outside door was closing. 'Well?' he said, suggesting that he was now willing to listen to my excuses.

I located the sheet of notepaper on to which I had copied out those four enigmatic lines of digits which I'd just sent back to their author. 'Barnabas, you know about these things: is this a code of some kind?'

My father considered the conundrum rather casually. 'Functionally, these numbers would identify four bank accounts – the branches and account numbers. Or so I would imagine.' When I objected that my own bank managed with a six-digit sort-code and an eight-digit account number, he laughed kindly. 'Have you never examined the cheques that we receive, from time to time, inconveniently drawn on foreign bank accounts? These numbers of course indicate *offshore* accounts.'

'Of course,' I said. The numbers would obviously identify four happy receptacles of the proceeds from Curwen's sales of books and other less innocent things.

'Possibly you ought to give somebody this information? Mr Grant comes to mind.'

I looked at my father with my eyes wide. 'But you're always telling me I should mind my own business.'

Barnabas threw me a dirty look and thought about it. All that he said was, 'That can never be entirely mistaken.'

Then I gave up and confessed everything while I tore the piece of paper into confetti and trickled it into my wastepaper basket. I was starting to think of more serious things.

'I suppose I'd better make some phone calls and try to find out where they've taken my van and how bad it is.'

'I don't think you should attempt to involve the insurance company financially, if it can possibly be avoided,' Barnabas commented.

That hadn't struck me before, but he could be right. I don't have a good relationship with my insurers, and it was true I'd incurred the damage deliberately. Maybe Curwen's cash would cover it? Almost certainly not.

And that was it, more or less. It wasn't until Saturday that Paul Grant dropped by to say that Lloyd Burke was dead, and that enough evidence had been found in his big house to incriminate both him and various associates – some of whom had been nicked, although the rest had disappeared.

When I asked him about Dona Helmer, Paul looked blank. 'You mean the solicitor? Oh, no – none of the employees there knew what was going on. He would have been crazy not to keep his real business strictly apart from his cover.' Burke had certainly not been mad. When I asked about Tim Curwen, he said ironically, 'Who's that? Oh – yes. Out of hospital, I think. Not under arrest. He claimed he was in fear of his life the other night and only trying to defend himself, so when one of his former friends tried to shoot him, he shot back. His story is perfectly credible, and he'll stick to it. He also says it was one of Burke's heavies, a man called Jimmy Ford, who killed McKane: Ford just happened to drop by and found Curwen and McKane together that night, and he – Curwen – barely managed to talk his way out of that with a whole skin. I decided to believe that story too, though he couldn't explain why Jimmy just happened to drop by Abbey House at the precise hour when McKane had gone there to lean on Curwen. Or how Ford could have known who McKane was. But the boss has decided it's best on all counts to reach what is called an "accommodation".'

'What does Jimmy Ford say?'

'By a surprising coincidence, Jimmy was the one who walked away from Mr Kennedy's car after you decided to stop it, and he never made it back to Burke's place. We'll come across him again, sooner or later, assuming he doesn't just retire to Salford, get plastic surgery, raise grandchildren and cultivate his allotment. We'd never get a conviction for this one. The CPS isn't even going to think of prosecuting with nothing by way of real evidence, and two villains contradicting each other on oath all the way. Luckily, Curwen's irrelevant now that Burke is dead.' I thought that Paul was looking shifty and wondered aloud what kind of 'accommodation' it was. He glowered at me. All right, so they had decided to put the message about that if you help the nice policeman, he will help you. He muttered, 'Maybe, eventually, we will be able to clear up this business – until another Lloyd Burke pops up. Who can afford to be finicky? All right?'

But Kennedy told me that Curwen had woken up in a hospital bed to the unwelcome sight of a detective called Grant looming over him. Apparently the two men had a long bedside chat which concluded with Mr Grant telling Mr Curwen to vanish – get himself not so much out of town as out of the country. Kennedy had delivered the new passport and *The Haunted Man* with its pencil notes. Apparently Curwen had thanked him for his offer of a thousand pounds to buy an air ticket, but said that he didn't need the money. Then he had discharged himself from hospital and limped off into the sunset. I suspect that Mrs Theresa Clark caught a taxi straight to the airport before anybody could change his mind. In her shoes, I would have done exactly that.

And, yes, I can't help wondering whether we all did the right thing. I don't suppose we'll ever find out.